CW01551797

THE BREAKTHROUGH

Aurélie Thiele

THE BREAKTHROUGH

"Look you here," Sancho retorted, "those over there aren't giants, they're windmills, and what look to you like arms are sails – when the wind turns them they make the millstones go round."

"It is perfectly clear," replied Don Quixote, "that you are but a raw novice in this matter of adventures."

Don Quixote, Part I Chapter VIII,
by Miguel de Cervantes Saavedra,
translation by John Rutherford.

1.

The plane landed in Boston half an hour late. André Darrieux grabbed his luggage, darted into the aisle as soon as the pilot turned off the 'fasten your seatbelt' sign – as if it mattered, really, that the red-eye from San Francisco had not quite kept to its schedule after six hours in the air, as if thirty-one minutes would make a difference. The other passengers stretched and unfolded their coats and retrieved their suitcases from overhead compartments, eyes bleary from the lack of sleep but glad to be home. A post-doc returning from the annual meeting of the American Physical Society, where André had given the plenary speech, later said that the M.I.T. professor had scribbled on a notepad throughout the flight, leaving his reading light on despite his neighbors' sighs; he always seemed busy, though, and from where he sat the post-doc had not noticed anything unusual. He insisted that there had been no hint, no clue, no warning.

One day earlier, several hundreds of physicists had crowded into the Continental ballroom at the Hilton to listen to André's speech. The Frenchman had risen to national prominence in the mid-nineteen nineties – among the members of his small research community – for postulating that the universe consisted of multidimensional objects called branes rather than point particles and had become a contender for the Nobel Prize almost overnight, although not everyone agreed on his odds. His fellow researchers had come back early from lunch to grab a good seat – front and center – near the short, stocky man mumbling at the lectern. André had lived in the United States for over three decades by then but still spoke with a thick French accent; the audience strained to follow him, hardly helped in this endeavor by handwritten transparencies full of notations he had not bothered to define. But no one could deny his command of the material, and the supersymmetry model he had developed with one of his graduate students elicited approving noises from the few in the room who understood it.

It held the promise of unifying the four forces of Nature at last – an achievement coveted by researchers for decades, the Holy Grail of their profession. That feat seemed within grasp because three of the four forces had already been brought together by quantum mechanics, back in the nineteen seventies – only gravity remained unexplained by such a framework. Why should it be treated any differently from the other three forces? That did not make sense. Team after team of scientists had attempted to find the missing piece in the grand unification theory, the "theory of everything," as it was called, in the hope of solving one of the most significant mysteries in their field and leaving their mark on theoretical physics. Some had come closer than others, but none had succeeded.

André had presented many of his arguments before, in a paper that had been circulating on the Internet – co-authored with the graduate student who had plowed through the minute calculations and deserved much of the credit. Neither wrote in the most straightforward manner, though, and most researchers who had ventured past the second page agreed they did not grasp all the intricacies of the model. Among the very few, listening to the talk, who supposedly understood the mathematics in the paper, no one raised any objection to André's approach. The rest of the audience sat in awe and asked him questions in a polite, respectful manner. While his theory could not yet be validated in experiments, it exhibited many appealing properties and André made a convincing case that its predictions would hold once technology caught up with theoretical advances. Colleagues and competitors alike gave him a sustained round of applause when he concluded his speech.

Attendees lined up by the podium afterwards to congratulate him. To his friends, André volunteered more details about the results and some of the extensions he was considering – careful not to give away too much information but obviously pleased with the work. What a pity the young man who had implemented his idea, labored over the equations, had left academia after his doctorate: untold promise, wasted by Wall Street's siren song. The other professors agreed heartily. André shook more hands – strangers' now that his acquaintances had stepped aside – nodded at graduate students gushing about the pleasure of meeting him, turned-over nametags dangling around their neck. The Hilton kept the meeting rooms heavily air-conditioned and André, who had complained about the cold before his speech, headed for the lounge to grab a cup of coffee with his admirers in tow. He was chatting with one of them when the technical sessions resumed; a colleague spotted the professor and a younger scientist hunched over a stack of papers while he hurried by their table. Shortly before nine o'clock, the same colleague caught a glimpse of André alone in front of the hotel, hailing a cab to the airport – he looked pale, as if he worried he was going to miss his flight, or as if enduring three days indoors at fifty-five degrees Fahrenheit had finally gotten the better of him, but the colleague did not think much of it. In hindsight he could not even tell exactly what André had done, that very last time he had seen him. Had he stood by his luggage? Talked on the phone? Scribbled on a notepad? It was all a blur in his colleague's mind.

Françoise sat by the baggage carrousel, hands in the pockets of her winter jacket. She had dreaded the morning traffic and left for the airport well in advance, only to learn from the television monitors at Logan that André's plane was not due on the ground before nine. Terminal B hummed with familiar sounds: announcements over the PA system, squeaks of trolley wheels. The last passengers of American Airlines Flight 4570 – non-stop service from Raleigh-Durham – waited for their suitcases, heaving sighs and looking at their watch while items they did not own glided on the conveyor belt.

A couple argued in hushed voices on the side. The woman, in her mid-thirties, waved her hands and rolled her eyes at her companion who, arms folded across a Tar Heels sweatshirt, stared straight ahead as if she did not exist. Françoise watched them from the corner of her eyes. Whenever she witnessed arguments, she often wondered whether she would have helped. In Lyon she had studied psychology while André attended the Ecole Normale Supérieure, and for years after settling down in Cambridge's graduate student housing, even later after buying the house in Belmont, she had introduced herself as a psychiatrist by training – using these exact words every time, as if anyone cared, really, that she had her own set of degrees, that she had not always been a stay-at-home wife. She would have opened her own practice if they had not moved abroad. André had agreed to help her pay the start-up costs, and so she had kept abreast of the developments in her field, lugged thick volumes through customs after transatlantic flights, taken notes and underlined relevant passages. Once André decided it was time for them to return to France for good, she would rent an office and put up a plaque by the door. Françoise Darrieux, licensed psychologist. Maybe this would all work to her advantage, she used to tell herself: she looked wiser now, and more knowledgeable. When she counseled clients, they would take her more seriously than a thirty-year-old. But André had received tenure and they had never left.

She daydreamed about her practice more often now that their son had moved to Southern California. She pictured the hardwood floors, the tall plants, the abstract paintings, and she liked to think that she would have been good at her job – she would have seen through people's white lies and demanded accountability. Really, the situation with Bernard could not be used to judge her competence. It was so much harder to raise one's own children.

André shoved his cell phone into his coat and rolled his suitcase in a straight line towards his wife, oblivious to the two children running around, their parents, the travelers from Raleigh-Durham, the limousine drivers holding signs with names on them. He was clenching his jaws and glaring into space. Françoise had expected her husband to look tired, annoyed perhaps at a crying infant or a talkative neighbor after the red-eye flight. Those things had happened before. His scowl did not alarm her.

"How was your trip?"

She handed him the car keys but he did not take them. "You drive."

In thirty-four years of marriage, he had never let her drive him, except for a month in the early nineteen nineties when his arm had been in a cast.

"What's going on?" Françoise hurried to keep up with André while he marched towards the exit. "Is everything alright?"

"I need to finish some work in the car. That's all."

"You've just spent six hours on a plane."

"It's a bit of an emergency."

Françoise tucked her chin into her scarf when they stepped outside. André buttoned his coat with one hand, dragged his suitcase behind him with the other, not bothering to stop to put his gloves on. The parking garage beckoned with its long rows of vehicles left head-in.

"We need to pay first."

André took another step despite hearing his wife's comment, sighed when the machine spat out the bill Françoise inserted. She tried again. At last the machine gave her the ticket back.

"Where did you park?"

"Level five."

André headed for the elevator, pressed the button to go up, then the one to close the doors.

"What happened? They didn't like your speech?" André shook his head. "So what's the matter then?"

The old, beaten-up station-wagon was parked in an empty corner of the lot, away from the other cars. André opened the hatch, pushed aside Buddy's toys – a chewed-on tennis ball, a plastic bone that squealed when squeezed in the middle, which the dog never tired of – and lifted his luggage with a grunt.

"I got you chocolates, though. Ghirardelli dark mint. They're in my suitcase."

Françoise smiled.

André walked to the passenger's door, retrieved his notepad and pencil from the laptop case before placing the bag at his feet. The driver's door opened and closed. Seat belts clicked. For a second, there was not a single noise in the car. Françoise clutched the wheel with both hands and looked at André. Her husband, bent over pages of formulas, paid her no attention at all. She turned the key into the ignition. A piano sonata crackled from the speakers.

André winced. "Do you mind?" He pointed at the radio.

Françoise switched it off, put the car in reverse. "Will you tell me what's going on?"

"I'm sorry. I just need to check something. It's urgent."

THE BREAKTHROUGH

"Surely it's not urgent enough that it can't wait until we get home."

Françoise proceeded slowly down the exit ramp – too narrow for her taste – found her way to the exit booth, fed her ticket to the machine. The gate opened.

"André?"

Her husband, his head turned toward the window, rubbed his temples with a frown on his face. Françoise eyed him, glanced at the road, eyed him again.

"What's wrong?"

André sighed. "It's been a long trip." He leaned back into his seat. "I'll get some rest after I take care of this. I didn't get any sleep on the flight."

Commuters had long reached their office by the time the Darrieux got on the East Boston Expressway. A line of trucks rumbled along, throwing mud onto Françoise's windshield and making it hard to pass, but after Government Center the northbound lanes of I-93 stretched lazily through the snow, traffic as fluid as ever. André pored over his notes and jotted words in the margin. Françoise caught herself peeking onto the bright yellow pages, as if the equations would ever make any sense to her, and then looked at the road again. She planned to run errands in the afternoon, hopeful that she would avoid the crowds of Thanksgiving shoppers at Whole Foods by a day or two. She also had to drop by the toy store. One of André's colleagues had recently become a father and it was bad manners not to buy a gift.

Bernard was flying in for the holiday. Françoise had expected him to wiggle out of making the trip, but – much to her surprise – he had bought plane tickets, emailed her his itinerary. Maybe the feast held some obscure meaning for him; after all, he had been born in the States, had grown up in that culture. Françoise could not have cared less about Indians and settlers, but she looked forward to seeing her son, in spite of everything. She knew her husband could be stubborn at times, and short-sighted, although he meant well and she agreed with him about Bernard. Perhaps this would be the beginning of, perhaps not a reconciliation, but at least a thaw in their relationship.

Françoise exited the highway. The first nor'easter of the season had dumped fifteen inches of snow on their suburbs the previous week, most of which – plowed up against the sidewalks in thigh-high mounds – was barely starting to melt.

"Welcome home."

André did not look up from his notes.

Françoise parked the car in front of the garage. She had salted the driveway herself – André had shoveled a path from the threshold to the mailbox before rushing out to Logan, promised he would do more when he came back, but by now there was nothing left for him to help with.

Françoise unlocked the front door. Buddy leapt out, drew happy circles around André, who stroked the top of his head.

"Come here." Françoise always worried the dog would run into the street just as a car raced by. He was only two, after all, and not as obedient as their previous German shepherd.

Buddy wagged his tail, then fell on his side and started rubbing his back into the snow. Françoise chuckled, turned toward her husband. "Look at that."

André trudged up the stairs. When he reached the house, he stumbled over the doormat and dropped his suitcase.

"Watch your step."

André gave his wife a blank stare. He opened his mouth but no word came out.

Françoise frowned. "Are you okay?" No answer. "Maybe you should lie down."

"I'm fine," André finally said. He wiped his brow and picked up his luggage. "I'll be in the study."

Françoise knocked on the office door around noon to ask her husband when he wanted to have lunch, peeked inside when she got no response. André was slumped at his desk, head leaning forward, eyes closed. He was still breathing but Françoise could not wake him up.

2.

Jim Calloway was not down on his luck. He did not look back on his first few years on the job as the high time of his life; he did not think he had already produced his best work. He had not given up his hope of winning a Pulitzer. He had not settled for mediocrity. Every morning he came prepared, with his notebook and his digital recorder, number-two pencils and extra memory cards, because he only needed one phone call to hear about the story that would make him famous, and the fact that he was already forty-five was of no importance whatsoever. By then, he had authored dozens of well-received articles – about early detection of brain tumors, the use of animals in biology experiments, issues of accuracy and usefulness in genetic testing – and hundreds more that had faded into oblivion right after being published, but he knew the tip would come eventually. Scientists liked to see themselves quoted in the pieces he wrote for the *Boston Globe*, and the day they had news to share, the day they wanted the world of non-scientists to learn about a breakthrough of theirs, they would remember him. That was his plan.

"I need something about a vaccine or a new drug." Jim turned the page, paused over the four-column account of a procurement scandal on Beacon Hill. "Fake data, unethical behavior. Pressure from higher-ups." He stared at the by-line. "Side effects people weren't told about."

Diane sipped her coffee, elbows on the table, hands wrapped around her cup, enjoying a slow start while she could. She worked as a nurse at Massachusetts General Hospital and the dramas of the day, big or small, would catch up with her soon enough.

"That kind of story doesn't come around too often," she said after a while.

"Sure, but I only need it once, and it'd put me on the map in no time. I've been waiting and waiting for my ten seconds in the limelight. At some point, it has to happen."

Jim sat with his back against the wall, his half-eaten bagel in one hand, the *Globe* spread over the table. Water rushed in the pipes above his head – the neighbors upstairs were washing the dishes, or running the shower. The first few nights in the apartment, after he had moved out of the house where he had slept for fifteen years and where Carol had raised their children, the noises in the building had kept him awake for hours, but now the heavy footsteps in the corridor and the doors slamming for no reason left him unruffled. He hardly seemed to hear them anymore.

One day, his daughters would understand that success in life, especially in a profession like journalism, required single-minded focus and absolute commitment. That was the price to be paid, but it would all be worth it in the end. His girls would take high pride in him. They would also, he hoped, be grateful for the lesson, which would help them thrive in any career path they chose, all thanks to his example.

Diane sank her nose into the cup. One gulp, two gulps. She rubbed her eyes.

"It might take five years before you get a story like that."

Jim glared at her. "That's the sort of story people care most about. They worry about big pharma endangering their loved ones. It might be happening as we speak. I just have to find the right source." He looked down at the paper, browsed through the Metro section. Diane watched in silence while he perused authors' names and gauged word counts. "What I need is access – a whistleblower who will feed me rock-solid information – and I won't get access without trust." Diane dug her spoon into her bowl of oatmeal, her long black hair falling in front of her face. Jim kept talking, his eyes on the newspaper. "Now, how do I build trust? That's the bottleneck. Once I've handled that, I've handled everything. Everybody in the business grapples with the same issue." He turned back to the long account of the procurement scandal involving state employees and sneered. "Of course, if your beat's Beacon Hill, then your life's much easier – you treat a couple officials to a beer or two and they spoon-feed you all the information you need. Covering state government is child's play. That's for amateurs."

Diane shrugged. "Absolutely." There was a hint of sarcasm in her voice, which Jim did not bother to comment on.

He opened the Health and Science section where, under the fold but on page one, the interested reader could learn about the attitudes of several Boston chefs toward trans fat. He had picked up the *Globe* on the steps outside his apartment building, torn the plastic wrap while he was walking back to the elevator and read the article in the hallway, anxious to see which cuts the editor had made before showing it to Diane. In front of his girlfriend, he pretended not to read his own work in print. He would insist, when pressed, that he did not care to know what had happened to his final draft.

"Look who has his byline in the paper today."

Diane's face lit up. She grabbed the page and pored over the first lines of Jim's work. "That's such a timely piece. People don't understand what that junk does to their body."

She read the rest in silence, her chin on her palm while her other hand kept a strand of hair tucked behind her ear. When she reached the end, she smiled and said: "Well done."

Jim bit into his bagel with a modest air on his face. He enjoyed the moment even after Diane got up to put her bowl into the sink and no longer looked at him. She did not need to stand up, could have reached the sink just by stretching her arm – the kitchen was so small that Jim's chair touched the wall whenever he pushed it back to leave – and it was understood that, although they both enjoyed the proximity to the Red Line, they would move to a bigger apartment once the divorce was finalized and the house was sold. Jim felt no desire to pack his belongings again so soon – he wanted to focus on his writing, do research for his assignments, and he did not mind working with his laptop on the kitchen table – but he had not yet broached the topic with Diane. There was no point in discussing those things anyway until the money sat in his bank account and Diane pressed him to take a decision.

He looked at his watch. "I'm going to be late."

The weather anchor on the New England Cable News channel had promised a rise in temperatures, but the wind blowing in gusts along Hamilton Avenue sent trash tumbling around heaps of snow, and if temperatures had inched up Jim certainly did not notice. He dropped a quarter into the Styrofoam cup of the homeless man sitting by the entrance to the T station and hurried down the stairs. A number of people were already waiting on the platform – neither too few nor too many but just enough to give newcomers hope that a train would arrive soon, and that when it did the cars would not be packed with hundreds of travelers who had languished at the previous stops. A man leaned over the tracks and stared into the tunnel, eager – it seemed – for two white, round lights to pierce the darkness. A short woman with curly hair was reading a self-help book. (Diane had read it too and tried to share some insights with Jim, who had pretended to listen and promptly forgotten everything she had said.) A few feet away, the upper body of a man in a business suit disappeared behind the *Wall Street Journal*. Near the emergency phone, someone was reading the *Boston Globe* at last, but Jim recognized the Health section under the man's armpit and did not investigate further. He spotted another *Globe* on the other side of the tracks – a college student standing next to the subway map was engrossed in the sports scoreboards.

A rumble grew from the depths of the tunnel. The commuters who had been reading tucked a bookmark into their paperback and folded their newspaper. They stepped closer to the edge of the platform while the train squealed to a stop. The car was already littered with dirty coffee cups and crumpled pages of tabloids; Jim was pleased to notice that no *Globe* lay around. In his mind, people who discarded the paper just after their morning commute could not possibly have read all the sections, and it was doubtful that they had reached the Health and Science articles before moving on with their day. That thought bothered him. The general public needed to be educated on the issues he was writing about and he was doing important work – he really was.

He stepped out of the train at the J.F.K./U. Mass. stop. The wind had let down slightly but the air remained biting cold. Jim turned his collar up, stuck his hands into his pockets and started walking, shoulders up to his ears.

He had not planned on becoming a science writer. He had not even planned on becoming a journalist – at Northwestern, he had studied biology. But he had enrolled in a writing course as an upper-classman and, when it had become clear that he had neither the patience nor the intellect to spend eight more years in school for a PhD, he had given science writing a try. To his surprise, he had found out that he was quite good at it. Physics he did not care about – except astrophysics of course, always a crowd-pleaser with its pretty pictures of stars, galaxies, distant planets – but he enjoyed explaining biology and chemistry to a lay audience, and anything with medical applications. Things had turned out well for him. He did not regret his choice. He did not wish he had gone to graduate school. He did not wish he had gone to medical school either. He did not long for more respect.

Carol had been wrong to suggest otherwise.

Jim headed toward the red-brick building and pulled the glass door, nodded at the security guard. The marble and granite of the lobby, which had been so typical of company headquarters built in the nineteen fifties, looked grandiose now, which suited Jim just fine. The newsroom stretched across the second floor – visitors always expected to find a room drenched with light, because of the large windows towering over the parking lot, but to Jim the place seemed cavernous and the interior showed its age. A handful of journalists sat at their desks, shuffled papers – the thirty-three-year-old who had broken the Beacon Hill story had not arrived yet. Two reporters on the metro beat discussed a football game they had watched the previous night, their chair tipped back against file cabinets and their hands folded behind their head. The newsroom rarely buzzed with activity before ten – many staff writers spent their morning in the field and made their entry after lunch.

Jim had barely hung his coat when his assigning editor stepped toward him.

"I was just going to see you." Jim grinned. "Did you hear about the drug trial that got suspended? You'd think that by now, big research labs wouldn't need trials any more, they'd use computer models or genetic testing, but it looks like we're stuck in the past on that one." He spoke fast, to make sure his editor would not interrupt him. "I was wondering how technology has changed the way big pharma brings its drugs to market. I'm sure it'd interest many of our readers."

Daniel Radinowski greeted this announcement with a pause.

"Hear me out first," he finally said.

Jim groaned. "Are we talking about the water reservoirs again? This is getting old."

"Give it your best shot."

"Dan, I promise you, Boston's water reservoirs are safe. I looked into it – the public can drink tap water in peace. There's no story."

"There's never any story until someone stumbles on something, and then there's one big story after all."

"Dan," Jim protested in a low voice. He glanced around, annoyed that other reporters might overhear the conversation and joke about Radinowski's only trusting him with low-impact assignments. But his two colleagues nearby were still engrossed in their discussion of the game, and there was nothing for him to worry about.

"Curtis wants to know more – give him more. Who tests the water, how old are the pipes, could the distribution system break down… Plenty of ideas right there."

Jim shook his head. "Can't you put one of the junior guys on it? That thing's a dead end."

The editor shrugged. "Find me something better and I'll think about it, but that big-pharma story is a no-go. Now, get to work."

3.

Olivia stepped out of the #1 bus and waited for the walk signal at the light – Massachusetts Avenue was not a street she dared to cross when it was not her turn, especially during the morning rush. The massive pillars guarding the entrance to the Rogers Building used to remind her of a Greek temple, back when she still paid attention to them; Killian Court, a short walk away, and the Widener Library at Harvard looked like temples too. Even the post office in Central Square, which had been built around the same period, seemed to long for grandeur. Olivia had found the recurring theme quite silly when she had arrived in town, but by now she had resigned herself to spending many years surrounded by architecture of dubious taste.

She followed the crowd in backpacks along the Infinite Corridor and strode past office doors and bulletin boards, hands in her pockets and chin in her scarf, indifferent to her surroundings. Students around her would occasionally recognize a friend, wave, shout a greeting – she could tell because of the smile that popped up on their face and their mouth opening wide, but her iPod drowned their chatter in the vocals of Esperanza Spalding and Norah Jones. She preferred her mornings that way. She increased her pace when she turned into a side corridor, unhampered by the handful of students strolling toward the library, and headed for the third floor.

André Darrieux's lab consisted of two rooms at the end of the hall, one for graduate students and one for post-doctoral fellows, both with drab interiors that had born witness to several generations of scholars toiling away on their research papers. Since the work did not involve any equipment, there was no reason to call the offices a lab, but the name had caught on anyway. This annoyed experimental physicists to no end. Darrieux himself sat on the other side of the hall, with other faculty members and the administrative assistant who made their travel arrangements for conferences, photocopied exams for their classes, made sure graduate students received their stipend on time. The graduate students did not dare play music on their computer until late at night, when the professors were gone, but the two post-docs liked Beethoven and Brahms and all kinds of piano sonatas, which they deemed suitable for daytime listening at full blast. Darrieux himself viewed Beethoven as a composer of unsurpassed genius and had been spotted more than once hovering in the corridor when Miguel and Xin played the Fifth Symphony. But everything was quiet that morning. The door to the post-docs' office was closed and the lights were off – they had left for California with Darrieux and were not due back from the annual meeting before the next day.

Olivia stopped in front of her office. Light streamed through the opaque glass, and she guessed correctly that Sergey would be at his desk when she entered. The room smelled of toasted bagel. Sergey kept everything he needed for breakfast in his corner of the room so that he would not have to wait in line at the coffee shop. He claimed it allowed him to spend more time working on his dissertation. He planned to finish in the spring, but he had had that plan for several springs now and his officemates had stopped asking him when he would graduate.

As the student with the most seniority in the room, he had taken over Matthew Johnson's desk after the latter had left – the farthest away from the door, with its own shelves. Hyong-Mo had decided to stay where he was, so Olivia had replaced Sergey by the wall that their office shared with the post-docs'. Patrick – the first-year student – sat by the entrance, forever distracted by the door opening and closing, catching colds in the draft. Neither Hyong-Mo nor Patrick had arrived yet.

Olivia put her keys back into her pocket. "Hi."

Sergey turned his head toward her and gave her a long look.

She frowned and removed one earphone of her iPod. "What?"

"Look on your desk."

Olivia lifted a yellow Post-It note off the table. Darrieux had called around nine. He wanted to see her as soon as he got in.

"But he's in California."

Sergey eyed her behind his glasses, with a mix of curiosity and displeasure at seeing a more junior student singled out.

"Did you answer the phone?"

He nodded.

"Well, what did he say?"

"Just that."

"So he's back, then? I thought the conference ended today."

Sergey stacked his books on top of each other and aligned their spine carefully. "He called from the airport. I heard some noise in the background – flight announcements, that sort of thing."

"But he's never called any of us before."

Sergey stared at her. "That can only mean one of two things, doesn't it?"

Olivia bit the inside of her cheeks. The news was either very good or very bad, and Darrieux would not have bothered to give her a call if the news had been very good. That would not have been urgent. He would have waited to tell her in person, that afternoon.

"I've got to go to class."

She crumpled the Post-It note and hurried outside, the earphone dangling in front of her chest.

"Do you know if Professor Darrieux has ever called students from the airport before?"

The administrative assistant, a pile of papers in her arms, raised a perfectly plucked eyebrow in the middle of the hallway. Olivia lowered her voice.

"To tell them he wanted to see them as soon as he got in?"

Evelyn squinted slightly. Then she pinched her lips and opened her door. "What happened?"

"I don't know." Olivia plopped into a chair. "I think I'm in trouble again."

"What makes you so sure?"

Evelyn placed the files next to her computer and leaned back into her seat. The poster of a recent Gauguin exhibition hung on the wall right above the screen; a plant in a woven basket spread its leaves onto the edge of the desk. Color-coded folders and manila envelopes lined up the "in" trays of the faculty members, each box carefully labeled so that no absent-minded professor would grab the forms another colleague had to sign. Evelyn had been working as an assistant in the department for about fifteen years, and there was not a single stray paper in sight. The tidiness of her office always impressed Olivia.

"He wouldn't have called otherwise."

"Maybe he had an idea for your work."

Olivia scoffed. "He really doesn't care about my work that much. Not after this past summer."

"He might've had some kind of breakthrough."

Olivia shook her head. "I'd say he found out we got scooped, but I don't have enough results." She reached for the bowl of Hershey kisses that Evelyn kept on her desk for occasions just like those, with a large box of Kleenex nearby.

Evelyn smiled reassuringly. "If someone wrote a paper on the same idea that you had, it shows it's an interesting topic. I'm sure there will always be something for you to write about."

"You don't know that." Olivia looked like she was going to cry.

"Maybe he was calling about something else altogether. Maybe he's decided to put you on a different research project and he wants you to start working on it right away. Wait until you talk to him."

Olivia unwrapped a piece of candy, and then a second one. "I'm trying to get results. I'm trying so hard. It's just that you don't extend Matt Johnson's work in a day. I don't even understand half his proofs." She ate the Hershey kisses and sighed. "I've got nothing to show for all the hours I've spent in the lab. The one thing I thought I'd found wasn't even true. That project's going nowhere, and I'm not getting any closer to graduating, and you can't do anything in science without a doctorate."

"That's not true."

Olivia grimaced. "You can't do research. You can't teach at a university. I want to have my own research group and mentor students and encourage girls to go into science." She curled into a ball on the chair, feet pushing against the edge, arms wrapped around her knees. "People say I'm really good at tutoring kids. That's one of my strengths. But I don't want to only explain things other people have discovered. I want to leave my own mark."

The computer beeped to announce incoming mail. Evelyn let her gaze drift toward her computer screen. Olivia paused as Evelyn read the message and typed a two-line reply.

"I've got that picture in my head of me sitting at a table with my graduate students, discussing the paper we want to submit to *Physical Review*. I've had that picture in my head since high school, except that back then I didn't know about the leading journals in the field. It's like golf, you know?" Evelyn frowned. "My father plays golf, and once in a while he lets me come along with him. He tells me to visualize where I want the ball to go before I make the swing, and if I can see it clearly enough it'll happen for real, no matter how difficult it seems."

"That sounds like good advice."

"But when does it become wishful thinking? Everybody says that if you have absolute faith in your goals and you don't compromise, you'll see your wildest dreams come true. I've wanted to become a professor for as long as I can remember. Some days, I'm convinced there's no way in the world it's not gonna happen, and then at other times, I sit there and think, oh my goodness, I'm going to fail and I have no plan B."

Evelyn looked at her, let a second go by. "Anyway, you sorted things out with Professor Darrieux in the summer, didn't you?"

"We talked. I still worry. If I change advisors now, I'll have wasted three years – three years and three months. I can't handle that. He knows it. I need him to get my degree."

"But everything's fine now."

"I hope so." Olivia threw the candy wrapper into the waste basket. "It's hard to tell." She looked at the clock. "I should get going. My class started a while ago."

4.

"My husband has had a heart attack and I want to see him."

Diane looked up from her paperwork. The woman, standing under the glaring lights of the hospital lobby, car keys in hand, stared at her with big, imploring eyes.

"What's your husband's name?"

"Darrieux. André Darrieux. He can't have arrived more than ten minutes ago. I tried to follow the ambulance in my car, but I couldn't keep up with it." The woman's chin quivered. She looked ashamed of herself, as if she had failed her husband by stopping at the red lights while the ambulance breezed through.

Diane smiled. "It's alright," she said gently. "We don't want you to get into an accident. Your husband did arrive a short time ago. You can't see him just now, but he's in good hands." Her eyes fell on the men's coat and woolen scarf in the woman's arms – brought along just in case, as if her husband would need them any time soon. Probable stroke, the EMT had said when he'd wheeled the patient in. Severe one at that. She fetched the admission forms. "The doctor will be right with you. Would you mind filling these out while you wait?"

"I want to see my husband." Françoise tucked her chin inside her turtleneck, pressed André's coat against her stomach. She did not take the forms.

"We'll let you know as soon as that's possible." Diane smiled again. Her voice softened. "In the meantime, why don't you have a seat?"

Françoise considered the request for a second, plodded toward a chair without adding a word. The waiting area of Massachusetts General Hospital was filled with its usual chaos – an elderly man worried he had broken his hip; a baby cried for no apparent reason; a bedraggled man talked to his feet. Coughs punctuated any lull in the conversations. A MedFlight helicopter had just landed with a motorist who had been injured in an accident on the turnpike. The staff hurried in and out of operating rooms. Someone yelled he had been waiting all morning.

"It'd be such a help if you could fill this out while you wait." Diane placed the sheets of paper in Françoise's lap, handed her a pen. André Darrieux's case was nothing she had not seen before, and she had work to do.

Françoise looked up.

"He's never had a problem with his heart. I don't understand what happened." She dropped André's coat on the forms. "I always thought his heart was stronger than mine. My family is the one with a history of heart problems."

Diane glanced around, in search of a resident who could enlighten the woman on her husband's condition, but doctors were nowhere in sight. The parents of a nineteen-year-old patient huddled in a corner, their eyes red from crying. The teen had crashed his father's pickup truck into a tree after driving over a sheet of ice and had been admitted in critical condition. The mother was having conversations with God under her breath – Diane had overheard her as she was walking by. She had spent the past hours handing scalpels to the surgeon who had stopped the son's internal bleeding and repaired some of the damage, but she wished she had been able to do more. The surgeon had done all the work. Even then, it was not clear whether the teen would survive.

She took a deep breath. "I believe your husband's heart is just fine." She spoke slowly, mindful of the woman's foreign accent. Françoise raised an eyebrow. "He was admitted with symptoms of a stroke. The doctors are running tests to confirm the diagnosis."

The woman frowned. She did not appear to understand what the word 'stroke' meant.

Diane looked around again, sighed, rubbed the bridge of her nose with her index finger. She felt drained after the teenager's surgery. A siren grew louder outside the building. A resident sprinted to the ambulance bay. "A stroke is what happens when a blood clot moves to a person's brain." She put her hands up around the top of her head, to show the woman where the brain was.

Françoise gaped. "But André's brain is his livelihood!" She looked hurt, offended even. "He's a scientist, a famous one. He can't have a problem with his brain."

Diane took a step back, surprised by the vehemence of the woman. "The doctors won't know for sure until they get the tests' results. Now, can you tell me if your husband seemed fine six hours ago?"

Françoise slumped into her chair, her arms folded under André's coat. "I don't know. Why?"

"It affects the type of treatment he should receive. According to the medic, you said he was already showing symptoms around nine o'clock this morning. Is that correct?"

Françoise let out a whimper. "I would've brought him here right away if I'd realized they were symptoms."

"I understand. It's not your fault. Now, did he exhibit any sort of abnormal behavior during the night? Slurred speech, problems with balance?"

"He was on a plane." Françoise stared at a point on the ground, about two feet away from her shoes. "He called me from the San Francisco airport just before I went to bed, to say he'd gone through security and the plane was on time."

"So he had no problems with his speech when you talked to him?"

Françoise shook her head. "He was upset, but he didn't tell me why. I knew from the tone of his voice that something was wrong, though."

Diane frowned. "Maybe a headache?"

"More like his research not going as planned. He was coming back from a conference."

"So you don't think he was showing symptoms on the plane."

Françoise gave the nurse a long, sad look. "I wish I knew." She paused. "Do you think he had a stroke because he was under stress?"

Diane blinked. "Strokes happen for all kinds of reasons."

"But could it be possible? He sounded so agitated on the phone." Françoise's voice wavered. "He usually tells me what's going on. I don't understand why he was being so mysterious. I asked him what was wrong, I asked him several times, but he wouldn't tell me. He just said, don't worry about it, I'll see you in the morning."

"You did the best you could."

Nurses and doctors surrounded a stretcher that had just been wheeled inside the hospital.

"But could it be stress?"

"It depends on the person. Strokes can be due to a lot of things. Sometimes, they even happen with no reason at all." Françoise grimaced, apparently not satisfied by the answer. "It could be stress, or it could be air travel, or a combination of travel and stress, or something completely different altogether."

"But André has been traveling for years. So many people invite him to give talks. They all want to hear what he has to say." Françoise made a faint smile. For a second, she seemed very proud, and then her smile vanished. "Air travel didn't give him a stroke." She stared at the nurse. "Something happened at that conference."

Diane did not know what to answer. She pointed at the forms. "Would you mind filling these out for me, please?"

Françoise took the pen, contemplated the first line and wrote André's name in the blank spaces at last. While she was filling the forms, Diane saw the attending physician walking toward them. He looked grim.

"The doctor will discuss your husband's condition with you now. Just bring the forms back when you're done."

She retreated to the nurse's station, shuffled papers while the doctor conferred with the woman. Françoise had gotten up when he had stretched his hand out to greet her, and she spent most of the conversation nodding, clutching her purse, pressing André's coat against her stomach. Her knees buckled at one point, and she asked the doctor something – Diane guessed it was a question because of her frown, which lingered after she heard the answer. She pressed her husband's coat a little more tightly, pinched her lips.

Then the doctor left and she sat back down.

"So?" Diane could not help asking the physician.

He glanced at her. "So what?"

Diane pointed at Françoise with her chin. "Is the husband going to make it?"

"It's too early to tell." The doctor checked behind his shoulder that Françoise remained out of earshot. "But even if he survives, he'll be lucky if he speaks normally again, or makes an addition. The brain scan didn't look good, to say the least."

"Does she know?"

The doctor shook his head. "There's no point in giving her the bad news all at once. I told her he had a severe stroke and will need extensive therapy. She'll figure out the rest soon enough." He sighed before walking to his next case. "I wish she'd brought him in earlier. Maybe we could've done something for him then."

Diane's gaze wandered back to Françoise. Now that the shock of the news had sunk in, she sat calmly, hands on her purse, ankles crossed under the chair, tips of the shoes pressing against the floor. She did not read magazines. She did not sneak out to make phone calls. She sat there, very straight, without moving, as if she was trying to conserve energy by feeling as little as possible – to keep her stamina for later, when her husband was discharged and allowed to return home. Diane thought she was going to wait a while.

"I'm going to take my break now."

The head nurse nodded, eyes on the computer screen. Diane met Françoise's stare before she reached the glass door, one arm in her jacket's sleeve and the other out. Then she headed out into the cold.

She did not have a hat and, after a few steps, covered her ears with her hands. Thankfully, the diner where she liked to buy her lunch was only a short distance away. The stereo system was always tuned to her favorite radio station – Kiss 108, which played mainstream pop music, easy, mindless fare that helped her forget the worst cases at the hospital, the wounds, the blood, the lives cut short. Diane did not need to listen to pop music when the prognosis was good – she did not even need to eat. She could waltz into the next surgery, fueled by Quaker's bars, and remain focused throughout. It was when the surgeon's efforts might come to naught that she needed the music. She was worried about the teenage driver.

THE BREAKTHROUGH

"Can't wait for spring to come," the store's cashier said when she saw Diane, who was a regular, "and it's not even New Year yet."

Diane chuckled. "I've been waiting for spring to come since Columbus Day." With the exception of one customer halfway through his sandwich, the store was empty – it was past most people's lunch time. "I'll have the half soup, half chicken Caesar combo, and a small coffee with that."

The employee was ringing her order when the door opened with a beep. Diane glanced behind her shoulder and recognized the wife of the stroke victim.

"Hi," Françoise Darrieux said with a tiny smile.

"Hi." Patients' relatives usually stayed on the M.G.H. campus, got their meals from one of the cafeterias – the few who ventured outside frequented the chain stores, with their familiar names that gave people an illusion of normalcy. Diane had never seen patients' relatives eating in the diner before. It seemed too much of a coincidence that Françoise stood there now. Diane did not like the thought she had been followed, although she felt sorry for the woman.

Françoise asked for a *latte* and came up to Diane, who was waiting for her order. "We met at the hospital earlier today. I'm the wife of a patient. A stroke victim."

"I know."

The employee placed Diane's and Françoise's drinks on the counter, then the soup and the salad. Diane motioned toward an empty table in the middle of the room.

"Do you mind if I join you?"

Diane raised an eyebrow, but Françoise kept smiling, and she could not find a graceful way to turn the woman down. She took two big gulps of coffee as they walked to the table and sat down.

Françoise looked around. "What a cozy little place." Diane plunged her spoon into her bowl of soup. The silence dragged on. "How long have you been a nurse?"

"Fourteen years."

Françoise seemed impressed. "It must be so rewarding to save people's lives."

Diane glanced up, pointed her spoon at her lunchmate. "That's what I thought too when I got into the field." She did not elaborate.

"You don't think that anymore?"

Diane shrugged. "In the end, doctors are the ones who save people's lives. I have more of a supporting role."

"But I'm sure a lot of people are very grateful."

"They are. But like I said, it's not a leading role. If you do this job for recognition, you're going to get disappointed." She took another gulp of coffee.

Françoise nodded with a sympathetic look on her face and waited for her to say more.

"When I started, I thought I'd have more of an impact on people. You know, me," Diane placed a hand on her heart, "alone, not as part of a team."

A white-haired man entered the diner and ordered a large cup of coffee. He picked a seat by the window, unfolded the newspaper. Diane's gaze drifted toward him. She recognized the front page of the *Boston Herald* and looked back at Françoise.

"If I could start again, I'd become a paramedic." She made a wry smile. "I would make more of a difference."

"I'm sure you're underestimating yourself."

Diane rolled her eyes, vaguely embarrassed by her own admission. "Anyway." The caffeine was starting to kick in. "You have a bit of an accent. Where are you from?"

"France."

"I've always wanted to go to Paris."

"I've heard it's beautiful." Françoise chuckled at her own comment. "I'm from Lyon. It's further south. Although I've been to Paris, of course. But most tourists have seen more of it than I ever will."

Diane chuckled too and pushed aside her empty bowl of soup. "You said at the hospital that your husband is a researcher. What kind of research does he do?"

"He works in theoretical physics at M.I.T. He says his goal is to understand how Nature works. Don't ask me what that means." Françoise leaned over the table and lowered her voice. "Some people even say he's a contender for the Nobel Prize." Diane gasped appreciatively. "And of course many M.I.T. professors are contenders for the Nobel Prize, but his odds are better than most." She stared at Diane. "That's why it's so important he recovers quickly. He has so much to contribute to the world."

Diane fidgeted on her seat. "Well, I think even people who don't have anything to contribute to the world should recover quickly. Everyone." She ate the morsels of chicken and the croutons first, leaving the salad leaves for later. Françoise did not touch her coffee.

"The doctor who's treating my husband – do you know him?"

Diane shrugged. "Sort of."

"Is he good? Because André needs the best doctor around."

Diane stared at her plate. "He's very good. He'll do everything he can, and if he can't help your husband, no one can."

Françoise seemed pleased by that answer. "How long do you think it'll take before André is back to normal?"

Diane drank her coffee.

"I don't know. I'm not a doctor."

"I'm just trying to get a second opinion." Françoise removed the lid from her coffee cup, put it back on again. "I'm sure he'll have to rest. I understand that, although it'll be hard for him. He never stops working." She smiled. "He doesn't see it as work. More like a giant playground he doesn't want to leave. And his course! He's going to be so upset that he has to miss lectures."

Diane forced herself to eat. Françoise continued talking.

"What kind of after-effects do you think he'll have while he recovers? Trouble to focus, perhaps, or irritability?"

"It depends on the area affected by the stroke. The doctor will be able to tell you more." Diane found one last morsel of chicken under the salad leaves and chewed slowly. "Do you have relatives in the area? Anyone who could wait with you?"

"My son lives in San Diego, and André and I are not very social. We're happy with each other. We don't need many friends." Françoise grinned.

Diane could not bear looking at her.

5.

Françoise pulled into the driveway and turned the engine off. Images flickered on the Hartwells' television screen in the house across the street. For a few seconds, Françoise squinted and tried to guess what her neighbors were so interested in, to take her mind off the events of the day, but she watched little television and did not recognize the program. Someone turned the light on in the Connors' kitchen and one of the teenage boys walked to the fridge. The street was quiet. Françoise sat in silence, hands on her lap, bracing herself for the emptiness of the house.

In a way, things had not changed. She had spent the previous evening without André, listening to Luciano Pavarotti hit high Cs in *La Fille du Régiment*; she could stay alone one more night. Perfectly reasonable explanations came to her mind. André had been delayed, or had extended his stay. Maybe he had decided to visit a colleague before heading back east. He could have missed his plane – that one had happened before. Those were all valid reasons for him not to be home by now.

Buddy greeted her with friendly yelps, then jumped about and ran to the kitchen. Françoise wondered whether the dog remembered the ambulance – she had expected him to lie down under the table with one of André's slippers, or to whimper in front of the door. Didn't he understand the gravity of the situation? She had read stories about dogs howling for hours after their owner had died, and could not help but feel hopeful. Maybe Buddy sensed there was nothing to worry about. Maybe André would recover soon.

Françoise dropped her keys on the counter and checked the answering machine. The nurse had promised to call if André's condition worsened – Françoise would not have left otherwise – but there was no message.

THE BREAKTHROUGH

Buddy sat down in front of his bowl and scratched the rim with his paw.

"You hungry, big boy?"

Françoise fed him a large serving of dog food, which he ate up within moments.

The medic had frowned when she had told him about the car drive. "Are you saying he was already showing symptoms three or four hours ago?" 'Yes' did not sound like the correct answer, and yet it was. She had chalked up André's behavior to the jetlag and his eagerness to figure out whatever had been preoccupying him – he could be very driven sometimes, overzealous, single-minded. But she should have known. Couples who had been married for decades were supposed to notice details like that, little things that eluded newlyweds – that was the whole point of sharing one's life with one another for so long. She had missed all the signals. What kind of spouse blundered like that? She should have checked on him, brought him a glass of water, insisted he take a nap. She would have found him in time and called an ambulance on the spot. Instead, she had blissfully gone about her business.

Buddy licked the bowl clean.

"You've got quite an appetite tonight." Grief-stricken dogs did not eat, according to those same stories she had read.

Buddy sat straight with his big expectant eyes that hoped the sentence meant 'second serving.'

Françoise sighed. "You've had enough."

As long as she kept the stroke for herself, André would remain healthy in the mind of everybody he knew. For these people at least, her husband was still doing just fine. He could be working in his study, bent over his books – once he had figured out the solution to the problem that had bothered him all day, he would step out and suggest they walk the dog together. His undergraduate students labored on their homework. His graduate students toiled on their dissertations. His colleagues planned on seeing him at his desk the next morning. For them, nothing had changed – the stroke had not happened. And if tens or hundreds of people believed André's brain functioned perfectly, didn't it make it so? Shouldn't the voice of the majority prevail?

Françoise looked at the dog. "I'm glad I have you." Buddy tilted his head to the side and raised one ear. Françoise patted him under the snout, the way he liked most. "We make a good team, Daddy, you and I."

Buddy wagged his tail.

She took good care of her husband. Nobody could deny that. She shopped at Whole Foods and cooked with olive oil and made her own bread in the little bread oven André had bought her for her birthday. She gave him fruits to eat, and multivitamins. She scheduled his doctor appointments. She had done everything she could – except checking on him that morning, because he liked to work without any disturbance.

"It might only be the two of us for a few days, but hopefully not for long."

The dog rolled onto his back so that Françoise would scratch his stomach.

André pushed himself too hard. He had nothing left to prove – he had tenure, he was famous – and yet he kept training students, put in twelve-hour days, strove relentlessly to uncover new findings. He loved science, but it had taken a toll.

Françoise opened the fridge and reached for the bottle of Chardonnay, leaned against the countertop to sip her glass of wine. What had bothered her husband, that morning at the airport? It had obviously to do with his research, and he had not behaved as if it had been good news. Maybe someone had beaten him to the punch on one of the research projects he had been working on – had figured out a way to prove the result André was after, and submitted his discovery for publication first. André was only involved in high-profile endeavors, the kind that forced Nobel Prize committee members to pause and take notice, and that naturally attracted media attention. A competitor's victory would have exasperated him, no doubt. But would it have made him adopt the mysterious behavior he had shown that morning? That seemed far-fetched.

Françoise tried to think about other explanations. If her husband had found a mistake in a paper, it would have had to be a really big mistake, in a really important paper. She could not imagine

André doing anything wrong when it came to his work, though. He was far too careful for that.

"We can simply tell ourselves that Daddy's staying in California longer than expected, but he'll be back soon."

She looked at Buddy, who hurried to the door, wagging his tail as if they were going to play. She sighed and let him out, but stayed inside.

After the dog came back – scratching the kitchen door to get her attention, his nose white from sniffing around in the snow – she changed her mind and called her son. Her call went to voicemail. The afternoon had not yet ended in San Diego, and Bernard might have turned his cell phone off while he sat in a meeting. She left a message. It occurred to her afterwards that her son, who did not use French except for weekly ten-minute chitchats with his parents, might struggle with the words she had chosen, mirroring her reaction to the nurse talking to her in English in the hospital. Would he know that '*attaque*' was French for stroke? How would he know? Had he even heard the word before? But of course he would call back. What choice did he have? He could not ignore her message – his own father, in the hospital. Françoise braced herself for the ring in the silent house.

Bernard would ask whether he should change his tickets and come immediately, but she would say no. There was no need. It would not help: Thanksgiving was only days away and he would arrive soon enough. He would agree with her, reluctantly. Françoise caught herself hoping that he would regret his move to California – André had paid for Harvard and then Harvard Business School, taken a second mortgage and co-signed his loans, and Bernard could not even rush to his father's bedside on short notice.

He should have thought about that earlier. Silly boy, who had relocated as far away from his parents as he could without leaving the country.

Françoise sat down on the sofa in the living-room. Buddy brought her his squeaky ball and let it drop on her feet.

"I don't want to play."

A pile of magazines and history books awaited André by his favorite armchair. Most of them had been left unread, but one had a bookmark stuck between the pages about halfway through. André liked to read, although he rarely found the time.

Françoise took another sip of Chardonnay. Her mind wandered back to the stroke and the conference, André scribbling notes in the car and then slumped at his desk – those details had to be related. The dog had lain down next to his squeaky ball but stood up as soon as she made a move toward the corridor, and followed her into the study.

Papers were stacked in uneven piles. Pens were scattered across the desk. The room lacked decoration: no painting, one small framed photograph of twelve-year-old Bernard with André's parents, one summer long ago in France. André complained that pictures distracted him. His degrees – the real doctorate and the honorary ones – hung in his office at M.I.T., where he got little work done beyond discussing research with students and sitting in meetings with colleagues. Françoise sat down in his armchair. Her gaze drifted over the small square of metal with blue dots that André assured her was a clock, a binary one, which could be used to tell time like any other clock. He had received it as a gift from a former student. Françoise found the present useless but appreciated the gesture: she liked it when former students showed themselves grateful for the time André had spent with them. She recognized the yellow notepad by the computer – the same one that André had taken to California – and leafed through it. The pages were covered with equations, which she was incapable of deciphering. Buddy curled up under the desk and put his nose on her ankle. She turned the computer on.

Students of course would be devastated. André spent more time with them than with Bernard, knew them better than his own son. He cared about them. He line-edited their papers, streamlined their proofs, advised them on their career options, wrote recommendation letters and even placed phone calls on their behalf when they looked for academic positions – they were lucky to have him. Evelyn would buy a get-well card for his colleagues to sign, and maybe some would pay him a visit while he remained at M.G.H. They would be shaken. Who would have expected him to have a stroke? He was not yet fifty-eight. Quite a few of his colleagues were older, and in worse health. Françoise could not help but think that the situation was unfair.

André had never hidden his password from his wife – he took pride in it consisting of her middle name and year of birth. About two dozen messages, identified by their bold letters, had found their way into his inbox since he had last checked his email: calls for abstracts, requests for reviews, and then a message from Olivia Reynolds. The name sounded familiar, but it took Françoise a second to place it.

"Olivia." Françoise clicked on the link. "Didn't she leave?"

The student was writing to apologize for missing his call that morning. She had waited until six o'clock – did he want to reschedule the meeting?

"Unbelievable." Buddy raised his head. Françoise turned to the dog. "Daddy's being too nice again."

André had announced three months earlier that he was going to cut the student off. If she could find another professor willing to advise her, he saw nothing wrong with her continuing at M.I.T., but in any case she would be someone else's problem. He did not think she had any future in his lab, although she insisted she did not want to leave. He had not mentioned her again and Françoise had not asked, but he had been so upset that day in the middle of the summer that she had assumed he had kept his word.

He had not.

Françoise read the message a second time and frowned – she was not aware of André's calling a student before. He would dial Evelyn's number to let her know that he was running late, but Françoise had never witnessed him call a student, or heard him say he would. And when had he found the time? There had been no noise coming out from the study. He might have used his cell phone when he had stepped off the plane, but she could not fathom why he would want to reach a student so quickly.

Something had been bothering him, he had been writing as fast as he could, and then he had called Olivia Reynolds, of all people, Olivia Reynolds who had apparently been achieving little despite her best efforts and who he was supposed to have let go over the summer?

This made no sense.

In hindsight, André's change of heart did not surprise Françoise as much as the fact that he had not told her about it. She remembered how conflicted he had been, how much he had wavered between terminating the student and giving her a one-semester reprieve. On paper, Olivia looked full of potential, bound to an exceptional career – André had been at a loss to explain why things had not worked out better for her. She had had difficulties understanding his previous work and he had suspected she might do better under someone else's supervision, on another research project. Or maybe she would turn out to be one of those college superstars who excelled at answering well-defined exam questions and never got used to the uncertainty of doing research. Those kept hoping for a thesis topic that would come neatly packaged with all the assumptions they would ever need, like a giant, years-long quiz, where they would prove whatever they were asked to prove and pick up their degree when they were done. But Olivia had been involved in small research projects as an undergraduate, and her supervisors had assured André that she had excelled at those. She should have thrived at M.I.T. Françoise could not blame her husband for giving her one last chance.

Dear Olivia, this is Professor Darrieux's wife writing. I am sorry to let you know that my husband suffered a stroke this morning and is now resting in the hospital. It is not clear when he will be able to meet with you.

Françoise stared at the last sentence and considered erasing it, but decided not to change a word – André always said that with students it was better to belabor the obvious. Otherwise, some might convince themselves that they were on track to graduate within a year, when in fact they had not completed half the research necessary to their thesis. It had happened before, and the story had not had a happy ending.

Françoise clicked on 'send' and leaned back in her chair.

6.

André opened his eyes. Françoise shut her book and grabbed his hand, kneeled by his side. "You're at the hospital. You had a stroke yesterday morning." She pressed his fingers. "But you're doing better now. It's going to be alright."

The man in the other bed mumbled in his sleep. André's gaze drifted along the wall. He had been transferred out of the emergency ward into the neurology department earlier in the day and while Françoise welcomed the greater privacy, she was not pleased that her husband had to share his room. But it would not last long, she kept telling herself. André would be released soon.

"Do you want more blankets or another pillow?" André gave her a blank stare. "Am I talking too fast?" He did not reply. "I guess I am. Diane warned me not to do that." Françoise pinched her lips. "I'm sorry. I'm glad you're awake."

She smiled.

André's face remained expressionless.

Did he remember what had preoccupied him in the car? Was he still worried? Françoise did not want to ask him questions until he felt better – she had spent the previous night, after she had emailed Olivia, reading on the Internet about blood clots in the brain and their after-effects, and she was determined to give André peace and quiet to speed up his recovery, although she did not believe that the sobering facts she had found online would apply to him. If athletes recovered from accidents more quickly than people who did not exercise, shouldn't André put his stroke behind him in a matter of days, weeks at most? His brain would minimize the damage. He was such an exceptional scholar.

"You gave me the scare of my life. When I saw you at your desk, I thought you were dead. Then I came to the hospital and was told you'd had a stroke. I couldn't even sleep last night because I was so upset."

André glanced at the apparatus in the room, the heart monitors and the IV drips. It was not clear that he had heard – let alone understood – what his wife had just said.

Françoise bit the inside of her cheeks.

"Hi," she tried in English, feeling very self-conscious. "Hello."

That did not help.

She rubbed her forehead with her free hand, keeping the other one on André's limp fingers, trying to hide her disappointment. Then she lowered her voice and, reverting to French, uttered the first thing that crossed her mind. "I'm your wife and we've been married for thirty-four years. Thirty-five in July."

A second went by.

The left corner of André's mouth twitched up.

Françoise gasped. She waited for a word, a whisper even, but no noise came out – she was about to doubt that she had seen André move when he raised his left hand, half an inch above the covers. Françoise hurried to the other side of the bed and clutched his wrist.

"Your right side seems asleep, but your left side is doing fine."

Tears pearled in her eyes.

She did not remember reading, because she had not thought it would matter, that the left hemisphere of the brain controlled the right side of most people's bodies and housed, among many cognitive functions, the ability to process mathematical symbols, equations, abstract formulas. She pretended not to know, because she had refused to listen when the resident had tried to tell her the bad news: this area had been severely affected by the stroke and the prognosis was not good. She did not realize that her husband's career was over. As far as she was concerned, André was awake and she would take her victories where she could.

7.

Françoise worried she would only get lost further if she kept wandering around – all these numbers confused her, and the fact that odd-numbered buildings were nowhere near even-numbered ones added to her bewilderment. She fished her cell phone out of her purse and called Evelyn.

"What do you mean, you're here?"

"I went to the library to research strokes, and then I decided to pick up papers for André before going to the hospital." She did not mention that she wanted to learn more about Olivia's project. André had not pronounced a word since he had woken up and even if he had, she would not have broached the topic with him – it was still too early, he was convalescing. But she had to find out in order to protect him from another stroke, although she did not know how she would manage that feat. "I'm on the first floor, between Building Four and Building Eight. I missed Building Six somehow, if you can believe it."

"Don't move," Evelyn said. "I'll be right down."

The students who came and went along the Infinite Corridor paid Françoise no attention, as if she blended right in – just one of many M.I.T. faculty members hurrying about. Françoise, who was terrible at all things technology-related – pored over user's manuals for hours to change the time on the television clock or the microwave – chuckled in spite of herself.

Evelyn tiptoed hurriedly on her high heels. The speed at which she moved forward more than made up for the shortness of her stride.

"You should've told me you were coming." She gave Françoise a hug.

"I'm sorry for the trouble. André showed me his office once, but I haven't been back in years. I didn't know whom else to call."

Evelyn waved the comment aside. "It's no problem at all. How is he doing?"

"Better." Françoise followed her into a side corridor, a stairwell. "He was moved out of the emergency room yesterday."

Evelyn's face brightened at the news. "I bought a get-well card, but most people have already left for Thanksgiving. They'll sign it next week." Françoise smiled while she climbed the steps.

A young woman – nineteen at most – sauntered down the stairs, notebook in arms. Evelyn waited until she had disappeared onto a lower floor to continue. "Everyone's in shock. Susanna Polits cried when she heard – she's the one who was almost denied tenure two years ago. The vote came down to the wire and André fought for her. She couldn't believe he had a stroke, kept repeating it couldn't be true. Without him she would no longer have a job here."

The two women stepped onto the third floor.

"I remember this hallway." Françoise seemed unsure, as if she would have made the same claim about any hallway she had been brought to. The corridor was empty and no noise filtered from the offices on either side, although a few had their lights on. Only the foreign students remained, and whoever did not have to travel for Thanksgiving.

"André's office is on the left. Would you like me to open the door for you?" Evelyn searched for the master key on her key chain.

They walked past the bulletin board, covered with seminar announcements and deadlines for fellowship applications. Françoise's gaze fell on the headshots of faculty members that were arranged in a glass case against the wall. She stepped closer and recognized her husband. The picture dated from a decade earlier – André wore his old pair of glasses and his hair did not show any grey.

"He looks so young there." Evelyn chuckled.

Françoise kept her eyes on the chubby, smiling face of her husband around age forty-five. "He does," she finally said. "He looks like he has his best work ahead of him."

"And he had, hadn't he? Two of his students got national awards. He received that prize from the European Physical Society."

Françoise grinned. She turned her head to the next display, which contained pictures of the graduate students with their name.

Her gaze wandered for a second, looking for someone. Then it stopped.

"What do you think of her?" Françoise pointed at the photograph of a young woman with curly, blond hair. .

"Olivia Reynolds? She's a nice girl. She puts too much pressure on herself, but she's a hard-worker."

Françoise stared at the picture, taking the news in. "What's her research about?"

"Not much at the moment, I believe." Françoise raised an eyebrow. "From what I understand, André pulled her off the project she'd been working. She says she's been reading papers and trying to find another topic since last summer. I don't have André's version of the story, though. He rarely talks to me about his students."

Françoise grinned. "So she hasn't really been doing any work, then?"

Her reaction puzzled Evelyn. "As far as I know."

Olivia could not have caused the stroke if she had nothing to upset André with. It was not her fault.

A door opened. A young, dark-haired man with a backpack and an enormous parka set a boot into the hallway but kept arguing with whoever remained inside.

"I'm telling you, he got bad news at that conference. He talked with that guy for way too long after his speech." There was a pause, most likely to let the other person answer, although Françoise could not hear a word of the reply. "Whatever it is, it's got to be huge. He had a stroke over it." The second pause was shorter. "Don't tell me those things aren't related. Maybe I should stop working on my project. Maybe he found out it's all worthless. And even if it's not, there's no one to mentor me anymore."

Evelyn's face had turned crimson. "Miguel!" she yelled. "Come and say hi to Professor Darrieux's wife."

The young man spun around, his eyes wide open, and blinked furiously. Another student poked his head out of the office.

"And Xin, you can come and say hi too." She leaned toward Françoise: "Those are André's post-docs. They were with him at the conference."

Françoise shook Miguel's hand, and then Xin's. "You saw him in San Francisco?"

Miguel nodded, shifted his weight from his left leg to the right, and then the left one again. "He gave a good talk."

"He didn't look sick on the plane," Xin said. "Very busy, though. Wrote the whole time."

"What about that person he spoke with after his speech?"

It was bad manners to show one had overheard a conversation, but Françoise could not resist asking.

Miguel cleared his throat and stared at his feet. "I don't know what they talked about. I saw them when I was going to another session after the break, and Professor Greenawalt saw them too." He made a vague gesture with his hand. "The other person was showing him something on his laptop. They must have sat there for at least twenty minutes, maybe more."

"And then he worked non-stop on the plane," Xin said. "That's not like him. When we travel, he likes to sleep. Or review papers. Nothing intense. Too many distractions, you understand."

A professor stepped out of his office – Françoise remembered seeing him at a faculty function but did not recall his name. He walked in the opposite direction and did not notice her.

"What about Olivia Reynolds?" she asked. "What does she have to do with this?"

The two post-docs glanced at each other.

"We've been asking ourselves the same question," Miguel said.

"Is she in today?"

Miguel shook his head. "She was here this morning, but she hasn't come back from lunch yet. She might have left for the long weekend. She didn't tell us about her plans." The silence dragged on. "I have to go," he added. "I was on my way out."

Françoise looked at her watch. "I don't have much time either. I have to pick my son up at the airport, and the roads are already jammed with Thanksgiving traffic."

The post-docs seemed relieved to see the meeting end. Xin returned to his office. Miguel buttoned his jacket and hurried away.

THE BREAKTHROUGH

Françoise walked to André's office – she could not pick the wrong one because her husband's name was painted across the door.

Evelyn inserted her master key into the lock. "Now, you know how he is. He feels he has more interesting things to do with his time than keeping his office neat and organized." She pushed the door open.

Françoise burst into laughter.

Manila folders were strewn about on the desk, the shelves, the floor even. The spine of a textbook added color here and there. Piles of documents – exams and handouts – had long crumbled and morphed into an ocean of paper from one corner to the next.

"This does look a lot like his home office. He doesn't let me touch a thing."

Evelyn grinned. "I don't think he uses any of this. He keeps everything in case he needs to consult his files later, but he doesn't remember where he put them." She pointed at a plant on a windowsill, which – with his large, healthy leaves and its long stems – looked like it had been left in the room by mistake. "I water the plant. That's why it's not dead. A student gave it to André when he graduated, so André doesn't want anything bad to happen to it." She paused. "Anyway, I'll be at my desk if you need me."

Françoise closed the door behind her. She had guessed, when she had seen the disarray in the room, that she would not find what she had come for, but it had been worth a try.

Since she was there, she did look for a folder labeled 'Olivia' – first a real one on the desk, then a virtual one on the hard drive of the computer – and unsurprisingly found neither. The student had not been doing any research. Her project had not worked out. André would not have bothered creating a folder about her unless she had had results to show for her work. Françoise dusted off the monitor with her sleeve, pushed the bread crumbs off the keypad (she had told André not to eat at his desk but he had not listened) and then stacked loose sheets of paper into a pile. They all contained information on her husband's studies, one way or another, but they were neither titled nor numbered and it was impossible to guess which ones – if any – held a clue to his stroke, his reason for calling Olivia on Monday morning.

Françoise sighed. The yellow notepad remained her best bet, although she could not decipher the equations it contained. Bernard's flight would land at the airport in less than an hour and she had no answers to the questions in her head.

She turned the lights off, waved at Evelyn as she walked by her office.

"Did you find what you were looking for?"

Françoise was unsure of how much to say. "Not really."

She must not have hidden her disappointment well, because Evelyn smiled and opened the top drawer of her desk. "Would you like to see the card? I can't give it to you right now, but you can have a sneak peek."

It was one of those cards people bought in crafts stores, with elaborate paper cut-outs on the cover and beautiful lettering. Françoise was pleased by Evelyn's choice. She held the card carefully, afraid to leave a smudge over the good wishes. *Get well soon. You're in my thoughts. I know you'll get through this. It's just a bump in the road.* Olivia had written: *Let me know if I can help.*

Françoise handed the card back to Evelyn, her fingers trembling a bit. "I don't understand why it happened. I really want to understand, but I don't know why."

"Maybe there's no reason." Evelyn pushed a box of tissues toward her.

Françoise pushed the box back.

"You heard his students. There's a reason, and I'm going to find it."

8.

"Hi, Dad. Mom says you're doing better."

André's eyes moved toward the voice. He showed no sign of recognizing the young man in front of him.

"Diane thinks it might help if you speak more slowly."

Bernard dragged a chair by the bed, turned his head toward his mother. "Enough with that nurse."

"She gives me good advice. She drops by all the time to see how André's doing."

Bernard leant toward his father, elbows on his thighs, right hand clasped over left fist. "I just arrived. We came straight from the airport."

He did make an effort to detach all the syllables. A smile fluttered on Françoise's lips.

Bernard wore his Harvard sweatshirt with a pair of jeans – he preferred comfortable clothes when he traveled, the kind of clothes that would not be ruined if he spilled his drink on himself in the middle of weather disturbances, although his mother disapproved of such attire. Twenty-nine-year-old French men did not go around in jogging clothes, except when they actually went jogging. But Bernard was more American than French, and Françoise had never become used to his casualness.

André's gaze drifted over the seven white letters on the crimson shirt. He did not seem to connect them to an actual word, a real-life entity, which happened to be the place where his son had gone to college and later attended business school. Françoise had dropped by the hospital that same morning, though, to prepare him for the visit. *Your son will be here later today…* She was not sure he had understood. Since the stroke, André had not reacted once to anything she had said.

"You'll get through this. It's going to be fine." Bernard choked on the last word.

The woman sitting by the other patient's bed shifted in her seat and whispered to her husband. Françoise glared at her. Couldn't she stay quiet? Didn't she see they were busy? But her reaction had little to do with noise. Instead, she resented the woman's husband for being older than André, and more alert – he nodded when his wife talked, uttered words once in a while. Françoise had hoped at first that they were grunts, but she had heard him ask for the time, and a glass of water. His forehead was lined with wrinkles. His hair was grey. Françoise gave him at least seventy years. And that man, André's senior by a decade and a half, sat up in bed by himself, ate lunch without help, conversed with his wife.

"We shouldn't stay much longer. We don't want him to get tired."

"Gotta go, Dad. But we'll be back tomorrow, alright? We'll sneak in some turkey for you."

"We'll put everything in plastic containers and have our little feast here, together, the three of us." Françoise made a big smile. "Won't that be fun?"

The other patient's wife glanced at André but he did not react. Mind your own business, Françoise wanted to snap at her. She felt the woman's gaze on her back as she exited the room.

A strong odor of detergent lingered in the hallway. A janitor who was cleaning the floor stepped aside when Françoise and Bernard walked by, careful not to slip.

"You didn't tell me it was that bad."

Françoise shrugged. "He had a stroke. He's not going to be up and about two days later." A doctor hurried past them, with a nurse following closely behind. Françoise called the elevator. "Wait until he's had a couple weeks of therapy and he'll be as good as new."

"I think it's going to take a bit longer than that."

Bernard spoke French with a slight accent, drawing his words while he searched for the next ones. Françoise rolled her eyes.

"Your French isn't getting any better."

"Mom." The two of them walked through the lobby, headed toward the glass doors. Françoise avoided looking at the people huddled in the waiting area. A baby wailed. Bernard shook his head. "What are you going to do when Christmas comes and Dad's still in the hospital?"

Françoise glared at her son. "How dare you give up on your father like that." Her voice had turned into a hiss.

"Lots of people need months to recover after a stroke. They go to rehab. That's part of the process."

They strode toward the garage on Parkman Street. A gust of wind bit their cheeks – Bernard shivered in the jacket he had brought from San Diego. He usually borrowed one of his father's coats when he visited his parents during the winter but Françoise had forgotten to grab one before leaving the house. She had had so many other things on her mind.

"I could come with you and visit nursing homes while I'm here, if you want."

Françoise stopped in the middle of the sidewalk. "André's not going to a nursing home. He's going back to his own home, where I'll take care of him, just like I've done for the past three decades and a half."

A passer-by glanced at Françoise and Bernard but kept walking.

"You can't handle all this by yourself, Mom."

"Don't tell me what I cannot handle. You're never even there."

A cab pulled over by the taxi stand. A young woman with curly hair stepped out, the white earphones of an iPod disappearing under her coat. She tucked her chin into her scarf and hurried toward the hospital.

Françoise frowned. "I've seen that woman before."

The stranger disappeared into the building.

Bernard let out a yawn. His flight had left San Diego at half past six in the morning, stopped in Arizona before continuing to Boston, and he had not been able to sleep. Françoise started walking again.

The two of them crossed the street and made their way to the parking garage's second floor. Row after row of compact cars, SUVs, station-wagons stretched in front of them. A pickup truck sported half a dozen stickers on its rear bumper, which made Bernard laugh. There was no beat-up Volvo in sight.

"Do you remember where I parked the car?"

Bernard shook his head. "We might be one floor up."

An old-model BMW drove past them, maneuvered into a slot. The driver turned off the engine and placed a parking ticket in his wallet.

Françoise sighed. "We forgot to validate parking."

"Give me the ticket. I'll take care of it while you look for the car."

"You've got to pay at the pay station on the first floor. It is on the right outside the stairwell." She handed him the ticket.

"I'll be back in a minute."

Bernard had not made more than five steps when Françoise shrieked. He turned around. His mother had covered her mouth with her hand.

"I know who that woman is. It's Olivia Reynolds. We've got to go back. Who knows how André is going to react when he sees her?"

"What are you talking about?"

Françoise was already rushing toward the hospital and Bernard had no choice but to follow along.

"She's one of your father's students. André called her as soon as his flight landed, apparently. I've never seen him as preoccupied as he was during the drive home. Something happened at that conference, and it has to do with her work." Françoise threw herself in the middle of moving traffic, ran between cars to cross the street faster. "Except that she has done nothing besides making mistakes, and he almost fired her last summer." She stumbled on a step by the hospital entrance but Bernard stopped her fall. They dashed through the lobby, Bernard slightly ahead, Françoise running out of breath behind him. "So maybe it doesn't have to do with her work, but she's linked to your father's stroke somehow." Two residents stepped out of the elevator, stethoscopes slung around their neck. Bernard reached the elevator first and blocked the door while his mother staggered in behind him. "What if he has another stroke when she shows up?"

"I don't think that's how strokes work, Mom."

"You don't know how strokes work any better than I do."

Bernard rolled his eyes. "What did Dad tell that student on Monday?"

"He didn't talk to her. He left her a message saying he wanted to meet."

"Then I bet she has no clue what's going on either."

"She knows something. And if there's a reason why your father has turned into this," she made a vague gesture with her hand, "I want to know what it is."

The doors opened on the neurology floor. Françoise charged toward her husband's room.

The other patient's wife looked surprised when she saw her. There was no other visitor.

Françoise panted. "Didn't a young woman come by?"

The woman nodded. "You just missed her. She only stayed for a minute." She eyed Françoise with curiosity while the latter collapsed onto the chair by André's bed. "Are you alright, honey?"

Her husband, his eyes open, breathed normally. The heart monitors displayed their usual wave pattern. André was exactly as Françoise had left him. Bernard chuckled with relief.

"I don't think he recognized her," the woman added. "She asked him how he was doing but he didn't reply. She said she hoped he'd feel better soon, and then they could talk about research. And then she left."

"She said that? That they could talk about research?" Françoise gaped in horror. "How did he react?"

The woman pursed her lips, obviously embarrassed. "He didn't. He didn't give any sign that he understood what she said."

Françoise struggled to regain her composure. "That's good. Thank you." She glanced at her husband again, calm, awake and perfectly unresponsive in his hospital bed. "We're going for good now, sweetheart." She forced herself to smile. "Get some rest. We'll see you tomorrow."

9.

"Things are alright."

Olivia plucked a morsel of turkey from her plate.

"How are your classes?"

"They're fine."

"She doesn't take that many classes any more. In graduate school you do mostly research."

The grandmother gave her son a blank stare, nodded anyway. Michael had told her several times what research was about, and yet she looked as confused as the afternoon after Commencement at the University of New Mexico, when Olivia had explained that she would stay in school a bit longer to think about physics problems that had not been solved before. Rosemary had asked her husband: didn't youngsters need real, concrete skills to succeed in the world today? Thinking about unsolved problems seemed awfully self-indulgent for someone who had lived through the Great Depression. Surely Olivia could find a well-paying job that did not require seven more years of schooling. That was what grown-ups did, in the grandmother's world.

Things were different in science, Michael had explained – there, no one would take a chance on you until you had proved your worth, and you proved your worth by earning a doctorate. In fact, if he had had the opportunity, he would gladly have done one himself. It would all pay off in the end. He knew, because he watched NOVA on PBS and bought all the books on popular science he could lay his hands on. He had offered Olivia a gift subscription to *Scientific American*, but generally read the magazine before she did. When she had moved to Cambridge, Olivia had not had the heart to update her address and deprive her father from his favorite reading material. Everything science-related fascinated him, but he was particularly intrigued by theoretical physics, and the question whether the forces of Nature could be unified in one elegant, deep, insightful "theory of everything." He had taught Olivia the standard model of particle physics when she was a teenager – the model that unified three of the four forces – although she had quickly understood quarks and gauge theories better than he ever could.

"Our little whiz kid." The grandfather smiled. "So how is your research going?"

"It's going okay." Olivia poured gravy on her vegetables.

The family was seated at Elizabeth's dining table. Olivia's parents had moved to Santa Fe after their only child's graduation from college and the sun-filled room, with its paintings and artifacts, its water fountain on the coffee table and its statue of the Buddha (her mother's, of course), bore no resemblance with the one Olivia had known when they were living in Albuquerque. She did not even have her own room anymore – she slept in the guest bedroom, suitably decorated to please any visitor. Her mother had stuffed her belongings into storage boxes and shoved them into a closet, where they remained, two years after the move.

This was no longer her home. She was on her own.

"Are you getting your proposal ready? Did you put your committee together?"

"Dad, you know I would've told you if I had."

Students did not "propose" – did not present their research topic to their doctoral committee – unless they had enough preliminary results to be confident they would not change directions along the way. Olivia did not have a research topic, let alone preliminary results.

"Don't wait too long."

Olivia shrugged. "There's no rush, Dad. I've got plenty of time."

She had not cared about her parents selling the house until the previous summer, when Darrieux had advised her to find another research group, another supervisor, and possibly another line of work. The latter he might not have meant – he had been angry when they had met. But it had occurred to her that, were she to leave Cambridge, she would have no place to come home to.

"You must have a topic by now. What's your dissertation about?"

Olivia impaled green beans on her fork. "It's a secret. My research advisor doesn't want me to talk about it until we're sure it works." She stuffed the beans into her mouth and chewed as slowly as possible.

Rosemary opened her eyes wide. Michael chuckled. "That's my girl, working on classified work!"

"That's not what she said." Elizabeth shook her head. "You always interpret things."

"Her advisor doesn't want her to talk about it because the project sponsor requires them to keep quiet. That's the way things work over there. Federal agencies want to know the impact their discovery will have on national security." Michael could not resist coming to his daughter's defense. Olivia took after him, with her round face and her big, brown eyes – guests always found the resemblance between them striking. Of her mother she was supposed to have the forehead, or perhaps the nose. A few friends of the family insisted they had the same chin.

"She's twenty-five and paid close to nothing, all that for the privilege to do research on a topic without any practical usefulness whatsoever." Elizabeth sighed. "In the meantime, people her age are getting married and moving up at work and signing their first mortgage papers."

Olivia emptied her glass of water in one long, drawn-out gulp.

The grandfather finally grinned from the end of the table, where he presided over the gathering. "She'll make good money once she's won the Nobel Prize."

Michael chuckled. "My thoughts exactly."

They said it as a joke, making it easy to dismiss their comments as the banter of overly proud relatives, but one suspected they were not kidding.

Olivia stared at the bottom of her glass. Her mother had bought new furniture after the move (a new sofa, new coffee table, new television), but she had kept everything she had had in the kitchen for some unknown reason – the one thing Olivia had paid no attention to when she lived in Albuquerque. That glass was at least ten years old.

"She would've made a good lawyer, though. She could've gone into patent law, or intellectual property. That would've been perfect for her, given her interests."

"And I'll make a good scientist." Olivia paused. "I am a good scientist." She scooped up a large serving of sweet potatoes.

Her mother rolled her eyes.

Olivia dumped the potatoes on her plate. "Research doesn't happen in a day, alright? Give me three months and I'll make a discovery that will floor every single one of you."

Her father beamed. It took a few seconds for Olivia to realize the enormity of what she had just said.

Elizabeth took a sip of wine. "I'll be looking forward to that."

Claire opened the door to the apartment and, finding the lights on, yelled to her roommate: "I'm back!"

Olivia was sprawled in front of the television with a bowl of cereals on her lap. "Hi there." She had thrown her jacket on the couch and was still wearing her boots.

"When did you arrive?"

"An hour ago."

Claire pushed her suitcase inside her room with her foot, washed her hands in the kitchenette.

"How was your trip?"

"Not so good." Olivia munched on a handful of Cheerios. "I didn't tell my parents about the stroke."

Claire wiped her hands on a towel. "Maybe it was too early. If Darrieux gets better soon, you'll feel stupid for worrying them."

"I went to the hospital on Wednesday after you left. Couldn't stay long because of my flight, but I saw him. He's not going to get better, let me tell you that. At least not better enough to go back to work."

"That bad?"

Olivia, her eyes on the television set, made a quick nod. "He can't speak, doesn't move, doesn't even remember me. And the only thing I could think about in New Mexico was, if I tell my mother she's going to laugh to my face and say: bad karma, you should've gone to law school."

The program was interrupted by a string of commercials. Claire returned to the kitchenette, opened a cupboard, and grabbed a bottle of whisky with two glasses.

"Extraordinary circumstances call for extraordinary drinking."

Olivia chuckled but waved her friend away. "I'm meeting with someone from the *Boston Globe* tomorrow. Can't be hung over."

"What's the meeting for?"

Olivia shrugged. "I'm not sure. A journalist emailed me over the break, saying he wanted to talk about Darrieux. I don't know why I accepted. I don't even know how he found me. I guess he's talking to everyone in the lab and I figured, he might as well talk to me too." She moved over on the couch to let Claire sit down. "I don't have anything to say, though. I don't even want to talk about Darrieux to begin with."

Claire poured the drinks, neat. "Then you're really going to need something to cheer you up."

Olivia took a gulp and winced. "It wasn't supposed to turn out like this, you know? I was going to make important discoveries and contribute to the advancement of science and all that."

She kept, quite predictably, a biography of Marie Curie on her shelves, all dog-eared from being read multiple times since her twelfth birthday, when her father had given her the book. In high school, she had won prize after prize at the science fairs. In college, she had been inducted into Sigma Pi Sigma – the physics honor society – graduated *summa cum laude*, conducted experiments for one of her professors and seen the results published. She had considered joining Teach for America after graduation, but that would have meant a two-year break to teach math or physics in low-income neighborhoods before going back to school, and her father had talked her out of it. She would forget much of the material she had studied in college, he had warned her, and it would hurt her ability to write a first-rate thesis. Now she served as an officer for the Boston chapter of the Graduate Women in Science group and tutored undergraduates. She had goals, worthy ones, that would serve the general public, yearned to leave her mark on the world, and it seemed so unfair – or at least counter-productive – to deprive her of that opportunity. Shouldn't her good intentions count for something?

"It'll happen eventually."

"I never thought about what it'd mean to spend twenty-six years straight in school, and I'm not even talking about doing a post-doc at this point."

Claire did the math and frowned. "You won't spend seven more years in school."

"Maybe I will. I need to find a new advisor. I have to start from scratch." Olivia put the empty bowl aside, leaned back on the couch and wrapped her hands around her knees. "Seven more years is not that outlandish, and I don't even know if it'll be worth it."

A door slammed in the hallway. The movie had resumed but neither Claire nor Olivia was paying it any attention.

"Maybe it's a sign, you know? Maybe graduate school isn't for me. Research isn't for me. I didn't want to admit it last summer, and look at the mess I'm in now." Olivia emptied her glass and poured herself another drink.

"We all face hurdles along the way. You're just facing a bigger-than-average one."

"Maybe bad things will keep hitting me in the face until I get it. It was a mistake not to go to law school."

Other female students labored on their doctorate throughout the country, hoped to become professors too. Some would encourage girls to study science, whether Olivia succeeded or not – in the grand scheme of things, she did not matter at all.

"Darrieux didn't have a stroke so you could see the light." Claire kicked her shoes off. "Bad stuff happens. Don't go looking for meaning when there's none."

Olivia looked dubious.

"I'm so mad at myself. If I'd picked another advisor, I'd be more than halfway done by now, or at least getting close."

The two roommates drank in silence, while the detective shot at the hit men who had been sent to kill him.

"I can't decide if I'm more upset at myself or at Darrieux," Olivia said once the hero had escaped his assailants.

"For having a stroke?"

"For letting me spend three years in his lab without anything to show for it." Claire sipped her whisky without a word. "For trying to kick me out too, but that's not the point. I would've nailed all the proofs a long time ago if he had advised me better. You don't let people trudge along for years with little guidance and then announce it's not going to work out."

"People have different advising styles. Some are more hands-off than others." Claire got up. "I should get something to eat before I drink some more. I'm going to be sick if I don't." She poured a bag of crackers onto a plate, retrieved a box of salsa from the fridge. Olivia nursed her glass of whisky on the couch. Her sullen expression was quickly turning into a scowl.

"I feel so used," she said when Claire came back. "Taken advantage of."

She could see, now, how she had been duped – how Darrieux had not cared one bit about her work – and that wasn't right. No it wasn't. She had hoped to accomplish great things, push back the frontiers of knowledge by joining his lab. She had weighed her options carefully. She had studied professors' publishing record on their department's websites and met with faculty members during Admits Weekend, when she had flown to Cambridge in March of her senior year. She was determined to work with someone established in his career but still on an upward trajectory, someone excited to come to work every morning, who would teach her the ropes and help her get started in her own career – someone who would mentor her and help her thrive. And she had convinced herself that Darrieux would play that role: surely, the great man would be thrilled to count such a capable student on his team. He had been so kind to her that weekend in March, giving her advice even though she had not yet accepted M.I.T.'s offer, suggesting papers she could read, offering to answer by email any questions she might have after the trip.

Olivia had arrived in Boston on a humid August afternoon with the intention to change the world, and fallen flat on her face.

"Darrieux was happy to waste my time when I didn't cost him a penny, and then once he had used up all my fellowship money, he couldn't get rid of me fast enough."

Claire dipped a cracker into the salsa. "He didn't, though. He changed his mind. And you got along well with him until last summer."

"You know what he was?" Olivia felt a bit dizzy from drinking too much alcohol in a short period of time. "A slave-driver. A pathetic slave-driver, and I'm glad he got a stroke. He deserved it."

10.

If Olivia had been honest with her mother, she would have told her that her research involved supersymmetry. The idea behind it was that each elementary particle that carried a force – each boson – could be associated to a particle that made up matter – a fermion – and vice-versa. Physicists had yet to observe the partners of the elementary particles they knew about, though, and the approximations they used to wrestle some sense out of their models led to five related, but different, "theories of everything." The world people lived in could only be governed by one model and, after a series of discoveries in the nineteen nineties had reinvigorated the field, André Darrieux had devoted most of his energy to finding the right one. His research group had tried to improve the approximations used by the rest of the community to eliminate some of the five models from consideration. The endeavor had proved fruitless, despite students' valiant efforts (Sergey pretended to have been much closer to a breakthrough than his labmates were willing to believe), and had marked the nadir of André's career. It was 1995; he was forty-nine and his research had stalled. But the second "revolution" in his field had given him another chance to leave his mark and, following a sudden trip to Lyon in the middle of the semester, he had redirected his group's research toward the eleven-dimensional spacetime postulated by string theory and the objects that populated it.

That had been a masterful idea.

In string theory, strings replaced point particles as the building blocks of theoretical physics. This idea had proved very popular with the general public, who found it amusing – in the popular press, all strings looked like spaghetti. André had wondered whether more complex quantities also came into play, with two, three or even more dimensions in a universe that counted so many, although the majority of those were invisible to the naked eye. With the help of his senior doctoral student, André had then showed that the theory indeed required the existence of such objects. The graduate student had called them branes, an abbreviation of the word "membranes." The name had stuck. Peter Neumann had ultimately won a prize for his dissertation, which suggested a connection between two types of theories of interest to researchers: string theories and gauge theories. This had taken the scientific community by surprise because the latter did not incorporate gravity but the former did. Perhaps a theory of everything had suddenly become within reach.

Under André's supervision, Matthew Johnson had then investigated the link between the two concepts in more detail. He had conjectured, and finally proved, the correspondence between a string theory defined on a certain type of curved space and a quantum field theory without gravity defined on the boundary of that space. His findings had brought gravity dramatically closer to the other forces, and offered promising techniques to study topics such as black holes and cosmology. Researchers sensed this deep, hidden connection would mark the beginning of a novel era. Pete's approach had aroused interest, but Matt's had truly broken new ground. It was thanks to both of them that André was rumored to be a serious contender for the Nobel Prize.

André had presented Matt's work at the conference.

11.

"I'm writing a feature on your husband, and I was wondering if you'd mind being interviewed."

Françoise thought about it for a second. "I'd rather wait until André gets better, if that's alright with you."

She did not ask the man how he had learnt about the stroke. That seemed to be what journalists did and she was not overly surprised by the phone call. Someone in the physics department must have told the *Boston Globe*. André was a prominent scholar, an impending Nobel-Prize winner – if she had worked in the news business, she would have found the story intriguing too. Although she had not intended to publicize her husband's medical problems, she was pleased that the world had taken notice.

Her decision was met by a long silence at the other end of the line.

"We're going to print in a few days. I think it'd be good to include your perspective. Of course, if you prefer to stay out of it, I'll just write about what your husband's colleagues and students said. That's perfectly fine." The man's tone indicated it was not. "I understand it's a difficult time for you. You might want to show us the more humane side of your husband, though. That'd make him a more likable figure."

Françoise pinched her lips.

At her door Jim Calloway looked harmless. He stood about an inch shorter than her and while André made up for his own lack of height with a heavy built and a well-regarded intellect, the journalist – slender, short and smiling – did not come across as the veteran Françoise had expected to find on her doorstep. Jim greeted her with a feeble handshake she would have advised her clients against, if she had become a therapist. Couldn't he at least play the part, fake confidence in his own abilities? She struggled to hide her disappointment. André deserved better.

Françoise showed Jim inside, hunching to keep one hand on Buddy's collar. Jim made a point of wiping his boots on the doormat, although the sidewalks had long been cleared of any melting snow.

"Would you like something to drink?"

She strolled into the kitchen with Buddy on her heels, prepared the cappuccinos and removed the pumpkin pie from the oven – still warm but not too hot. She had not forgiven the reporter for his words on the phone (that was not a way to talk to the wife of a famous researcher, especially under the circumstances), and she took her time arranging cups and plates on a tray.

When she returned, Jim had sat down by the coffee table – in the one armchair that allowed him a full, unobstructed view of the living-room. Françoise grinned when she saw him there. That was exactly where she had hoped he would sit. She had dusted off the family pictures on the mantelpiece, borrowed frames from the bedroom – André carrying four-year-old Bernard during a trip to Disneyland, dressed as Batman for Halloween with his ten-year-old son as Robin, holding one side of the teenager's high school diploma while Bernard held the other one. From the seat he had chosen, the reporter could not fail to notice André's devotion to his child. Françoise had also placed his books within arm's reach, spine out, to showcase her husband's broad range of interests – not every French-born physicist read about American statesmen and the Vietnam War and Lyndon Johnson's role in the civil rights movement. The journalist would be impressed. Didn't he find André much more likable already?

"How is your husband doing?"

"A lot better. He was moved out of the I.C.U. a few days ago."

"I'm glad to hear that."

Jim's voice was flat, but he seemed to mean what he had said. He placed a digital recorder on the table and asked Françoise to state her name.

"Françoise Darrieux."

The reporter chuckled. "I wouldn't have pronounced it quite that way." He paused. "I took four years of French in high school and don't remember a thing. I mean, I can still say '*bonjour*' and '*comment allez-vous*', but that's about it."

His hostess nodded with an indulgent smile. "That's a good start."

Buddy lay down at her feet but kept his eyes on the table, as if the pumpkin pie would fall from the edge if he stared hard enough.

The journalist cleared his throat. "As I told you on the phone, I'd like to get a better sense of what your husband is like outside work. I think it'd be interesting to compare that with the image he gives at M.I.T."

Françoise did not take the bait, did not inquire about the image the man was referring to. She put her cup down. "At home André spends most of his time in his study, editing papers for his students or preparing slides for his talks." Her face brightened. "He's a bit of a perfectionist." Jim scribbled something on his notepad. Françoise pointed at the volumes piled up by the man's elbow. "When he does relax, though, he likes history books." André had finished them years earlier but the journalist did not need to know that. He had loved those books, especially the biography of Harry Truman that she had placed on top of the pile, and they helped give a better sense of him. "Have you read that book by David McCullough? André speaks highly of it."

Jim glanced at the book but did not take notes. "What else does he like to do?"

"He listens to classical music. Mostly Beethoven. But not any Beethoven, mind you." Françoise could not resist sharing details about her husband, although she had promised herself she would remain on her guard. "If he decides to listen to the Fifth Symphony, for instance, he needs the recording by the Wiener Philharmoniker for Deutsche Grammophon, with Carlos Kleiber conducting. Only the best." She chuckled.

"That goes along with his perfectionism, doesn't it?"

Françoise's opinion of the journalist leapt upward. "Yes, indeed. I guess that's why I never converted him to opera. If we lived in New York, he would be a regular at Lincoln Center, but if he can't go to the Met, he's not that interested." She frowned. "Is your drink too hot?"

Jim had barely touched his cappuccino.

"No, it's fine. It's very good."

André had bought her a state-of-the-art coffee machine that rivaled the equipment in French *cafés*. Didn't the man notice the better taste? the stronger smell? In the States, freshly-brewed coffee had no smell, and so little taste, in the big Styrofoam cups baristas poured it into.

"It's excellent, really." Jim took a gulp and pointed at the photographs in her back. "Is that your son?"

Françoise glanced behind her shoulder, as if she was not sure.

"Yes, it is."

"How old is he now?"

"Twenty-nine."

"Oh." The journalist gave the pictures a hard look.

"We haven't framed the more recent ones yet."

The truth was, Françoise had taken all the recent ones down after learning of Bernard's relocation to San Diego. Her son had retrenched behind the platitudes of a unique job opportunity and a short-term move (he did not plan to stay in California forever), but it was obvious to Françoise that he had wanted to put some distance between him and his father – she still resented him for that. All that talk about proving himself and having responsibilities given to few people his age rang hollow. He could have proved himself in the Boston area. He did not have to move.

Jim re-read his notes. "You were saying, your husband's a perfectionist. That must be reflected in the way he interacts with students, right?"

I know what you're getting at, Françoise thought.

"He expects the best of them. That's very empowering for young people, to have someone display so much confidence in their abilities." She took another sip of cappuccino. "Most people who achieve any kind of success in life met early on someone who believed in them and showed them the way." Jim tapped his pencil against the notebook. Françoise resented his frown. "He's opened doors for them, helped them obtain post-doctoral fellowships and faculty positions. I'm told the letters of recommendation he writes carry a lot of weight." André had explained the process to her many times over the years, and she sounded like she knew what she was talking about.

"So his students' future depends on his writing a good letter."

Françoise nodded. "It makes sense, when you think about it. He's the person who spends by far the most time with them. He knows better than anyone whether they have a chance of making it on their own or not."

"That must frighten students, to have someone hold so much power over them."

Françoise shrugged. "It's like that everywhere. If you want to get a doctorate, your advisor must agree to sign the dissertation. That's a lot of power right there."

Jim tried the pumpkin pie at last and seemed to enjoy it, chewing slowly, taking his time. Buddy's ears pointed up.

"Is it true that when a student is about to graduate, he has become the true expert in his topic, more knowledgeable even than his own advisor?"

"That's possible." Françoise looked skeptical. "The advisor knows more about a broader range of fields, though."

"But in this one narrow topic, the advisor does come to rely on his student for insights, doesn't he? After all, the student spent all these hours on the project, struggling with proofs, trying methods that didn't work. What ends up in the dissertation is only the tip of the iceberg."

A truck rumbled down the street. Buddy raised his head, lowered it back onto Françoise's foot.

"Maybe."

"So what happens when the dissertation is ready, but the advisor wants to take advantage of the student's expertise a little while longer?"

Someone had told him about Pete.

"I don't know." Françoise smiled. "Usually the dissertation isn't ready, but the student convinces himself it is because he wants to leave. Then he complains when his advisor doesn't see it that way."

THE BREAKTHROUGH

"But what makes a dissertation ready? I mean, you can't hope that one student will solve all the open problems in the world. Research never ends. What makes a specific dissertation ready?"

Françoise's smile hardened. "You need to have a claim that can stand on its own. As long as your advisor can poke holes in your theory, you have to keep working."

André had used these exact words in his letter to the department chair, refuting Pete's allegations with more care, Françoise felt, than Pete had spent on thinking his arguments through. How did he dare attacking her husband, who had spent countless hours by his side? André maintained he was not hurt – those things happened, he often said, and Pete had a history of not handling setbacks well. The storm had been brewing for a long time. Françoise found his reaction hard to believe, though. He should have felt betrayed – she certainly did. André taught students everything he knew, assigned them to cutting-edge projects, helped them get jobs at top universities when they graduated. They owed him their careers. He did not deserve to become the target of baseless attacks. Those students were his academic children.

The department chair had ruled that André should have clarified his expectations but did not have to sign the thesis if he did not find it met his standards. Pete had earned his doctorate one year later. Every evening during those twelve months, André had braced himself for scratches on his car doors, slashes on his tires, broken eggs on his windshield when he approached the Volvo in M.I.T.'s parking lot. But Pete had behaved. His dissertation had even won an award in the end, although by then he had left academia and had not bothered to claim his prize. He worked for a consulting company now, where he made no use whatsoever of his training in theoretical physics but hopefully impressed clients with his analytical skills.

Every single faculty member in the department knew about his accusations, and most of the students too.

Jim reached toward the pumpkin pie. "Do you mind?" He grabbed another slice. Buddy wagged his tail – that dog always wanted to eat. "Don't you think it's possible that your husband pushed one of his students too hard and the kid crumbled under pressure? For instance, that he cut corners to graduate and made up some results?"

Pete! André will never forgive you.

Françoise leaned over the table, her gaze hard. "Mr. Calloway, I have no idea what his students did or didn't do, but I can tell you my husband cares about them a lot. He wants them to do the very best work he knows they're capable of. He doesn't push them too hard. If you want proof, you should ask former members of his group. I can give you names, if you'd like."

"That would be very helpful." Calloway smiled.

Françoise marched into the study. Buddy hesitated for a second but stayed by the table, holding watch over the pumpkin pie. Françoise fetched half a dozen dissertations from the shelves and dropped the books in front of her guest. "If you need more, just let me know."

"I'm sure that'll clear everything up." Jim shared his slice of pie with the dog.

"I think he's had enough." Françoise dragged Buddy to her side of the table.

Jim stretched out his hand to let the dog grab one last bite. Françoise pursed her lips. She had looked him up on the Internet and read one of his recent articles, about the attitude of Boston chefs toward trans-fat. The topic had struck her as pedestrian for someone writing about a M.I.T. professor and Nobel-Prize hopeful, but she had reasoned that he would use his latest assignment to gain respect from his more established colleagues, the ones who eyed Pulitzer Prizes and reprints in the *Best American Science Writing*. Maybe his article would surpass anything the *Globe*'s star reporters could have written, because André's story would matter more to him, would have more of an impact on his advancement prospects.

Sitting face to face with the journalist in her living-room, Françoise scolded herself for her naïveté. That man would never, ever write the story André deserved.

"People who saw him in California said your husband appeared agitated toward the end of the conference. Any idea what that was about?"

THE BREAKTHROUGH

Without the slightest hesitation, Françoise fed an enormous slice of pumpkin pie to the dog. She had not known others had witnessed André's odd behavior. She had not known it had lasted that long.

Buddy rose and sat upright by the table, thrilled by his luck, waiting for more.

"No," Françoise said, both to the dog and the journalist.

Jim leant back in his chair, eyes on his notes. A frown barred his forehead again – that was not a good sign. He finally looked up. "Do you think your husband is a slave-driver?"

"I beg your pardon?"

Françoise had raised her voice in surprise. The dog barked.

"That's the expression I've heard used about him. Do you think he is?"

"Of course not. That's ridiculous. Nobody in their right mind would ever call my husband a slave-driver." She struggled for words that would convey the full extent of her outrage. "He's devoted to his students. They're like family to him."

Buddy edged closer to the table, lurked by the dish for a second or two, and then snatched a slice of pie before Françoise had a chance to pull him back.

Françoise shrieked. Calloway laughed. "You should take it as a compliment. He really loves your cooking." The dog licked his chops.

"He's acting out because André isn't here. He usually behaves better than this."

Jim finished eating under the dog's watchful eye. "Don't you wonder why your husband was acting so bizarrely at the conference, whether it triggered the stroke?"

Françoise shrugged. "We'll have to ask him when he gets better." She was relieved the journalist did not pursue the 'slave-driver' angle. That sounded like something a student would say – a young, immature, disgruntled student – and she did not want to think about one of André's protégés badmouthing him to a journalist while he lay in the hospital, unable to defend himself. They were like family, for God's sake.

"If I could figure out why he was so preoccupied, my readers would get a better sense of what matters to him. We'd understand so much more."

"I wish I could help" – Françoise pretended to mean that – "but André never discusses his work with me. He knows there's no point. He'd be speaking a foreign language, as far as I'm concerned."

"What about his study? Could I see it?"

"Of course, but he didn't have the time to do anything before the stroke. He just sat down and slumped forward. He didn't even turn his computer on."

"Did he bring any papers back with him from the conference?"

"No, nothing." Françoise folded her hands on her lap and made a wistful smile. "André keeps a lot in his head. His memory is better than most."

12.

The Darrieuxs arrived in Cambridge on a hot, humid afternoon in August of 1971. They had been married for five weeks and viewed the trip as their honeymoon – an interlude in an exotic place before they resumed their life in France. André had applied to graduate school on his professors' advice but doubted that he would be admitted; the acceptance letter had come as a shock. A research assistantship would cover his tuition and living expenses, provided that he work for the faculty member who had signed at the bottom of the page. André had never heard of Hans-Hermann Walzenberger but the opportunity had seemed too good to pass up. The fact that both André and Françoise spoke mediocre English did not matter – he understood the language well enough to write a thesis and she stuffed her suitcases with French paperbacks.

As it turned out, Walzenberger was a thirty-four-year-old wunderkind with a baby face, who had joined the faculty the previous fall and had yet to advise a single graduate student.

"He's young."

André did not mean that as a compliment. In France, professors needed to do research by themselves or with senior colleagues for years before they earned the right to supervise theses. When they finally did, they looked much older than their students and a lot more knowledgeable.

"I'm sure he's very qualified. M.I.T. wouldn't have hired him otherwise."

Françoise and André were walking toward Central Square, where they had been told they would find cheap hardware stores. Their studio lacked lamps, shelves, dishes, and – more importantly – it lacked fans in the sweltering late-summer heat.

"He writes a lot on the board, hops from one corner to the next. And he speaks so fast I can barely understand him."

"It's better if he writes, then." Françoise smiled.

They stopped at the intersection with Main Street, hurried to the other side when they saw a gap in traffic.

"He figures things out on the fly, right there, in front of me. I'm the one who's supposed to figure things out."

"He's just trying to help you get started."

"How can he help me if he's about my age?"

"You're blowing this out of proportion. He's ten years older than you."

Françoise walked close to the buildings to stay in the shade, waved her map in her face to get a bit of fresh air. In Lyon, summers were hot and dry – 'heavy' was the word people used. The heat overwhelmed you, oppressed you, but did not make you sweat. She had not understood how summers could be humid until she had stepped out of Logan Airport.

"He even wants me to call him Hans. Can you believe that?"

"Americans are more casual. It's a cultural thing."

"People shouldn't call professors by their first name. We're not friends." André shook his head.

"Don't call him Hans if you don't want to." Françoise wiped her brow. "Nobody's forcing you."

They walked in silence along the rows of decrepit houses and vacant lots. A patron was enjoying a late lunch in the diner by Brookline Street. Two students carried a chest of drawers, stopping every few steps to rest their arms, while others stumbled back to their dorm with household items stacked up to their chin. Françoise's new sandals were hurting her feet. A homeless man sitting against a fence held out a baseball cap in her direction – he could not have been older than twenty-five but was missing a leg. Françoise clutched André's arm and stared straight ahead. To her dismay, André slowed down, unrolled a one-dollar bill and dropped it in the cap.

"He must have served in Vietnam."

Françoise peeked behind her shoulder. The man had turned his head toward the next group of people walking in his direction, and she could not get a good look at his face.

THE BREAKTHROUGH

"Perhaps, or perhaps he just likes that people think that way."
A Bob Dylan song drifted from a car passing by. "Is the project any
good, at least?"

André nodded. "It's a bit outlandish, but if it works, it'll make
us famous."

Every three months or so, Walzenberger organized dinner parties at
his house that stretched well into the early morning. He invited
friends from his Harvard days – writers, artists, the occasional phi-
losopher – and André, his lone student, whom he called his "partner
in crime." His guests all found the expression highly amusing, except André who fought an urge to roll his eyes. At first, he had
wondered whether he should attend, in case it violated some kind of
ethical code. Françoise, though, relished any opportunity to socialize. Befriending one's advisor was not wrong. It would have been
rude to say no. Her only acquaintances were the other wives she
chatted with in the elevator or the laundry room at the residence
hall, and their conversation revolved around the weather and the
best brands of detergent. She had gone to the Museum of Fine Arts.
She had strolled along Newbury Street. She had stared at every
single monument about the Declaration of Independence. She had
shopped at Faneuil Hall and eaten in the North End. She had sat on
the steps of the Widener Library and read in the sun while Harvard
students trudged toward the circulation desk. She had ambled along
Memorial Drive and watched the rowboats glide on the Charles
River. She was getting bored. André gave in every time.

Walzenberger lived in Brookline. The trip took about fifty
minutes using public transportation – the Green Line in particular
rumbled along with excruciating slowness – and then the Darrieuxs
would trot through a quiet, residential neighborhood, Françoise
holding the bouquet of flowers and André the bottle of wine, until
the small two-storied house appeared behind a fence. They could
not miss it, even when they disagreed on the house number – se-
dans and station-wagons and one or two Ford Mustangs were always parked along the curb. In the summer, conversation snippets
and saxophone solos greeted visitors before they reached the mailbox. Walzenberger's wife loved jazz and played John Coltrane re-

cordings through the night. Her children hid under the table and sauntered amidst the two dozen guests until the baby-sitter caught hold of them and dragged them back to bed.

Walzenberger debated with his friends about politics, the economy, anything but work. Science was only discussed in relation to the Cold War and the race to beat the Soviets. Françoise struggled to follow the discussion, but she could tell when she heard the word 'Nixon' that the guests hoped he would not stay in the White House much longer – and indeed after the President's resignation, Walzenberger had thrown an extravagant party at his house, complete with champagne, streamers and confetti. The mood in the room darkened at the first mention of Vietnam. Brigit Walzenberger would retreat on the patio and light a cigarette, refuse to come back in until she had drawn the last puff. Françoise had been an occasional smoker in Lyon but had kicked the habit after moving to the States – she worried that was the reason why she could not fall pregnant. Nonetheless, she kept Brigit company, sitting with her back against the wind, explaining the smoke hurt her eyes. Walzenberger's wife spoke English with a heavy German accent that, for some reason, made it easier – at least for a French person – to understand the words she was trying to pronounce. Françoise preferred listening to her than to her American guests, crowded around the buffet in the warmth of the house.

"He should do more to stop the war. He's a professor at M.I.T. His opinion would carry some weight." Brigit stared straight ahead. "Who cares that he doesn't have tenure? So many people will be dead by the time he gets a job for life."

Françoise glanced over her shoulder into the living-room, where "Hans" gesticulated in front of his friends, some nodding vigorously, some interrupting with their own wide arm movements.

"He seems quite outspoken already."

"That's not enough."

André stood one step back, his head turned toward whoever happened to be speaking, his lips always closed except to sip some wine. He did smile every so often but refused to participate more. The only topic he wanted to discuss was the theory of quantum chromodynamics, which had recently emerged out of Princeton and explained why quarks behaved like free particles in high-energy reactions. André had broached the discovery once and Walzenberger had burst into laughter, slapped him on the back. "No work here!"

Françoise nibbled on a cracker. "I think maybe it makes more sense for Americans to speak out."

The Walzenbergers were permanent residents, but they did not have American citizenship. They did not have the right to vote. They had no say in the outcome of the war.

Brigit tapped lightly on her cigarette to make the ashes fall off. A record by Duke Ellington was playing in the living-room. She closed her eyes. "Isn't this music beautiful?"

Françoise preferred opera.

"It is."

"That's one thing I like about the States – so much great music. I'll miss that when we return to Germany."

"When do you think you'll go back?" Françoise's voice betrayed her alarm.

Brigit opened her eyes and drew another puff. "In a couple of years. Don't worry – André will have graduated by then." The silence dragged on. "It's difficult not to have family around, you know. You can't ask your relatives to look after your children when you need to run errands or go to the doctor's. You're too far away to help your parents as they get older." Brigit took her time exhaling the smoke. "You can't be there for them, and they can't be there for you. It becomes hard after a while."

Françoise nodded. "We're just like you. We plan to go back to Europe after André gets his doctorate. Nothing matters more to us than family."

Brigit looked at her and made a faint smile.

Françoise reached for the alarm clock and raised herself on an elbow. Half past two. "You should come to bed. You need to sleep. You can't do anything good if you're tired."

The lamp drew circles of light around the table while the rest of the studio disappeared in darkness. André was working by the window with his back to the room, his pen scratching against the page. Françoise heard no other noise – no car cruising along Memorial Drive, no footstep above her head, no water running down the pipes, as if she was alone in the world with her husband, in that eerie silence that only fell upon the town in the middle of the night or right after a snowstorm.

"I have to get results before the meeting. Otherwise I'll end up watching Walzie scribble equations for hours on the board again." Shortening his advisor's last name was André's sole compromise with American casualness.

Françoise yawned. "Come to bed. You're just going to make mistakes."

"The more interesting things get, the more he keeps me on a tight leash."

"He's sending you to that conference in June."

André crossed out what he had written with long, determined strokes of his pencil, then crumpled the sheet and threw it in direction of the wastebasket. He missed.

"You'll have to re-do everything in the morning. There's no point in staying up so late."

"I need every moment I can find. When we meet, I don't have time to think his arguments through. I just take notes of what he writes. I'm nothing more than a secretary to him." André pushed his glasses up his nose. "We've been working together for over three years now. How am I ever going to prove myself if he doesn't let me do a thing?"

Back in 1973, a professor at Princeton and his graduate student had established that the strong nuclear force was – like the electromagnetic and the weak nuclear forces before it – governed by something called a gauge field. That provided the basis for the theory of quantum chromodynamics, for which André showed unbridled enthusiasm and which unified three of the four forces of Nature in a convincing whole. A number of Nobel hopefuls, wishing they had made that discovery themselves, had jumped into action, albeit a little late. Neither Walzenberger nor Darrieux harbored the slightest illusion that they alone toiled away to bring the fourth force into the fold – eyeing a grand unification scheme that would assure them a spot in the Pantheon of the best scientists. At any given time, dozens of researchers throughout the country strove to achieve that same goal. This was a race and competition was fierce. André did not quite know whom he was competing against, but Walzenberger framed the situation in no uncertain terms: of course, he could take Sunday off to go sailing on the Charles River with his wife but when he came back, someone else might have beaten him to the finish line. Someone might have submitted a paper with the results he had hoped to derive, and André – Walzenberger never forgot in moments like those that he already had a doctorate and did not need a second one – would be left with the task of finding another topic suitable for a dissertation. Now obviously he could do whatever he wanted. Walzenberger, for one, would spend Sunday in his office.

"You know what I'm worried about?" Françoise responded to André's question with a shrug and rubbed her eyes. "What if there's nothing left to prove?"

"Not again." Françoise buried her head in the pillows.

"I mean, nothing worthwhile? What if there are only crumbs left, after the standard model?"

"I'm sure you'll find something to write on."

"I'm not kidding. What if physics is like a big bucket full of stuff, and after every discovery we take an item out, and one day there's nothing left to find?"

Françoise pushed the covers back. "People have been making discoveries for years. They're not going to stop now just because two people have published a paper with a nice theory in it."

"But what if there's nothing left except marginal improvements, and hugely difficult problems that won't be solved in our lifetime? What if the grand unification theory doesn't go anywhere? What will I do then?" André paused but Françoise did not have anything to say. "There are too many doctoral students in physics for the number of discoveries that can be made each year. What if I am one of those who never find anything? How will I make a difference then?"

13.

"Is Daddy having an idea?"

Diane looked at Jim, tilted her head to the side, and pretended to analyze the matter.

"Not right now, no. He's not."

Jim shrugged. Diane held Michelle and Tricia by the hand – right hand for Tricia, who was particular about those things, and left hand for Michelle, to make sure she would not wander away. The girl had developed a taste for independence now that her mother let her walk to the bus stop by herself.

"Daddy's funny when he's having an idea."

"Daddy's hilarious."

Michelle never missed an occasion to show that her vocabulary extended beyond her little sister's. The girls had spent Thanksgiving with their mother but Jim had custody for the weekend. This had been decided weeks earlier, before André Darrieux's stroke and Jim's decision to write about it, but – as he had told Diane while they waited for his ex-wife to drop off the girls – as much as he looked forward to seeing his daughters, the timing could not have been worse. The deadline for the Sunday edition loomed ahead and his editor had yet to be convinced that the story had any value.

The group strolled to the next exhibit. Michelle and Tricia squeezed into an empty spot in the crowd of on-lookers – the aquarium always attracted plenty of families with children, especially on weekends, and the Thanksgiving holiday proved to be no exception.

"Look at them! Look at them!" Tricia pointed at the little blue penguins, her nose pressed against the glass.

Jim trailed behind. He sneaked a notebook out of his pocket and scribbled a few words. Carol had announced hours earlier that she had been promoted head of the human resources department at her company, in that casual way of hers she always used when she wanted to share news without seeming to care: *the girls might tell you we had a little celebration last night. My boss is leaving and I'm getting her job.* She had been wearing expensive clothes – even Jim had noticed the difference with the blouses and skirts she usually bought at Kohl's. Her career had blossomed since the divorce. His was stuck in the same quagmire it had been bogged down in for the past twenty years and it was hard not to conclude that Carol had done well to part ways with him. He could hear her father say: he'd been dragging you down. Look at all you've accomplished since he moved out. You deserve so much better.

The lead of Jim's pencil broke on the page.

Michelle frowned. "What are you doing?"

Her sister turned her head away from the animals. "See, Daddy is having an idea. I knew it." She sounded triumphant. "Daddy always has ideas when we're with him. Like when we went to see the paintings."

Diane smiled. "You're right. That was at the Museum of Fine Arts. Did you like it?" The girl nodded. "Which painting did you like most?" She tried to drag Tricia forward so that she would not see her father absorbed in work.

"The painting with the four daughters."

"It's my favorite too. When I was a student in nursing school I used to come to the museum every chance I got and look at it first thing. John Singer Sargent. *The Daughters of Edward Darley Boit.* What a remarkable painting." Tricia was not paying attention anymore. She had turned her head and was glancing at her father. Diane followed her gaze. Of course, Jim was hunched over his notebook, writing something down. "You liked the youngest girl, didn't you? The one who sat on the carpet in the foreground with her doll."

Tricia did not listen anymore. "Dad," she said.

Jim had not even glanced at Sargent's masterpiece before disappearing into a side gallery, eager to jot down a couple of sentences about a story he had been working on. The lead paragraph had come to him all of a sudden. He had worried he would forget the words if he did not write them down on the spot. Needless to say, that explanation had not convinced Diane at all when she had found him half an hour later, revising his draft on a bench of the American wing.

"Dad," Michelle repeated, more forcefully than her sister. "We're over here."

"I'm coming, sweetie." Jim took a step forward but did not put the notebook away.

Michelle eyed him suspiciously. "What are you writing?"

"The name of the fish."

Diane gave Jim a long look. Tricia, happy that her father had joined the group, waved at the penguins.

The apartment in Quincy was no match for two bouncing children – they could not play hide-and-seek because there were so few hiding places, they could not jump on the couch because either the springs would give way or the downstairs neighbor would tap on the ceiling with a broom, and they lost interest in their brand-new Crayola pencils within seconds. Diane had come up with the idea of visiting tourist attractions – it would give father and daughters quality time together and much-needed happy memories, of which they were in short supply after the contentious divorce and endless accusations. They had made repeat trips to the Museum of Fine Arts, the Museum of Science. This was their third visit to the Aquarium in a year and neither Tricia nor Michelle was growing tired of it, When Jim had suggested that maybe he did not need to go and stare at fish again – he would meet them afterward, buy his girls a giant cup of hot chocolate and a pumpkin muffin – Diane had refused to entertain the thought he could walk away from them, even for a moment.

At that moment in the Aquarium, surrounded by rockhopper and little blue penguins squawking by the water, she glared at Jim with the same determination as before.

"You will not work on that article of yours before they're in bed." Diane spoke in a whisper, her face so close to Jim's that they almost touched. Jim opened his mouth. "And don't talk to me about deadlines. You still have a week."

"Five days, and I don't have a story." Jim whispered back, although his daughters, who had turned their head up toward the adults, obviously heard every single word. Jim's piece was scheduled to run in the Sunday edition – a source of pride for him because of the higher readership. People would pause and take notice.

"A couple more hours won't make a difference."

Jim lowered his voice even further. "I really need to make this happen." And then: "I can't be a third-rate journalist when Carol's raking up bonuses and promotions."

Diane rolled her eyes but did not protest. She had put on eyeliner and a touch of lip gloss for the woman's visit, like every time, although they never interacted for more than a minute while Jim lifted the girls' bags out of his ex-wife's car. Her own words of congratulations, when she had heard the big news, had sounded more heartfelt than Jim's – he could tell she had been impressed. Maybe she wondered whether Carol had made the right move in signing the divorce papers – whether Jim was such a catch after all. If the thought had not yet crossed her mind, it certainly would in the coming weeks, or days. The article on that M.I.T. professor represented Jim's only opportunity to restore the balance before that happened.

"Those two don't get along," a little boy said, about penguins who appeared to be ignoring each other on the far side of the exhibit.

"Maybe they had a falling out." The woman must have been the boy's mother.

Tricia tugged on Diane's sleeve. Diane smiled and tapped her finger against the glass. "Did you see that? He jumped in the water! Let's see if he does it again."

Tricia followed her gaze, but Michelle's interest had dwindled. "What's your article about?" she asked her father.

Jim made a sweeping gesture with his hand. "It's complicated." He did not mind letting other visitors know that he worked for a newspaper, but none of them seemed to be paying him any attention. They had not come to listen to him. The penguin dove into the water a second time and kids shrieked happily.

"But what is it about?" Michelle insisted.

"You wouldn't understand."

Michelle pursed her lips and stared down.

Diane sighed. "Come on now. Tell her what it's about." The boy and his mother walked out of earshot, oblivious to the suspense

– what was Jim Calloway writing about? – or completely uninterested.

There was a moment of silence before he caved in. "A famous scientist had a stroke and people are trying to figure out why."

To his dismay, no head turned in his direction. People preferred the penguins.

"What's a stroke?"

Jim glanced at his girlfriend, as if to say: I told you so. Diane bent down toward the child. "He had a problem with the functioning of his brain. Some parts didn't get the blood and oxygen they needed for a while."

Tricia, distracted from the animals at long last, looked at her with big eyes. "Is he doing better now?"

Diane blinked. "A little."

He was conscious, awake. He did not talk but his eyes sometimes followed Diane when she walked across the room. That was something.

A middle-aged couple strolled into the hall while three four young children, all boys, galloped ahead. The older one snapped a picture of the penguins with a disposable camera. The other two shoved each other playfully and burst into laughter before their mother could shush them.

"Why did the functioning of his brain have a problem?"

"We don't know. That's what your father's trying to understand."

"I think he'd been flying too much, and he got a blood clot that went to his brain. That happens. It's rare, but it happens." Jim pointed at Diane, indifferent to the fact that neither of his girls was able to comprehend what a blood clot entailed. "She wants to believe he had a breakthrough. She talks with the man's wife too much."

Tricia glanced at him with bewilderment.

"A breakthrough is a discovery, and your Dad doesn't mean what he says." Diane grinned. "It's a fine story. I like it."

Jim had seen the professor once, when he had come to pick up Diane at the end of her shift – at least that was what the pair had told the other nurses. It was agreed that Jim would not mention the visit in his article, not even drop the slightest hint, but he refused to describe André's condition to his readers if he had not seen it. Diane, who had peeked into his file while residents busied themselves elsewhere, was at a loss to give any details about left-hemisphere stroke and aphasia. Jim had to meet the man in person and see for himself.

He had stood in the doorway the whole time, in case the wife dropped by, making small talk with Diane while she checked on the patient. (*I'm glad it's not snowing anymore.*) His eyes, though, had remained set on the person lying in the hospital bed, pale and tired. His fingers itched to take notes, although he realized that it would have attracted too much attention. André's skin sagged in long wrinkles around his cheeks, which had come as a surprise because he appeared chubby – rotund even – in every single picture of his on the Internet. Jim had read that the left part of most people's brain controlled their ability to communicate, as well as the movements of their right side; that did not bode well for André's future as an academic. As a matter of fact, that did not bode well for André's future, period. He pointed at a plastic cup when he was thirsty, half his face perked up when Diane stepped into the room, but he gave no hint that he followed conversations or remembered a thing about science. The monographs on quantum mechanics and string theory that his wife had brought remained unopened on the nightstand. Diane found that heartrending.

"I hope he had a breakthrough." She liked that idea.

"Come on. That makes no sense."

Michelle looked puzzled. "Why?"

Jim answered before Diane could. "Because people who make discoveries get excited. They're happy. They don't get upset and have a stroke."

Diane shook his head. "He could've found a mistake somewhere. That'd count as a breakthrough if it was in an important work, and that'd certainly make him upset."

"Maybe it's like that Knight of the Round Table," Michelle announced. "The one who sees the Holy Grail and dies." She had learned about knights in class the previous year.

"That's right." Diane nodded. "He saw a breakthrough and had a stroke."

"Who dies?" Tricia's voice betrayed a sudden anxiety.

"Galahad, but it's just a legend." Jim put his notebook in his pocket and stepped closer to the glass. "These penguins are amazing."

No one talked for a minute or two.

"It's a fine story."

"I heard you the first time around."

"I'm just trying to help."

Jim scoffed. "A scientist's finding a mistake doesn't count as a story. It's so trivial. I'm going to be laughed out of the newsroom if I try to get that into print."

"But it could be a big mistake that makes his whole theory crumble. Maybe he trusted his students and then he realized he shouldn't have. Betrayal always sells."

"I don't write fiction. You should write a novel about this, though. Sounds like you've got everything figured out."

Jim's voice had been steadily rising and a man cast him a disapproving glance.

"And you could show a bit more empathy."

"I don't feel sorry for the guy. He was a slave-driver."

The group ambled to the next exhibit, Tricia and Michelle more sullen now that the adults were talking about work.

"I doubt that's the way he viewed himself."

"Who cares? His student didn't mince words about him. 'He was a slave-driver, and I am glad he got a stroke. There's a justice after all.'"

"A lot of good, hard-working people get strokes every year and they haven't done a thing to deserve them."

"I'm not going to ignore his student's comments and pretend he was a saint." Jim stood in front of the bay window, his hands deep in his pockets. The family with the three sons shuffled out of sight. "Let's say, for the sake of the argument, that he found a mistake. He was working on fixing it, and then he had a stroke." Jim paused. "He could've died in a car crash and people would've said we lost the next Einstein, but he had a stroke and his students said he was a slave-driver." Michelle tugged hard on Diane's arm. Diane grabbed her hand, which she squeezed while looking at Jim. "So what is this about? Comeuppance? Bad luck? A smear campaign? What's the right angle?"

Tricia started sucking her thumb – a sure sign she was getting tired, and bored with her father's speech.

Jim thought again about Carol in her expensive clothes, her smile, her obvious happiness without him. Her friends would agree that the divorce had done wonders on her career, although she might have been promoted anyway if she had stayed married. He did not want anyone to think he had been dragging her down – he had not. They had grown apart over the years and her becoming successful once she had moved away from him was purely a coincidence.

Wasn't it?

14.

The seminar speaker stood by his laptop while a faculty member checked the connection with the LCD projector. His guest's slides appeared on the screen, too small; Thomas Greenawalt fumbled with the settings to resize them. Students lined by the table where Evelyn had set up the food and refreshments. They loaded their plastic plate with cookies and mini-pretzels, grabbed a drink and lowered themselves into their seat, careful not to let anything drop.

The speaker's slides matched the size of the screen at last. Tom stood up with a beaming smile.

"We're having a good turnout today." Kevin Rodrik nodded, pleased that so many students and professors had found the time to attend. "How do you like working at Argonne? I'm sure you'd find another faculty position easily, if you went on the job market."

"It's good not to have to teach. I can do more research now. Of course, I miss the interaction with the students – Princeton students are really very good – but definitely not preparing exams and homework assignments."

The men chuckled. Olivia, who sat on the opposite side of the room – too far away to follow their conversation – stared at them with the sullen look of people left out of a joke. Kevin looked boyish, especially from a distance – it was easy for Olivia to believe he was only a few years older than her but enormously more successful. She bit into her chocolate-chip cookie and chewed it with vigor. The speaker scanned the room, counting the attendees. His gaze paused on Olivia and then drifted away.

Sergey sauntered down the stairs, dumped his backpack in the front row. He snubbed the food table and headed for the lectern with a grin.

"Kevin, let me introduce you to my new student, Sergey Malienkov."

Sergey stretched out his arm. "I've read so many of your papers. It's great to put a face on the name."

Kevin smiled.

"Sergey's one of André's students. He was getting ready to graduate when this all happened." The guest nodded. There was no need to explain. "So I've adopted him, and hopefully we can soon send him on his way."

"I'm glad to hear things are working out. I was wondering what would happen to his students."

"The department is giving the others Teaching Assistantships for the coming semester."

"That's good. I saw André on the last day of that conference, two weeks ago. He looked pale, but I would never have guessed he was about to have a stroke."

"Nobody expected it."

Kevin sighed. "That was after his plenary talk – I thought he might just be tired. Of course, in hindsight, it's obvious he'd gotten bad news. You should've seen his face." There was a pause. "Did you ever find out what he was so upset about?"

Tom shook his head.

A voice rose to his left. "Whatever it was, he called Olivia about it as soon as he got off the plane."

The two men turned toward Sergey, surprised to find him still standing next to them.

"Who's Olivia?"

Tom pointed at the young woman munching a cookie in the back of the room. She seemed lost in thoughts until a classmate, who was making her way toward an empty chair in the same row, touched her lightly on the arm. Olivia shifted her legs to the side without acknowledging the woman.

Tom looked at Sergey. "You should take your seat. We're going to start any moment now." He waited until his new student had stepped aside to continue. "The year Olivia applied, we all wanted to fund her. She was one of those students who just stand out." Kevin nodded – he knew the type. "Grades, recommendations – everything was perfect. I was so annoyed that André got to hire her first.

And now? She's in her fourth year and hasn't published a thing. Isn't even close to submitting."

Kevin glanced at his host, unsure of the reaction the man was hoping for. "Supersymmetry isn't for the faint of heart."

"Working with André hasn't done her any good, let me tell you that. He almost kicked her out last summer. They had a big argument in August." Tom checked the time on the large wall clock – no hurry. He turned back toward the seminar speaker. "André was screaming at her in his office. You could hear him from the stair-well. She even ran out in tears."

The line by the refreshments had dwindled. Two lone cookies lay on the table. Susanna Polits hurried into the room and claimed the last bottle of water. She smiled at the seminar speaker and shook his hand.

"I still don't understand why she got tenure," a voice whis-pered behind Olivia. "She doesn't have that many publications in top journals and she's a tough grader. I avoid all of her classes."

"She's not even a good role model," Olivia whispered back without as much as a glance behind her shoulder. She did not care who it was. "She's not married and works all the time."

The voice chuckled. "Of course you'd do a lot better, given the chance."

Olivia's cheeks reddened. She stared straight ahead. The semi-nar speaker and Professor Greenawalt remained standing by the lectern, while Sergey had finally taken his seat – reluctantly.

"What was André screaming about?" Kevin could not resist asking.

"He was upset at a mistake she'd made. She wasn't getting the right result, but she couldn't see what she was doing wrong."

"I guess they patched things up if he called her as soon as he got off the plane. What is she working on now?"

Tom shrugged. "I wish I knew."

Hans-Hermann Walzenberger appeared by the door, proceed-ed to the front of the room. He was in his late sixties by then but still resembled the baby-faced wunderkind André had met in 1971, with his big cheeks and his round head, only partially covered by thin blond hair. He had gained weight, though, and walked more slowly.

"How was your trip?" He shook the guest's hand.

"I almost got snowed in on my way here, but my flight made it out before the worst of the storm. I heard temperatures in Chicago dropped to minus twenty last night."

The old professor chuckled. "That's a problem New Jersey didn't have."

"Hans." Tom rolled his eyes.

Kevin smiled. "Winters are hard, but Chicago is beautiful." Hans did not appear to realize that he had not left Princeton willingly, or perhaps he did not mind rubbing salt in the wound.

"I'll go sit down now."

Tom nodded. "We'll give the latecomers a minute or two before we start."

Hans picked his usual spot in the front row, two seats away from Sergey, who fidgeted about on his chair and waited for an opportunity to say hi. Hans ignored him.

"I thought he had retired."

"He? Not a chance. Comes at eight every morning and leaves at seven. He's at his desk more often than most. I think he also comes on weekends."

Kevin frowned. "Is he widowed?"

Tom shook his head. "Married to the same woman for the last forty-five years. And he'd set up a camp bed in his office if we let him."

His colleague's research output had trickled down to one review paper a year. He no longer worked with graduate students. The department had him teach the introductory physics courses, advise the undergraduate majors on their course load, mostly because it had no other use for him and the former wunderkind needed a reason to keep his office space.

"It's hard to believe he used to be one of the most famous members of the department. Every single conjecture he made after 1975 was disproved, or failed to catch on. He never got over the fact that his ideas about preons didn't work – and that was after all the hoopla on the SU(5) symmetry, which didn't work either."

"He lost his drive."

"He sunk into irrelevance, while André's star rose with every symposium."

Kevin shrugged. "Those things come and go. Fame is a curious thing."

Hyong-Mo took a seat toward the middle of the room. Daniel was nowhere to be seen, although he had attended every single seminar this semester. He had enrolled at M.I.T. with the sole purpose of working with André Darrieux and his absence suggested one of two possibilities: he was either struggling with his disappointment, somewhere by himself, or preparing his transfer application to Caltech. Tom had tried to recruit him before taking Sergey on, to no avail.

Kevin kept talking. "The Large Hadron Collider is going to crush a number of dreams, let me tell you that."

It was time to get started. Before stepping forward to introduce the speaker, piece of paper in hand, Tom turned to his guest and made a little smile that seemed good-natured enough. "Hopefully not mine."

"We might all retire before some of those issues are resolved." Kevin looked nowhere near retirement. "If string theory loses its appeal, we'll all have spent decades building castles in the air. Give us a few years, and we might all look like Hans."

Tom's smile hardened a little. "Hopefully not me."

He caught up with Olivia in the hallway after the seminar.

15

Bernard was born in 1976, long after Françoise had lost any hope to have a child. André expected to graduate within a year and his wife had begun a silent countdown: the last fireworks for the Fourth of July, the last barbecue for Labor Day. The Darrieuxs had lived in Cambridge for five years by then and it was time for a change.

"It'll be good to have you back, see Bernard more."

Françoise smiled at her mother, who had come from Lyon to help with the newborn.

"He's growing up fast," Valentine said.

Françoise put the bag of groceries on the counter, placed the eggs in the fridge. "He sure is."

Bernard made cooing noises in his crib and kicked his legs in the air.

Valentine tickled the soles of his feet, to the baby's delight. "Hello, dear. Hello." She was shorter than her daughter, with a round face and long grey hair she always tied into a bun. Françoise did not look like her at all – she took after her father. Her sister was the one who looked like their mother.

"Next thing you know, he's going to start crawling." Valentine let out a sigh. "He might even walk before you get back."

The silence dragged on one, two, three seconds. Françoise crumpled a paper bag and threw it into the wastebasket. "Did I tell you André's teaching him how to count? He shows him numbers and repeats them for him. He says that'll help Bernard when he starts to talk. Isn't that sweet?"

"I'm glad to see André finds time for him, especially with that schedule of his."

Françoise reached for a grocery bag and bumped into her mother when she turned around – two people could not stand in the kitchenette without getting into each other's way.

"He's busy, I'm not going to pretend otherwise. He's trying to graduate. But he plays with Bernard and reads him bedtime stories almost every night."

Françoise carried a basket of apples into the living area, placed it by the television set – a present of André's before the pregnancy, because she complained of loneliness so often and he insisted on working late. The sofa, covered with blankets and pillows, had been turned into a makeshift bed for Valentine. At night, Bernard slept in a crib by her side so that Françoise did not have to get up when he cried and André could steal a few hours' rest. The arrangement would have worked better in a real apartment instead of a studio but Valentine had wanted to help. She would have helped if her daughter and son-in-law had lived nearby and she would help now that they lived a continent away. That was what grandmothers did.

She glanced at the Boston skyline, stretching on the other side of the river. "You do have a nice view." Françoise shrugged. She had stopped paying attention to the view years earlier. "You won't have a view like that when you get back, but there's some nice land south of Lyon."

"I'm not sure if André wants to have a house built at this point." Françoise stacked cases of baby formula in the pantry. "He doesn't like to talk about it, keeps postponing any discussion to whenever he doesn't have so much work."

"You might have to wait a while, then." Bernard fussed in the stroller. Valentine picked up her grandson and rocked him gently. The child tugged on her bracelet. "That boy's getting strong."

Françoise waved her fingers in front of Bernard so that he would let go of her mother's jewelry, grab her hand instead. "He only has a couple months left. There's still time."

"But he'll finish in June, right?" Valentine asked prudently. "It looks like he's struggling to wrap things up."

"He says the final stretch's always hard, but he'll make it happen. He's been very clear he wants to graduate this spring." Françoise retrieved her son from her mother's arms. "If he didn't mind staying longer, he wouldn't put in sixteen-hour days now."

"The sooner we have you back, the better."

Françoise nodded. "We'll be home for Bastille Day."

Brigit bought clothes for the baby, late.

"I'm sorry I didn't bring you this earlier. Things have been so hectic." She smiled sheepishly.

"But you already got us a present. Blue pajamas. Your husband gave them to André months ago."

Brigit stared at Françoise, and then burst into laughter. "Of course. How could I forget?" She took a gulp of Cabernet Sauvignon, her grin frozen on her lips. Françoise could not stop looking at her – her skin sagged around the neck, her cheeks had become puffy, and a faint smell of cigarette lingered around her shoulders. She was not aging well. "Anyway, you can't have enough baby clothes."

Françoise tore the wrapping paper and gazed at another set of pajamas, white this time with little ducks making happy faces. "That's perfect. Thank you so much."

They sat at an outside table on Newbury Street, enjoying the sun. Brigit had picked the restaurant and recommended a couple of dishes on the menu with the assurance of patrons who have tasted every item. Françoise had planned to order a garden salad, but Brigit would have none of it: one does not go all the way to Newbury Street to order a garden salad, she had told Françoise. Let me order something for you. It's on me. Françoise had caved in and selected the pan-seared salmon with mashed potatoes on the side – this would not help her shed the pounds she had gained during the pregnancy but the order had pleased Brigit beyond words. Françoise chewed on morsels of bread while she waited. Walzenberger's wife stayed away from the bread but had already sipped half her wine.

Françoise gazed at her son, asleep in the stroller. "He's going to be so excited when he wakes up. He loves ducks. I'm sure he won't let me put any other pajamas on him until he gets too big for them." She folded the clothes back, tucked them in next to Bernard's bottle and his diapers.

Brigit smiled, her eyes on the baby. "They're cute at that age."

The shadows of passers-by ambling on the sidewalk glided over them. Newbury Street, with its upscale eateries and fancy shops, was a popular destination for tourists and locals alike.

Groups chatted mindlessly; Françoise tried not to pay attention to them. She winced when she heard a woman talk in French. The man by her side suggested they walk down one more block before deciding where to eat. Françoise observed the couple as they sauntered away – it was not unusual to run into French people in Boston; the consulate employed many of them and the town, with its reputation for being a "European city", attracted more than its share of French-speaking vacationers. Françoise owed them the wide selection of magazines at the Out of Town newsstand in Harvard Square, which supplied expatriates with news in print from their country. Whenever she felt homesick, she hopped onto the T and picked up a two-week-old issue of *Paris-Match* from the racks, its celebrity news hopelessly stale but entertaining nonetheless, and read the magazine on the steps of the Widener Library. But Bernard did not leave her any time to miss France anymore – her feeling of aching loneliness was quickly fading away. Now that she had become a mother and her sojourn in New England was drawing to an end, she found herself much more willing to agree with André: things had not been so bad after all. She would be glad to return home, but she would bring fond memories of Cambridge back with her.

Brigit pointed at the infant. "He must be keeping you busy."

Françoise shrugged. "I don't mind." She relished every minute with her son. She wanted to watch him rest, watch him wake up, watch him giggle, watch him crawl. She showed little interest in anything else. Valentine had returned to Lyon by then, and Françoise stumbled happily out of bed every night when the baby fussed for his bottle. He needed her! He needed her!

"Enjoy this while you can. Things become more complicated when they grow up." Brigit waved at the waiter for another glass of wine. "Once they develop a personality of their own, that's when trouble starts."

Françoise stared at her with pity and a tinge of disgust – poor Walzenberger children, she thought, straddled with a resentful mother who wished they had remained helpless little things. She pushed a crumb of bread off the table, keeping her eyes down to hide her dismay. She would never end up like that.

THE BREAKTHROUGH

"Maybe I should do a post-doc. That would increase my chances of getting a good job when we go back to France. There aren't too many faculty openings, you know." Françoise, who had been warming up a casserole, put down her wooden spoon and gave her husband a long, alarmed look. "Since we're already here, we might as well stay two more years."

André spoke without emotion, as if he was only describing a minor delay, a tiny postponement, a microscopic snag in the time-table they had agreed upon.

Françoise added a sprinkle of pepper and wiped her hands on the towel, although they were neither wet nor dirty. Elizabeth Schwarzkopf sang in the background, in a recording of *Der Rosenkavalier* André had bought his wife for her birthday.

"You're getting a PhD from M.I.T. Isn't that enough for the people in Lyon to give you a job?"

"They don't have a vacancy every year. We might have to go somewhere else. And the more papers I publish before we move back, the more likely it is that I'll get accredited to supervise theses right away."

Françoise carried the pot to the table. "But you can work with other professors from day one, can't you? It doesn't matter that you won't be able to have your own research group from the moment you start."

André leant back in his chair. "A lot of graduate students take eight years to finish or more. It'd be as if it had taken me longer than expected to write my dissertation. That happens." A ladle of food splashed onto his plate. "It'll pay off in two years."

"What makes you so sure you'll be done then? Why not three years, or five? Aren't there post-docs who stay five years too?"

Françoise had raised her voice and immediately regretted it, but there was no noise, no movement coming from the bedroom where Bernard rested in his crib. The boy had not woken up. It was late – André had labored in his office until ten – and Françoise had played with her son, bathed him, read him a story and tucked him into bed hours earlier.

"Walzie only got a two-year grant. He won't sponsor me for more than that."

"I thought you didn't like him." Françoise sat down opposite her husband and unfolded a napkin.

André reached for his fork and knife. "He's alright. He's got good ideas, and he's helping me get recognized. That's worth putting up with his failings just a bit longer."

"My mother thinks we're coming back at the end of June. Your parents do too. Everybody's expecting us. Your brothers haven't even seen their nephew yet."

André rubbed his eyes. He had not slept more than five hours a night that week or the week before that. "We'll have them over."

"That's not the same thing. It costs a lot of money to come here."

"And I want to put all the chances on my side to get the best job I can find. What's wrong with that?"

Françoise avoided her husband's gaze.

"Two more years," André said. "Bernard will start pre-school in France. That'll leave your mother and my parents and everybody else plenty of time to see him grow up."

André received his degree on a hot June afternoon in Killian Court, alongside fifteen hundred graduating students. The seating area was packed with relatives – parents, grandparents, siblings, aunts and uncles – cheering the procession, while graduates in cap and gown proceeded to the folding chairs lined up in the middle of the lawn. Françoise sat in the shade next to André's parents, worried that they would disapprove of her mothering skills if Bernard broke into tears for any reason and she could not calm him down. To her relief, her son showed no inclination whatsoever to throw a tantrum – those strange people in black garb and odd hats fascinated him, and he could not take his eyes off them. Students waiting by the stage to receive their degrees cooed at the boy, waved to get a smile – the cute toddler reveled in all the attention. He repeated students' greetings: 'hello', 'hi', 'hello', raised his tiny hand at the graduates and made a big grin.

"That boy's quite a people person." André's father chuckled. "He'll make a good businessman someday, or a politician."

André's mother nodded. "He's got his own personality already. Who knows how he'll have changed the next time we see him." Françoise fanned herself with the program and, her eyes on Bernard tottering about, pretended not to hear. Solange touched her elbow. Françoise turned to her with an innocent smile. "So when do you think you'll come to visit us?"

Françoise blinked. "You'd have to ask André. It depends on his schedule."

"I sure hope you know what you're doing." Solange had used the plural "*vous*" for 'you', as if her daughter-in-law had played any role in André's decision to extend their stay, debated alternatives with her husband before agreeing that he should accept the post-doctoral position – as if he had given her a choice. Françoise opened her mouth to protest, but André and the graduates around him were just leaving their seats to stand by the stage (straightening their caps, adjusting their tassels), and there was no point in starting an argument now.

A school official mispronounced André's name into the microphone. The young man strode up the ramp to receive his diploma. The three Darrieuxs sitting in the audience clapped feverishly while the fourth one tugged at his mother's skirt. André's father snapped a picture.

Françoise bit her bottom lip, disappointed that the ceremony would not mark the end of her stay in the States.

16.

"M.I.T. made me an offer," André announced one evening. The Darrieuxs had been renting a small house in Inman Square for a year and a half, and Françoise had not expected them to renew the lease.

"An offer for what?"

"A faculty position."

Françoise gaped. "I wasn't aware you had applied." The couple sat on the carpet in the living-room, legs crossed, with Bernard between them. Cubes were lined in front of the boy; each sported a letter of the alphabet painted in bright color on its side. Bernard's task was to arrange the cubes in alphabetical order. The boy had reached the letter F – six cubes out of twenty-six – and Françoise beamed every time he said the correct answer. It was as good a time as any to break the news.

"I didn't. Not really." André looked down.

Françoise was so astonished she could not even bring herself to scoff, simply glared at her husband. After years of fourteen-hour workdays, the fine lines around his eyes had deepened into wrinkles, and he had recently bought a new pair of prescription glasses because he could no longer read small fonts with the old one. Otherwise, his appearance had not changed in the seven years Françoise had been married to him, if one forgot an ill-advised period of three months in 1975 when he had tried to grow a beard, and it was easy to believe he remained the same person she had met in Lyon – easy but obviously wrong, because the André of those years long past would have returned home after his doctorate, just like he had said he would.

Bernard, oblivious to his father's announcement, read aloud the letters he had already found. A… B… C… D… E… F… He clenched his little fists. What came after F? Although the game had been Françoise's idea, André attached a lot more importance to the outcome than his wife – his son needed to know the alphabet forward and backward before any other child, because that was his son – and the boy was eager to please. F… F…

"I wanted to get some practice interviewing. I didn't think they would give me the job."

"G!"

Bernard clapped his hands. His father leaned forward and handed him the cube, but did not glance at him. His mother looked as if the blood had been sucked out of her face. Strands of hair fell in front of her eyes – the hairdresser had tempted her into trying a shorter cut than usual, adding layers to her plain trim below the jaw line – but she did not push them back. Bernard held the cube against his chest and stared at his parents. "It's a good offer. I'd be well-paid. There's no comparison with academic salaries in France."

The pain in Françoise's eyes was unmistakable. "You could've told me you'd applied."

"I didn't want you to read too much into it."

"What do you mean by too much? You have no intention of ever leaving Boston. That's very clear." She paused, but André did not protest. "I'm reading just the right amount into it."

Bernard grabbed the cube with a G and pressed it against his mother's thigh, to gain her attention. Françoise did not look at him.

The bottom shelf on the wall was filled with her psychology books, marked and annotated – case studies of troubled children and thick volumes about experimental therapies. They had gathered dust for years, but now she had started reading them again in preparation for the move. She was going to open her own practice. She was going to work three days a week once Bernard had begun preschool, which would put her free time to good use – and her advanced degree too. That had been their plan for years. She had waited long enough to make a difference in people's lives.

"I haven't given M.I.T. an answer yet. If you really want to leave, we'll leave." Françoise's face lit up in spite of her best efforts to remain impassive. "The universities in Lyon aren't hiring, though. The ones in Grenoble aren't either. The competition to get a job in Paris is fierce, and Walzie isn't connected well enough with the folks over there to give me an in." André spoke matter-of-factly; Françoise could not gather her thoughts fast enough to interrupt him and offer counter-arguments. "We won't see our families either if I teach in Bordeaux or Lille. It won't make a difference if we stay here instead." But of course it did, because Bordeaux and Lyon lay in the same time zone and one could place phone calls from one city to the other without racking up eye-popping international charges. "We could wait to move back until something opens in the Rhône-Alpes area."

Françoise fought back tears. "You could ask your former professors at Normale Sup for help."

"I will, when a position opens. But it'd boost my career if I worked here for a while first. I'd get a big start-up package to build my research group. I'd teach the best students in the world."

"We'd agreed we'd be back home by the time Bernard starts preschool," Françoise blurted out, because André obviously needed to be reminded of what he had committed to. The boy, hearing his name, turned his head toward his mother and offered her the G cube again. Françoise did not take it. "I don't have friends here. I barely speak English. There are only so many shirts I can iron before my brain goes numb. Days are going to be really long when Bernard's in kindergarten."

André rubbed his forehead. "Maybe you could find a volunteer job, be a French tutor somewhere."

"I don't care about teaching people French."

"We could get you a dog, then." Françoise rolled her eyes, although it was not a bad idea – she liked dogs and André knew it. Bernard threw his cube on the floor but his parents ignored him. "We don't have to stay if that makes you unhappy. On the other hand, if we do stick around for a few years, we can save money and then buy ourselves a nice, big house when we go back to France."

Françoise let out a whimper. "You don't want to go back. Don't pretend otherwise. I'm going to be stuck in this country forever."

"That's not true. I have no interest in staying in the States more than a couple of years. But M.I.T. is giving me the resources to do great work, work that can change our understanding of physics and the laws of Nature and what the world is made of. We'll only stay long enough for me to get some momentum going in my research, and then we'll move back to Lyon."

Bernard ran around in the yard with his friends. He played a game that could have been baseball, if Françoise had known enough about the rules to identify the sport with certainty. The boy had invited two of his buddies from elementary school – Steven and Mike – and they hollered at each other, "Great save!" or "Willie Mays at the bat!" Françoise, who watched them from the kitchen window, had no clue who Willie Mays was. The kids were throwing and receiving the ball, throwing and receiving, while Nestor jumped around them.

"Nestor, sit!" The Labrador sat down. He obeyed Bernard better than he did Françoise. Both the child and the dog seemed to relish the larger garden, and the bigger house, which André had bought in Belmont after his second year on the faculty. Now they could play without stumbling into the furniture or the fence.

Françoise filled a glass with soapy water, rubbed a sponge against its bottom.

Steven handed the glove to Mike and exchanged places with him. French boys that age played soccer, but one could not find a single soccer ball in the toy stores of the Boston area. When the Darrieuxs returned to Lyon for the summer, Bernard stayed away from his cousins kicking the ball, although they had invited him to play with them once. They had called it football. The boy had frowned, protested that was not football – American football bore no resemblance with soccer, and from a Yankee perspective, the latter amounted to nothing more than a group of boys hurrying back and forth on a field, a bit like cross-country running. His cousins had never heard about American football, which was not broadcast on French television, and struggled to make sense of the tackles and touchdowns Bernard had described for them – in soccer, yellow and red cards were issued if you used your hands. That was against the spirit of the game, the kids had tried to explain Bernard.

Françoise placed the glass on the draining rack, reached for another one. Her son was at the bat.

"World Series, bottom of the ninth!" he yelled, and threw the ball into a tree.

"Home run!" The three boys guffawed.

Bernard raised his fists in the air. "We're champions!"

He spoke with the fluency of an American – and he was one, by birth, while his parents had yet to apply for citizenship. Françoise could not explain why her son was able to pronounce English words to perfection when his parents struggled with the foreign language, although she had heard that it occurred frequently among young children. She held that against her kid – Bernard should have spoken English with a French accent, like his mother. When she listened to him talk, she felt he wasn't really hers.

17.

Matthew Johnson gathered the pages of notes spread over his desk, fastened them with a paper clip and took a deep breath.

"How do you think it'll go?"

Matt glanced to the side, where Sergey was peering over his shoulder. He shrugged. "I didn't make a lot of progress."

"I hope he's in a good mood. I didn't make a lot of progress either."

Both students glanced at Darrieux's office, across the hallway. They had left their door open so that Matt could catch his advisor as soon as he arrived for their meeting; Sergey would see him about an hour later.

"You've got a couple of years ahead of you. At this rate, I'm not going to graduate in June, or even in August."

"That's still months away. You'll figure something out."

Matt stifled a yawn. He should have made that last cup of coffee a double shot. Empty Styrofoam cups piled into the wastebasket – one was Sergey's, three were Matt's, and several more would find their way into the trash by the end of the day. Ever since Matt had bought an espresso machine for the office, he no longer wasted time trudging down the corridor, plodding down the stairs, standing in line to get his caffeine fix, but he now drank coffee all day long to compensate for his lack of sleep. It was so tempting – the machine sat right there, perched on top of the empty desk by the door. Some days, when Matt's hands began to shake, Sergey would disappear for twenty minutes and come back with bottles of water from the convenience store. Then he would tease his friend to see who could gulp one down faster.

Matt glanced at his watch – the boss was running late. "I can't imagine being still here in the fall. I'm so tired of this life."

He puffed out his cheeks and underlined the equation at the bottom of the last page.

"How close are you?"

"Close enough, but I need that last result to tie everything together. Otherwise it's like a puzzle that's missing a piece. I can't leave it like that." He drew a second underline, joined both in a long, thin rectangle, which he filled out with diagonal strokes. Sergey chuckled. "Or rather I could, but then I wouldn't graduate."

Matt pushed his papers away, tucked a foot under his desk and leaned back, balancing on two of the chair's legs. That vantage point gave him a better view, through the one dirty window in the office, of the courtyard and the large, leafless oak trees under the overcast sky. A woman hurried in the cold – she looked like Susanna Polits, with her blue parka and white woolen hat. Matt had heard the professor might not be granted tenure and leaned back a little more, to see if that was indeed her. Polits sat on his dissertation committee; he hoped to graduate before she left. Otherwise, he would need to find someone else to take her spot. That would complicate matters.

His foot slipped. He lost his balance, grabbed the edge of the desk while Sergey got hold of the chair.

"Careful."

"I think I saw Polits outside." Sergey turned to the window but the woman was gone. "Maybe I could ask her for help. She might have some ideas."

"Why don't you ask Darrieux?"

Matt grimaced. "I'd rather not tell him I'm struggling." He slid his wedding band up and down his finger. "He might not even let me schedule my defense. If he doesn't believe I can get that last result in time for Commencement, he'll say there's no point."

A door opened and closed; someone strode toward the other end of the corridor. The footsteps faded in the distance.

"What's the worst that can happen? Even if you have to postpone graduation, that'll just delay the start of your post-doc. I'm sure the lab director will understand, wherever you go."

Matt gave Sergey a long look but did not reply.

Sergey frowned. "What?" Matt reached for his notes and began to read them intently, as if he had never seen them before.

"You're not planning to do a post-doc?" Sergey opened his eyes wide. "You're leaving academia?"

Matt shook his head. "I don't know yet."

"But everyone in the department expects you to become a professor at a top university. Darrieux himself praises you as his best student of the decade, and he doesn't give out many compliments." Matt shrugged. Sergey leaned back. "I always thought only the weakest students left science for an industry job. I thought the others stuck it out. At least, I thought you'd stick it out, of all people." He paused. "Are you interviewing for industry positions?"

Matt nodded. "We could use the cash. Kate's been the bread-winner for long enough. Especially when the baby comes, I want her to take as much time off as she'd like." He kept toying with his wedding band. "There's no need to tell Darrieux now, though. I don't even have an offer."

"Do you think you'll get one?"

Matt's face brightened. "I made it to the last round at Goldman Sachs." Sergey whistled. "But that remains between us, alright? If Darrieux hears about it, he'll say I won't have time to revise our papers once I'm in the real world, so I might as well stay here until I've submitted everything."

"He's certainly under a lot of pressure to publish."

Sergey and Matt had known what they were getting into when they had applied to join his lab; back then, they had been drawn to the excitement of cutting-edge research, the prospect of momentous discoveries. It did not seem so glamorous any more, now that they had spent tens of thousands of hours toiling in a dreary office with no breakthrough to show for their hard work.

"You know what's strange? Pete told me once that Darrieux didn't start squeezing him until he was halfway done. One day Darrieux came back from a last-minute trip he'd taken to Europe, and that was it. Research had been important before, but overnight it became urgent, and it stayed like that until Pete got his degree."

Sergey raised an eyebrow. "Go figure."

"Pete could never understand what had happened."

Footsteps echoed in the hallway. Sergey sat straight on his chair and listened carefully.

Matt shook his head. "That's not him."

The footsteps grew nearer. Thomas Greenawalt strode by.

Matt did not speak again until the professor had entered his office and closed the door. "That guy's a jerk," he said, referring to Greenawalt. "I almost worked with him, and I'm so glad I didn't. I've taken two of his courses and he doesn't even acknowledge me when he sees me in the corridor." Sergey nodded – that had happened to him as well. "We were only five in class. There's no way he doesn't remember me."

"He doesn't like that Darrieux's research overshadows his. I hope I never turn out like that, disgruntled and bitter." The silence dragged on. "But it's all going to be alright. We're going to sort everything out and find whatever there's to find and this research's going to make us famous."

Matt laughed.

The door to the stairwell swung open; someone with heavy footsteps hurried down the corridor. Matt grabbed his papers and got up. "Here comes the boss."

André Darrieux wore a long, dark coat that fit tightly around his midsection, and the red woolen scarf his wife had given him for his birthday. He was shorter than Matt, larger too, with a rotund face that smiled often but which, at that particular moment, showed only intense focus as he power-walked toward his office, leather briefcase in one hand and key ring in the other.

"Sorry I'm late." André pushed his eyeglasses up his nose and, bent over the doorknob, fumbled with his keys. "Come on in."

Matt paused on the threshold. The clutter always seemed most daunting when he was about to enter – when he had not seen his advisor's office for a week and was suddenly reminded of its disarray. He would forget his surroundings within minutes, discuss Type IIB string theory or D-branes without paying the slightest attention to the mess, but first he stared at the piles of documents that threatened to merge into an ocean of paper under the frames of André's honorary degrees.

"I didn't get a chance to tidy things up since last time," André said sheepishly as he untied his scarf and hung his coat. "I'll get around to it when the semester's over." Matt suppressed a chuckle. André smiled. "I've said that before, haven't I?" He cradled a pile of handouts and placed it on the floor, so that Matt would have space on the desk for his papers.

André plopped onto the swivel chair. Matt sat down opposite him. Their relationship had not taken the best start, six years earlier – Pete had filed his complaint shortly after Matt had joined the group, which had made for very tense weeks. André, already cautious around students, had taken extra care not to give the new hire any hope. The project would not be easy; he would not graduate soon. André had mellowed, though, after the department chair ruled in his favor. Maybe he felt a tinge of guilt at treating Matt so coldly, since the student had done nothing wrong. Maybe Matt reminded him of his son, who was only three years younger. Maybe Matt even reminded André of himself and his own eagerness to leave his mark when he had first arrived on campus. In any case, they got along quite well, for a graduate student and his supervisor.

"Any news on the baby?"

"So far so good. A couple more weeks to go."

André smiled. "I'm sure you can't wait." He paused. "So what do you have for me today?"

Matt tapped his pencil on the page. "I've been working on the thing we talked about. It's been hard. I think I'm on the right track, though. It's just a lot of equations." André extended his arm toward the papers. Matt handed them to him. "I'm getting there."

André pored over the notes. Matt eyed him over the table, eager to catch a glimpse of approval, but André's face betrayed no expression. Matt's gaze drifted to the desk, then the shelves, as he waited for his advisor to comment on his work. With the exception of a small boom box and a stack of classical CDs by the computer, the office was devoid of personal items, had been so as far back as Matt could remember. He had not even known his advisor had a son until that afternoon in June, when André had arrived for their meeting pale with anger.

The professor made an approving noise. Matt looked at him but André seemed absorbed in his reading. He had never talked about Bernard again. Matt wondered, sometimes, whether he had lent him the money.

André turned to the last page and Matt pointed at the line at the bottom. "I was wondering what to do there, with the compactification. I've looked at the vector moduli half a dozen different ways, but I haven't managed to prove yet that our theory doesn't depend on their initial values."

André read the paragraph Matt was showing him. "Your approach looks fine. We're not going to solve this problem in a day."

"I'd just really like to be done in June. I'll be set back by at least a semester if this doesn't work."

"What matters is to make a strong contribution. In the grand scheme of things, six more months isn't that big of a deal." Matt winced; André gave him a long look. He reached for a pencil and, after a moment of hesitation, added a few lines at the bottom of Matt's page. "I'd use this property if I were you, and inject it over there, and also plug the result you had last week, the last one we talked about." He scribbled while he spoke. "Why don't you try that? See what you come up with. The preprint I gave you might be helpful too, although you have to be careful with the assumptions." He handed the papers back to Matt. "I can't picture our conjecture not being true. It ties everything together too perfectly not to be correct."

Matt nodded without vigor. "Do you think I'll graduate in June?"

"You can graduate as soon as you get this done. You're almost there." André's eyes twinkled with excitement. "I'm not sure you understand how important this is. It'll bring us so much closer to unifying the four forces. It's going to open up a whole new area of research, give physicists new tools to approach problems. People will talk about this for years."

Matt forced himself to smile. "I'll make it happen."

18

The article was published on the first Sunday in December. Françoise would never have known, or at least not known for days, if the wife of another faculty member had not called.

"I haven't seen it. I haven't even gotten out of the house yet."

"I'm so glad. Don't buy it. Don't waste your money. Everyone in the department has the highest opinion of André. That journalist is just trying to sell copies."

Françoise hopped into the Volvo and headed for the news-stand outside the Alewife train station. She could have bought the *Globe* at CVS or Starbucks, but André insisted they patronize small, independent businesses, and he liked the family selling the papers – first-generation immigrants, trying to make a life for themselves. Françoise hurried back to the car, locked the doors, and unfolded the Health and Science section.

"Anything interesting in the paper today?"

Jim shrugged. "Not that I'm aware of."

Diane, still in her pajamas and with her black hair tied up in a ponytail, sat down on the couch. She folded her legs under her, careful not to spill her tea while she moved about. "Can I have what you've already read?"

Jim retrieved the Metro pages, which he had tucked between a cushion and the armrest, and handed them to his girlfriend. That was out of character for him – he usually browsed through the Health and Science section first, commented on the writing of the other reporters on his beat, compared the placement and size of the articles before looking at the rest.

Diane frowned. "What happened to the Health section?"

"I don't remember where I left it." Jim kept his eyes on the sports results.

Diane raised an eyebrow but did not comment. She unfolded the Metro pages, brought her cup to her lips, winced immediately. "I'll go and put in some more milk." She got up slowly – she did not want tea to drip onto the carpet – and disappeared into the kitchen.

The fridge door opened and closed and, after a few seconds, opened and closed again. Diane returned.

"What's that under the couch?" She pointed at the space behind Jim's feet.

Jim bent down. "That's the newspaper." He grabbed the bundle of pages and, without giving it a second glance, tucked it under the cushion where the Metro pages had been.

Diane stood motionless for a second. She took another sip of tea – perfect now with the extra milk – before striding toward the couch and leaning over the armrest. Jim, his eyes on the football scores, clenched his jaws but did not stop her as she plucked the Health and Science section out of its hiding place.

Diane stared at the headline on the front page. Her face turned white. "That's about André Darrieux," she said. Jim's eyes narrowed on the long list of touchdowns and interceptions that had occurred during the weekend games. "They printed your article. Why didn't you tell me?"

Diane placed her cup of tea on the table and, clutching the newspaper with both hands, read the lead paragraph as fast as she could.

"I don't think you're going to like it. It was a difficult decision to make, but in the end I owed it to my readers to tell the real story."

"What real story?" Diane, browsing through the story, gaped at something he had written. "The story that his student's spreading around? The story that makes someone who can't defend himself look bad because it sells papers?"

"I don't write to sell papers."

Diane shook her head and plopped into an armchair, started reading again. She covered her hand with her mouth when she reached the last column of text.

Jim eyed her across the room. "It's not that bad," he finally said. "The article's fair. It's not, you know, a hatchet job." Diane looked like she was going to cry. She rested her elbows on her thighs and massaged her temples, eyes half-closed, chin quivering. "The man's not a saint. I presented all sides of him."

"You parroted what a disgruntled student told you." Diane's mouth twisted with disgust.

The couple's neighbors turned the television on. The set was probably placed right against the wall; Jim and Diane, if they had bothered to listen, could have followed the actors' entire conversation. Jim raised his voice above the TV's chatter. "The fact that she doesn't like him doesn't mean she's disgruntled. It just means she doesn't like him, and she gave me valid reasons for that."

"You only know her version of what happened. Besides, maybe she got carried away. People say all kinds of things they don't mean to look good in the newspaper."

Jim shook his head. "She meant every single word." Diane pinched her lips. The neighbor changed the channel. "Anyway, it's my article. You're not responsible for what I wrote. Stop making a big deal about this."

"You don't understand." Diane waved the paper in the air. "Without me you wouldn't even have known André Darrieux existed. I made this happen."

It took Françoise several minutes, when she was done reading, to feel able to drive without risking an accident – without forgetting to stop at a red light or ignoring a 'yield' sign. She sat in the car and breathed, in and out, in and out. A young man parked his pickup truck next to the Volvo and hopped out; two teenagers who had been waiting by the glass doors of the T Station slapped hands with him before they all disappeared inside. Françoise waited for the moment she would cry. It did not come – the shock had drained her of all her energy. She felt too numb to even stretch her arm, turn the key into the ignition, put the gear in reverse. A wave of Red Line passengers spilled onto the sidewalk and scurried away in the cold winter morning. The same sentence kept tumbling in Françoise's head: she had thought the interview had gone well.

How naïve she had been.

She stared at the photograph of André's empty office on the front page, read the beginning of the article again.

"What a bunch of nonsense." Françoise leaned her head against the headrest. She often thought aloud in her car, although most days she limited her comments to other people's driving. "I should call that journalist and complain, but he's not going to care." The engine was still off and the temperature in the Volvo was dropping fast despite the bright morning sun. Françoise folded her arms across her chest. "I can write a letter to the editor. I guess that's what people do. They write letters." Her writing skills in English would not impress anybody but at least she would set the record straight. "The *Globe*'s readers must expect me to defend André no matter what, though. They'll never believe me over that journalist." Françoise tapped her foot against the car floor. Her breath condensed into a little cloud in front of her mouth. "André would know what to do." He would contact the right people, pen a convincing letter, turn public opinion around. "He would fix this."

She wanted to see him.

Françoise turned the key into the ignition and, cranking up the heat, maneuvered out of the parking spot.

The rehabilitation center faced the Charles River, half a mile from M.G.H.; Françoise had not even needed to learn a new route to get there. She used the same highway, the same exit. Once, she had even forgotten that she was not driving to Massachusetts General anymore and kept left on the exit ramp instead of going right, missed her turn onto Nashua Street. She had not made that mistake again.

Françoise left the *Globe* on the passenger seat and scanned the lounge on the first floor – no copy of the news rag lay around. Good, she thought. Very good. She was pleased with the facility and found the physicians extremely helpful, but she missed chatting with the M.G.H. nurse who had often dropped by to see how André was doing. She had been so nice. Diane, her name had been. Françoise had promised to let her know of all the milestones in André's recovery. She seemed to have grown quite fond of him.

Françoise made a large smile at the staff members who hurried along the corridor, unsure of who cared for André but eager to make a good impression – she needed to build a lot of goodwill now to counterbalance the picture that the *Globe* had drawn of her husband. Hopefully, everybody at the clinic read the *Boston Herald*.

André was alone. He lay in bed and looked at nothing in particular.

"Surprise!"

André turned his head in the direction of the voice. Françoise thought his eyes widened when he saw her. "I know I told you I'd come around three, but I figured I'd do something different for once." She tried to sound light-hearted. André liked to joke about her routines: how she ordered the same dishes at their favorite restaurant each and every time, prepared a pot of herbal tea whenever they came back from a walk, could not start her day without NPR in the background, and refused – adamantly refused – to change the route she took to go to Whole Foods, although André knew a shorter way. He did not appear to remember any of this now. She had told him she would come at three, and the André she had been married to would have known right away that her showing up much earlier meant there was an issue.

"Did you have a good night's sleep?" Françoise could not decipher her husband's reaction. "It's a beautiful day outside. Cold but sunny, and not a single cloud in the sky." She propped up the pillows. "I hope we won't get another snowstorm before Christmas. I've had enough bad weather for a while." André did not move in his hospital bed. Diane claimed his ability to process facial expressions remained intact, because it was housed in the hemisphere that had not been affected by the stroke – she had looked it up on the Internet in her free time and shared the news with Françoise the next morning. He can tell if you're upset, she had warned her. He can't ask you what's wrong, but he'll know if something's bothering you. André had never distinguished himself when it came to reading people but Françoise did not want to risk worrying him. She grinned. "Actually, I hope we won't get another snowstorm before you're discharged. I want you on shovel duty." The muscles on one side of André's face twitched. His wife decided he found her comment funny.

"I wonder if you'll have any visitors today."

Françoise hoped not. André had not received many visits since he had been transferred to the clinic, except for Evelyn who had brought a get-well card from the physics department. Most of the time, acquaintances left André alone, which was just as well. If they came after reading the *Globe*, they would not remember to fake cheerfulness. He might notice their pity. He recognized concrete words – the speech therapist held items and pronounced their name, day after day, to bring his memory back – and Françoise was certain that he would understand "article in the newspaper." His visitors' faces would tell him the media coverage was not putting him in a good light.

What would people say? Françoise knew what she wanted to hear: it was not the first time a reporter distorted the facts to get attention; M.I.T. made an easy target. It had nothing to do with André. But Jim Calloway had quoted a real person – a real, anonymous person uttering those awful statements while André could not defend himself – and as much as Françoise wanted to believe everyone liked her husband, she doubted that the journalist had made the quote up. No, it came from a member of André's circle.

Françoise pulled her husband's blanket up. "Would you like to watch television?" She grabbed the remote. *Meet the Press* was about to end. "You can change the channel if you want." She pressed the remote's buttons a few times, trying to elicit a grunt from André – a sign that this or that program interested him more than the others. When the sign did not come, she returned to NBC. The anchor and his guests spoke too fast for her to make sense of their words. At home she relied on closed captioning to follow what happened on the screen – she understood English better when it was written than spoken – but at the clinic she had not figured out how to turn the feature on. "Do you remember that undergraduate student of yours, the one who racked up three thousand dollars in debt from playing poker and was worried to tell his parents? I wonder what happened to him." She paused. "I was convinced he'd never pay you back, but he did." She smoothed the blanket. "He was very thankful."

The program broke to commercials. The cheerful tone of the actress praising cough syrup annoyed Françoise.

"And the one who called you from the police station after he got caught for underage drinking and started to fight with the officer, a couple of years ago? He was happy you bailed him out." Françoise chuckled. "Those are good memories. You had an impact on all these kids."

André did not move, but his eyelids fluttered. Françoise hoped a speck of dust was not bothering him. She wanted to believe he had been listening to her speech.

"I read an article in the *New York Times* the other day, about a famous mathematician people call a slave-driver. They say his research is in trouble, but it sounds like they're jealous." She eyed André's reaction. He had none. "I wonder what the mathematician's going to do. Maybe it'd be a good idea for him to write a letter to the editor." Silence. "Or he could simply focus on his research. You know, prove them wrong on the facts. If people have decided he's a slave-driver without any evidence, they won't change their mind simply because he says he isn't." Françoise took a deep breath. "What do you think?"

André did not reply.

He rarely got upset, but the rumor that he had received devastating news at the conference – that his legacy was at risk, his reputation endangered – would have made him bang his fist against the dinner table and utter all the French curse words he knew. Françoise sensed as much. The article raised more questions than it answered. Jim Calloway did not explain what the bad news were about, but he strongly suggested that M.I.T. would benefit from counting fewer slave-drivers in its midst, and that André had met his comeuppance for bursting with ambition and treating students poorly.

Françoise ground her teeth before she remembered Diane's warning – he can tell if you're upset. She slapped a smile on her face.

"Thankfully, you're not that mathematician. Your colleagues hold you in high esteem. Nobody would ever call you a slave-driver."

One of André's eyebrows arched into a frown. He seemed so helpless, with half his face that did not move, in that white, foreign room he could not leave. Françoise had run to him just like eight years earlier, when Bernard had been rushed to a trauma-one hospital in Vermont after a skiing accident – she had not managed to reach her husband by phone, had grabbed her car keys and headed for Cambridge. André had been sitting in a faculty meeting; they had entered the Burlington city limits two and a half hours later, anxious to see their son and relieved not to have met the state police along the way. Françoise had relied on him back then, to decide they would drive to Vermont and make sizable forays above the speed limit, while she hoped they would not crash but was grateful she did not have to drive. She had relied on him for thirty-four years. He could not help her now.

Françoise patted André's hand. "Your research's going great. Your reputation's well-established. I'm so proud of you."

He would not devise a plan to set the record straight. The doctors did not even agree about the damage the stroke had done to his brain – she kept asking them, and they kept eluding her questions. He might not have understood what she was trying to say. He watched the images flickering on the television set but showed no sign of recognizing the news anchor.

"You focus on getting better, alright? I'll take care of the rest. Don't worry about a thing."

She was on her own.

19.

André's father died in October 1995. He had been working in the yard when he fell; the paramedics were unable to revive him. Françoise picked up the phone in the kitchen and knew right away that something had happened – calling from France to the United States cost a small fortune and Michel would not have bothered if there had not been an emergency.

Françoise held the handset out to her husband. "It's your brother."

On the East Coast, the Saturday afternoon had just begun; The Darrieuxs were still eating their lunch. A platter of cheese lay on the table, bracketed by two long-stemmed glasses, André's empty and Françoise's about a third full with Cabernet Sauvignon. Rex sniffed around with his nose up, in the hope that a morsel of bread had been left within his reach. Françoise leaned against the countertop and looked at her husband.

André cradled the phone between his neck and shoulder, rubbed the bridge of his nose. He turned pale all of a sudden. The dog sat very straight and stared at his owner with big, inquisitive eyes.

"I'll see if we can get on tomorrow's flight. If not, we'll leave on Monday evening, Tuesday at the latest. I'll call you back when I have our tickets." André hung up. "My father died."

Françoise covered her mouth with her hand. For a second, nobody talked.

"What happened?"

"He had a heart attack." André wiped his forehead, took a few steps.

"I'm so sorry."

André waved her aside and reached for the dog's leash. "I'll be back in an hour."

Rex barked happily, thrilled by the surprise outing. André put on his shoes and grabbed a jacket; the patio door closed behind the two of them. Françoise hurried into the living-room and watched as they walked away – Rex trotting along and pulling André forward, André looking down and paying his surroundings no attention. Françoise stood by the window until her husband and their dog had disappeared out of her sight.

She tried to reach Bernard at Harvard, but the phone rang and rang in his dorm room without anyone picking up. That did not surprise her – in addition to his coursework, her son juggled saxophone practice with the jazz band, meetings of the College Democrats and sessions of the International Relations Council. He had promised Françoise to give the French Club a try, although she could not hold it against him that he had yet to find the time. She left a message on the answering machine he shared with a roommate in Lowell House. Bernard returned her call forty-five minutes later; by then she had cleared the table, washed the dishes, dragged a suitcase out of the closet and spread over the bed all the clothes she owned in black. André had not returned from his walk.

"Your grandfather died." Bernard did not say a thing. "André's father. He had a heart attack. We're flying out tomorrow or Monday for the funeral. Needless to say, you're coming with us." She paused, but her son did not comment. "I've got to call the people at the kennel to see if they can take Rex for a few nights."

Françoise grabbed a pen and scribbled 'kennel' on the to-do list she kept by her nightstand. The silence dragged on at the other end of the line.

"Hello?"

"I'm still there."

"You have to tell your professors. Make sure you get the notes for the lectures you're going to miss, and the assignments too."

Françoise stretched a dress across the bedcover – long-sleeved with a bateau neck – placed a hat on top, took a step back to gauge the result. This would be perfect for the church.

Bernard sighed. "I've got a project presentation on Thursday. We haven't finished writing the report. I don't want to ditch my teammates."

"It's a death in the family. I'm sure they'll understand."

"And I've got rehearsals for the jazz band. Our big concert's coming up. How's the band going to practice without me? What about the exam I've got to study for?"

Françoise blinked, wondered whether her son was saying what she thought he was. "He was your grandfather. You have to come. You'll only miss a couple of days."

"But I barely knew him. I had no connection to him. I saw him once a year, and he wasn't even nice."

Françoise glanced behind her – worried that André would appear by the door, back from his walk at last, and overhear the conversation – but her husband was nowhere in sight.

"He was upset with your father because we live so far away. That had nothing to do with you. He loved you very much."

"He had a strange way to show it."

"He was your grandfather all the same. You're coming with us."

"No one will notice if I'm not there. I've got so many things to do."

Françoise wound the phone cord around her index finger, closed her eyes, pressed her lips together. She did not blame her son for his indifference. He had developed no bond with his relatives across the ocean; she could not expect him to miss his grandfather. Miss him for what? They had shared so little – vague words about Bernard's courses and the importance of education in today's world, before Gustave returned to his greenhouse and Bernard flopped onto a deckchair with a book. Invariably, that book would be in English; the boy struggled with his French, which in the States he only spoke with his parents. He barely glanced at the model boats that his grandfather had built over the years, never asked about his former job at the geophysics institute. For him, the man was a stranger alive and an annoyance dead, wreaking havoc on his schedule, threatening his good grades.

"He was very proud of you. He told all his neighbors that his grandson was going to Harvard."

"I spent more time with my friends' parents in high school when I went over to their home than I ever spent with him. I see the janitors and the kitchen staff at Lowell House more often. And if they died, I wouldn't be invited to their memorial service."

"You're invited to this one, and you're coming with us." Bernard scoffed. Françoise, tugging on the phone cord, wondered what kind of mother she had been. "I raised you better than that." She pretended to believe her own words. What had she done, she thought. What had André done.

Michel picked them up at the airport and drove them to his and André's mother's house. Solange hurried outside when her younger son stepped out of the Renault Laguna. Her hair was gray and her face wrinkled; she walked with a cane and, while she had once been only a few inches shorter than Françoise, she now looked diminutive next to the rest of the family. Françoise never became more aware of time passing by than when she saw her mother-in-law after a long absence.

Solange, leaning on her son's arm, took small steps toward the front door; Françoise followed right behind them. Michel and Bernard retrieved the suitcases from the car's trunk and entered the house last. When the Darrieux men stood side by side, one could not fail to notice the prominent forehead they all shared – Bernard struggled to communicate with his relatives, kept his sentences in French short and to the point, but he was part of the family without a doubt. On photographs, Françoise was the one who looked like she did not belong.

Michel's wife, Lise, emerged from the kitchen. "How was your flight?"

André shrugged. "It was alright. Uneventful." Françoise stifled a yawn. She had rested about ninety minutes on the plane – or rather, had closed her eyes and pretended to relax. Whenever she had glanced at her husband, she had found him staring at the back of the seat in front of him, oblivious to the television monitors, the noise, the stewardesses pushing carts in the aisles and passing food around. André, it seemed, had kept his eyes wide open the whole time.

"Do you want to eat something? We brought croissants."

The group moved into the dining room. Michel helped his mother onto an armchair and took a seat by her side. Solange and

THE BREAKTHROUGH

Gustave had lived in the same house for the past fifty-five years; their children had grown up in that dining room, toiling on their homework, watching television, playing cards. Gustave had taught his children *bridge* and *belote* during the long summer holidays – André in particular showed a talent for card games. Father and son always won when they teamed together against Solange and Michel, to Gustave's never-ending delight. The Darrieuxs would be missing a fourth player now.

But, despite André's efforts to squeeze a game in his schedule when he was in town, they had been missing one for decades.

The room was plain, a bit small for six people, with the furniture taking most of the space – the dining table, the coffee table, the sofa and two armchairs, the television set, and cupboards of various sizes. Lise brought a pot of coffee and china cups on a tray, together with a paper bag full of croissants.

Solange looked at André. "He seemed fine. I wish you'd seen him. He seemed absolutely fine when he said he was going to do some gardening. There was no way to tell this was going to happen." She crumbled a handkerchief into her palm. Michel patted his mother's hand. "He was looking forward to seeing you this summer. He even bought a physics book to better understand what you were doing." Solange sniffled. "An American wrote it. Someone at the bookstore said it was a best-seller in the States. It's about recent advances in theoretical physics and what it means for the Universe and how Nature works. It sounded really impressive." André, elbows resting on his thighs, stared at the floor. Françoise felt he knew exactly which book his mother was referring to and did not want to talk about it. "Let me show you."

Solange gripped the armrests and tried to lift herself up.

"I'll get it, Mom." Michel disappeared into the corridor, returned almost immediately, gave his mother the book.

"See. That's it." Solange placed the thick volume on her son's lap. The book, written by a Harvard professor, had already won many awards.

André stared at the cover page. "That sounds interesting."

"He was disappointed not to find your name mentioned anywhere. He read the index three times to make sure there was no mistake."

"People write that kind of books to showcase their achievements. They don't write them to give their competitors free publicity."

Lise filled the cups with coffee. "Tell me when to stop. The milk's over there. And please, have some croissants."

"That's not what the book's about. You didn't even read the back cover." Solange paused. "But maybe you can write a book too, about your big discovery, when you finally make it. We've all been looking forward to that."

Michel stepped outside and lit a cigarette on the patio with his back to the house. Lise handed another croissant to Bernard; Françoise blinked furiously.

Solange stared at her son. "Gus always thought you were going to leave your mark. It was never in question for him. He wanted so much to see your day in the limelight."

20.

"Have you read it?"

"What – oh, that? No, I haven't. I've been studying for my test tomorrow. Besides, I don't know the guy. Haven't even taken a class with him."

"I haven't either, but I read the article. Everyone in the building is talking about it. I wanted to see for myself."

"I took his particle physics class last spring. He wasn't a bad teacher. Not the best one either but good enough, and less arrogant than most. I only went through the first few paragraphs of the article before I gave up. It just didn't seem to be about anyone I knew."

"A hatchet job, if you ask me. You really have to read the whole thing to understand that, though."

"Have you interacted with him outside class? Everyone can seem nice enough in a lecture hall. That doesn't mean a thing."

"I never talked to him besides saying hi when I ran into him in the hallway. But he didn't seem any worse than the other professors. A lot of students wanted to work with him."

"And those who did regretted it. That much is clear, isn't it? One filed a complaint with the physics department and another made all those comments to the reporter."

"That's only two. He's had many more. If it was some other professor in his situation, who knows what that person's students would say?"

"I was surprised the journalist knew about Pete. That happened years ago. He was just wrapping things up when I came. Not on friendly terms with anybody, ever, as far as I can tell. Between Pete and Darrieux, I'd think twice before taking Pete's side."

"Darrieux doesn't particularly come across as someone who, what was the quote, let me get the paper, *pressures his students for results, without any concern for their well-being, and lords his power over them.*"

"But that's the whole point. That's why there's a story. Because you don't expect it."

"I feel this is getting awfully close to slandering him."

"The reporter wouldn't dare. He doesn't work for a tabloid. He must have very solid sources he knows he can trust."

"And this one – an anonymous quote. *He was a slave-driver and I am glad he got a stroke – there's a justice after all.*"

"Terrible. That's the worst one, I think."

"Yeah, that one really gets to me. It just seems, I don't know, awfully disloyal."

"Friends of mine are already taking bets trying to guess who said it. It'll probably be the favorite game in town for a while. Pete has an early lead."

"Well, I looked up him in the alumni directory, and he lives in Singapore at the moment. He seems to be doing quite well. He has no reason to hold a grudge so many years later. It's doubtful the journalist was even able to get ahold of him."

"Who made those comments, then? They don't sound like something the journalist would pluck out of thin air without proof."

"For what it's worth, he's right on the statistics about strokes – perhaps that counts for something. My uncle had one last year. An ischemic one, like Darrieux's, when the blood flow is interrupted in the brain. It took him months to re-learn how to speak and understand what we were saying. He still can't make simple additions in his mind. We don't let him calculate tips. And yet things look a lot worse for Darrieux than for him."

"Is that because Darrieux missed the three-hour window for treatment, because the damage in his brain couldn't be addressed in time?"

"That, and the fact that he earns a living from mathematical models. If he loses those skills, what will be left?"

"So the journalist is telling the truth. Darrieux's prognosis is dire."

"Of course the journalist is telling the truth about that. It's something everyone can check. That's how he builds credibility. It doesn't mean a thing about the rest."

"I can't understand how that garbage ended up in the *Globe*."

THE BREAKTHROUGH

"Controversy sells."

"The *Globe* usually does far better work that that, though. It has received so many Pulitzer Prizes – in criticism, in reporting, also in public service. It has high standards. There's got to be more behind this article than an interest in selling papers."

"Maybe the writer is a newbie, trying to leave his mark. Always worry about the hotshots. They hog the spotlight."

"Darrieux isn't nearly famous enough to be worth creating controversy around. A tempest in a fish bowl, at most."

"Isn't he a contender for the Nobel Prize?"

"He's as much a contender for the Nobel Prize as I'm one for the dissertation-of-the-year award at the annual meeting. I'd love it if it happened, but at least I'm not kidding myself. He's imagining things."

"I can name several other profs in the department who deserve the prize more than he does."

"I like the work he's published over the past few years. He's written some really good papers."

"What bothers me the most is that the journalist visited Darrieux's wife at their house. He knew he wasn't going to put Darrieux in a good light, and yet he sat in the woman's living room and interviewed her at length and then quoted her many times."

"Why not? What she said sounded harmless."

"It reinforces the image of him as a crazed perfectionist. All that talk about Beethoven's Fifth that has to be played by the Wiener Philharmoniker for Darrieux to even listen to it. *Only the best.*"

"I bet she regrets talking to that journalist now."

"If I were her, I'd be fuming about what he wrote on my family rather than what he quoted me on. The guy did everything to make Darrieux sound estranged from his only son. And his analysis about the choice of pictures on the chimney! What sort of pop psychology was that?"

"I agree – completely over the top."

"But isn't it true, that Darrieux is estranged from his son?"

"I think it is."

"You're kidding me."

"I'm not. His son relocated to San Diego to move away from him. I can't remember who told me that. Maybe Evelyn?"

"She talks too much."

"But Darrieux is indeed absent-minded. There was nothing mean-spirited in her admitting that, or telling the journalist that little mundane tasks bore him to no end."

"They do bore him. They really do."

"If that part is true, why not the rest? *Any distraction that takes time away from research is unwelcome, and students who cannot exhibit such dedication are discouraged from joining his research team.*"

"That's hot air."

"That journalist has some numbers on the average time Darrieux's students take to get their degree. It has increased markedly over the past ten years, and it's not like they graduated fast before."

"I wonder what could've triggered such an increase."

"Maybe the journalist rounded some numbers up, or cherry-picked the students to compute his statistics."

"Anyway, there's no point in debating that now. You read the article. Odds are, he won't return to work."

"That last paragraph got to me, man. It really did. That was cold on the journalist's part."

"What does it say?"

"You can read it if you want."

"Here. *In his hospital room, André Darrieux has the vacant gaze of those who have seen their legacy crumble in front of them. He does not appear to recognize the day nurse when she opens the door. One thinks about all the discoveries that used to be within his reach and that he will never make.*"

"Enough. You're going to make me feel sorry for the guy, and he doesn't sound like someone I want to feel sorry for."

"You don't know if the accusations are true."

"We'll never know for sure. He has his supporters and his detractors, like everyone else. People will believe what they want."

"And the last sentence! It punched me in the stomach."

"*Instead, the Nobel-Prize contender who pushed his students so hard stares ahead in his hospital bed, motionless, his days of glory behind him.*"

"Can we drop the matter now? I've got work to do."

21.

Françoise decided against going back to the house – Buddy would wag his tail and jump about, expect a second person to step out of the car; she would stroke his head and whisper: not today. Instead, she drove to Cambridge and parked the station wagon in the garage on Eliot Street, wandered around Harvard Square in the cold afternoon sun. She had seldom returned to the area while André was a young assistant professor, but she used to have lunch with Bernard every other week near campus during her son's college years. They would talk about his courses, his friends, anything that was on his mind. Françoise had taken great pride from her relationship with her child. That had been before Harvard Business School, before Bernard's foray into entrepreneurship, before the start-up he had funded with three friends, before his money problems.

Two students finished a late lunch on the steps of the Widener Library, their fingers red from the cold. A group of undergraduates huddled in front of Sever Hall. The wind had picked up and Françoise buttoned her coat. She read the announcements on the bulletin boards to distract herself – a room would become available near Central Square after the finals, the last student concert of the year would feature works by Tchaikovsky and Brahms, it was not too late to sign up for a prep course before taking the GMAT. But her thoughts kept wandering back to André. He had never received so much attention from the press, even after the European Physical Society had awarded him its High Energy and Particle Physics Prize. The article in the *Globe* was what people would remember him for, until his condition improved and he could defend himself – an article that portrayed him as an insecure, ruthless individual who relentlessly pressured his students for results without any concern for their well-being, written by someone who had not even talked to him.

Françoise had forgotten her gloves in her haste to get out of the house and folded her arms across her chest, hand inside opposite sleeve, to warm her fingers. Students hurried against the wind, chin tucked into their scarf. Françoise made a large circle through the yard for lack of anything better to do. She tried to collect herself but could not come up with a plan of action. She was not used to dealing with her husband's professional world. She did not know how to fight the critics.

That much she knew: André had not brought this upon himself. He did not deserve what had happened. The Darrieuxs had been married for almost thirty-five years, though, and Françoise had never seen her husband as preoccupied as in the car, after his flight had landed at Logan – maybe the journalist's claims contained a grain of truth, buried under all the exaggerations. André had received bad news at the conference. He would not have spent the ride home scribbling on his notepad otherwise.

Françoise's heart sank. What had her husband learnt that could endanger his reputation and put his legacy at risk?

She caught herself using the journalist's words. Surely he had been trying to sell more copies. She should not believe what she had read. Yet, she could not help but worry.

The cold was seeping through her clothes. She crossed Massachusetts Avenue, pushed her way through the crowd strolling down the sidewalk, pulled the large glass doors of Au Bon Pain. The coffee shop was bustling with patrons, like every weekend afternoon. She grabbed a latte, although she disliked American coffee and American chains with French names – no self-respecting French establishment would ever serve coffee in extra-large paper cups. At least her purchase would postpone the drive back to Belmont by fifteen more minutes. She looked for an empty table near the bay window and, when she could not find any, retreated to the back of the store in search of a spot. Her gaze fell on a young woman with curly hair who sat alone, a book open in front of her, an iPod by her side. Françoise started when she recognized Olivia Reynolds.

"Do you mind if I join you? It's so hard to find a seat." Olivia looked up from her book and gave her a blank stare. "I'm Françoise

Darrieux. My husband told me so much about you. I've seen your picture. It's so nice to meet you in person."

Olivia opened her eyes wide. Her cheeks turned bright red in a matter of seconds. She shook her head – no, she did not mind at all. Françoise plopped onto a chair while Olivia put her book away and slid the plate with a half-eaten muffin toward her side of the table.

The silence dragged on.

"I'm sorry about the article," Olivia said.

Françoise forced herself to smile. "It's not your fault. Do you live around here?"

"Ten minutes away down Mass Ave." Olivia paused. "I really didn't expect the article to come out the way it did. I was shocked when I read it."

"You're lucky to be so close to Harvard Square. I love this area."

Olivia nodded and took a sip of her drink. An employee had checked the 'hot chocolate' box on the side of the cup.

"How are things going for you?"

"They're going alright." Olivia kept her eyes down.

"My husband would've hated putting you in this situation." Françoise poured a packet of sweetener into her latte. At home she preferred her drinks without sugar, but there was no point in pretending that this beverage tasted anything like her *café au lait*. "I'm sure that, given the circumstances, one of his colleagues will agree to supervise your dissertation until he comes back to work."

Olivia shrugged. "Actually, I'm thinking about taking some time off."

Françoise waited for her to say more, but Olivia did not add a word.

"I guess it's as good a time as any to get some rest, before diving back into the thick of things." Françoise congratulated herself in silence for using an English idiom. André would have been proud.

"It's not just because Professor Darrieux is in the hospital. My research project isn't getting anywhere." Olivia bit into her muffin and stared at the crumbs. "It wasn't supposed to be that hard. I only had to extend someone else's work, but I can't even understand most of the proofs." She sighed. "I wish I'd done better, you know?"

"It's a difficult topic. Your parents must be proud. Not everyone goes to M.I.T."

Olivia scoffed. "My mother wanted me to go to law school." She tore off the top of the muffin. "Maybe I'm not cut out for this thing. I thought I was, but maybe I was wrong. In New Mexico, I was a big fish in a small pond. I wanted to try the big leagues. I should've stayed where I was." She pinched her lips. At the counter, an employee shouted for someone named Esther to pick up her mozzarella chicken sandwich. "I didn't do a lot of research my first two years because I was taking so many classes, but last year I got serious about it. I wanted to impress Professor Darrieux so badly." She looked at Françoise again. "I'm really sorry about the article."

They sat in silence. Next to them, a redhead with freckles browsed through a magazine, her chair surrounded by Crate & Barrel bags; a couple discussed the movie they had just watched at the Brattle Theatre. A middle-aged woman across the room burst into laughter – a high-pitched laughter that made patrons chuckle, although no one could figure out what the woman was laughing about.

"It's alright," Françoise finally said.

"I wish I could help. I feel really bad about the whole thing."

Françoise made a vague gesture with her hand – there was not much left to do. Olivia looked disappointed.

"I remember when I first met Professor Darrieux. It was Admits weekend my senior year. I'd gone to Paris for Spring break – nothing fancy, I stayed in youth hostels with my friends, but the city was fabulous – and I thought we could talk about that. He laughed because he wasn't from Paris. He was from Lyon." Françoise smiled. "He said that for the last thirty years about the only thing he'd seen from Paris was the Charles-de-Gaulle airport and I knew more about Paris than he did. He also joked I shouldn't ask him anything about wines except to drink them."

"That sounds like him." Françoise chuckled.

"We were similar, in a way." Olivia corrected herself quickly. "Are similar. When I tell people I'm from New Mexico, they always look me up and down, me and my fair skin, as if I really mean I'm from Minnesota." Olivia and Françoise laughed together. "So he isn't the typical Frenchman and I'm not the typical New Mexican and we get along well."

The couple who had seen a movie at the Brattle got up and put their coats on. A woman carrying a bulging plastic bag from Harvard Book Store hurried toward their table and claimed it before anyone else had a chance to.

"What are you doing, then, if you don't have an advisor?"

"Studying for my classes. The department chair told everyone in Professor Darrieux's group that we'll be taken care of for the spring semester. We'll be on Teaching Assistantships. That leaves us a couple of months to figure out what to do."

"By June, André will probably be back at work."

Olivia blinked. "That'd be nice."

The woman with the bag from Harvard Book Store cracked open the hardcover she had just bought.

Françoise wrapped her hands around her latte while she searched for the right words. "Maybe you can do a little something for me, if you have time on your hands. It's really for André more than for me." She paused to gauge Olivia's reaction. The young woman raised an eyebrow. "I think André got bad news at that conference, but I can't understand a thing of what he wrote after I picked him up from the airport. It's a lot of equations. There aren't even that many words." Olivia leaned over the table, her mouth slightly open. "I need someone to read his notes and tell me what they're about."

Olivia's face lit up. "I'd be happy to." She giggled on her seat.

"André had a student named Pete Neumann a while back. The two didn't have the best relationship, especially toward the end. I wonder if maybe what happened has something to do with him."

"But didn't Pete leave, like, ten years ago?" Olivia frowned. "I read his dissertation when I started in the lab."

"Maybe. I don't know." Françoise shrugged. "He wouldn't have been above faking a few proofs in order to graduate."

In the corner, a mother and her son leaned against the wall, sandwiches in hand, and waited for a table to become available.

"Someone would have figured it out by now." Olivia grimaced. "It wouldn't have taken ten years. I mean, Pete even got a prize for his dissertation. His work got triple-checked. If there'd been a mistake somewhere, Matt Johnson for one would have caught it."

Françoise tilted her head to the side. "What makes you so sure?"

"Matt worked on the project for years after Pete graduated."

"Then maybe Pete fooled a lot of people. My husband would certainly have been devastated if he'd found out a decade later."

Olivia bit into her muffin, chewed slowly. "I can't imagine anyone fooling both Matt Johnson and Professor Darrieux for so long."

"I guess it'll be easy to check. Either my husband's notes are related to Pete's work or they aren't. It'd be so helpful if you could drop by one afternoon and take a look."

Olivia nodded vigorously. "What about this week? I don't have class on Tuesday." She finished eating her muffin and lifted the plastic lid from her cup, peeked inside to check how much hot chocolate remained. After a moment of hesitation, she took a last gulp.

"Tuesday would be perfect. I'll pick you up at the T station. Just give me a call when you get there." Françoise scribbled her phone number on the back of a Whole Foods receipt.

Olivia pocketed the piece of paper and pushed her chair back. "I'd love to stay longer but I've got to get going." She wriggled into her jacket, a bit tight around the shoulders, and shook Françoise's hand. "It was nice meeting you."

Françoise allowed herself a smile while Olivia sauntered toward the exit. She had promised André she would take care of everything – he only had to focus on getting better – and she was keeping her word.

22.

Françoise picked up Olivia at Alewife and thanked her for coming.

"It's nothing, really. I've got some time on my hands." Olivia dropped her umbrella at her feet, fastened her seatbelt. The back of her jeans had soaked in the rain while she was hurrying to the T station in Central Square. Françoise cranked up the heat.

"How are your classes?"

Olivia shrugged. "Good. Almost over." And then: "I'm too old to be taking classes."

"You don't have much of a choice, now, do you?" Françoise smiled. Olivia did not reply. "Are you staying in Cambridge over the break?"

"I'm going to New Mexico for two weeks, coming back the first week of January."

The car's wipers squealed across the windshield. Olivia leaned back in her seat and watched the landscape. She had never been to Belmont – it was a residential area and she had not had any reason to go.

"New Mexico must be nice during the winter."

"Nicer than here, that's for sure."

"What do you like most?"

Olivia sighed. "There are too many things to count. Sometimes I think I should've never left."

"You can always move back after you graduate." Françoise checked her rearview mirror and glared at a SUV that was following her too closely. "I'm so glad I ran into you the other day. André's notes are Chinese to me. It bothers me to think the clues to his stroke might be right there and I can't see them."

"Physics is Chinese to a lot of people." Olivia chuckled while looking out the window, at the trees and road signs, the houses in the background.

"I was hoping to get André out of the nursing home for the day, but the staff said it was too soon. He wouldn't have been able to help. He's got everything in his head, though. It's just hard for him to express himself."

Olivia blinked and untied her woolen scarf. Her cheeks were glowing pink all of a sudden. Françoise turned the heat down.

"I didn't expect him to be there anyway," Olivia finally said. Françoise left the Concord Turnpike at the Route 60 exit, her foot on the brake pedal. "I can ask him for help later if I need to, but I doubt it'll come to that. I know the topic well. I can do this." She sounded like she was giving herself a pep talk as much as trying to convince Françoise.

"I'm sure you can. André thought highly of you."

Olivia opened her eyes wide. "He did?"

"Absolutely. He said so many times."

"I wish he'd told me that."

Françoise stopped at a red light. The rain was not letting up; water puddles stretched across the roadway. A pickup truck idled at the intersection. "That article's making me sick. André's done so much for his students, and this is what he'll be remembered for." She bit her bottom lip. "I keep wondering what people think about him now. They probably believe what they read in the paper. I don't blame them. I would do the same."

Olivia tucked a strand of hair behind her ear, twice, and looked away. "Maybe they'll forget about it. The Sunday edition's pretty thick. There's a lot of information. Besides, other journalists will write about him. In the grand scheme of things, this article isn't going to matter."

"His colleagues won't forget. People who work in his area will find the article on the Internet when they search for his papers. It'll never go away." Françoise grimaced. "Even our son in San Diego will find out sooner or later."

The light turned to green.

Olivia tugged on the sleeves of her jacket. "Do you have other children?"

"No, just him."

"San Diego's a nice place to live."

"I don't understand why that reporter had to write such awful things. I mean, I know controversy sells, but André's a good man. He's devoted his career to training students and advancing science. Doesn't that count for something?"

"I'm sure the part on the fallen giant moved a lot of people," Olivia said after a while.

Françoise gave her a dubious look. "The article describes my husband as a slave-driver who deserves every bit of misfortune heaped on him."

Olivia fidgeted on her seat. "Maybe you should write a letter to the editor."

"No one reads those." Françoise pulled into a driveway. "No, I have to do more than writing a letter. I just haven't figured out what yet." She turned the engine off and removed the key from the ignition. "Here we are."

Olivia got out of the car, her hand raised to protect her eyes from the rain. The house had two floors, with a white front and dark tiles on the roof. It did not appear as massive as some of the others on the block, although it was certainly large enough to fit two bedrooms with their own baths and walk-in closets, maybe an office as well – a family with children would not have found it luxurious, but it offered plenty of space for empty-nesters.

"We've been living here almost thirty years now. Hopefully long enough for our neighbors to know that article is worthless."

Olivia exhaled sharply.

Buddy leapt out when Françoise opened the door and wagged his tail at the stranger.

"Hello, you," Olivia said.

Françoise grabbed the dog by his collar, dragged him back inside. "He likes to lunge at people to wish them welcome. We don't have the best weather for that sort of things."

Olivia chuckled and wiped her feet on the doormat. She peeked into the living room, glimpsed at the pictures on the mantelpiece, the books on the coffee table, the plants by the window. It could have been anyone's home, neat and well-decorated.

Françoise headed for the study with Olivia following closely behind. "I hope you figure out what was bothering André. That

Globe reporter has his story wrong and I'm going to make sure the world knows, one way or another."

She stepped inside. Olivia lingered on the threshold. The room was filled with papers, stacked in crumbling piles on the table and on the floor – that room she recognized as her advisor's, without a doubt. At M.I.T., Darrieux (that was how she always called him when he was not in the room, instead of using "Professor" or referring to him by his first name) had made one pile for the courses he taught, one for the papers drafted by his students, one for the journal submissions he had to review; they never looked particularly stable and sometimes collapsed in the middle of a meeting. Darrieux would interrupt himself to straighten them out, dig out an old piece of campus mail – an advertisement for a talk long past maybe, or a conference held months earlier – that he would sheepishly throw away while Olivia tried not to laugh. Her advisor disliked anything that took time away from science, which included tidying up his office.

"This is what he was working on." Françoise picked up the yellow notepad on the desk. "Please, have a seat. Do you want something to drink? I've also got some pound cake if you'd like." Olivia perched herself on the edge of the armchair and stared at the legal pad with big, hungry eyes. Françoise watched her for a second. "I'll let you work, then. If you need anything, I'll be in the kitchen."

23.

"Is everything alright?"

André looked behind his shoulder. His wife was standing in the doorway, poking her head inside his study. It was three in the morning and Françoise struggled to keep her eyes open.

"I'm fine. I couldn't sleep, so I decided to get some work done." André paused. "The jetlag's been harder on me this time around."

The program of his father's memorial service still lay on the corner of his desk. Françoise knew very well that André's insomnia had nothing to do with time zones but let the white lie slide. "Do you need anything? Something to drink, maybe?"

André shook his head. Françoise sighed. Rex curled himself at her feet and waited.

"I'm going to make myself a cup of warm milk. I'll prepare one for you too." This time, André nodded.

In the kitchen, Françoise dropped a handful of croquettes into Rex's bowl. The dog wolfed them down, barked for more.

"You're going to get fat. It's bad for your heart."

"That dog might well enjoy life while he can." André plopped onto a chair by the kitchen table. "My father had stopped smoking years ago and was watching his cholesterol. It didn't do him any good."

"Maybe he would have died earlier otherwise."

"He died early enough."

Françoise placed two cups on the table and returned to the stove, where the milk was slowly warming up. "So what were you working on?"

"Something for Pete. I'm meeting with him this afternoon."

Françoise frowned. "Didn't you already meet with him two days ago, right after we returned?"

She turned the stove off and poured the milk into the cups. André raised the bowl to his face, stared at the liquid. "I'm refocusing his thesis. We're changing directions. That's why I have to meet with him more."

"I hadn't realized his research wasn't going well."

"It was going okay, but I got a better idea. The topic is more cutting-edge. His dissertation will have more impact." Rex, resigned to the thought he would not have a second serving, curled into a ball at Françoise's feet and rested his snout on her slippers. "Do you remember that conference I went to in March, the one in Los Angeles? A researcher from the Institute for Advanced Study in Princeton gave a talk that blew everybody's mind. He turned the playing field upside down." André made sweeping gestures as he spoke and raised his voice. The dog raised his head under the table and looked in André's direction. "I want Pete to work on some ideas I got while I was listening to him, see where that leads us. String theory is obviously our best shot at unifying the four forces. I might as well jump into the fray now, before too many people have joined in." André paused. "I wished I'd made that discovery myself. That researcher has his legacy etched in stone now. I should've been working on this since day one." He paused a second time. "I have some catching up to do, but I can handle it. String theory is a relatively new research area. I can get up to speed quickly."

Françoise rubbed her eyes. Not a noise was coming from the street – no car driving by, no bird chirping in, just the most complete silence in the middle of the night while two people sat around a kitchen table. The dishes of the previous evening's meal were aligned on the draining rack by the sink, dry already. Unread magazines were stacked in a neat pile next to the spice rack. Rex let out a heavy sigh.

"That conference was a while back, though. You've never mentioned changing Pete's thesis topic before."

André shrugged. "I thought I'd have my next graduate student work on it. I changed my mind."

"When did that happen?"

"A couple of days ago."

THE BREAKTHROUGH

"You mean, after we got back from Lyon?" André looked down at his cup, elbows on the table. "You were successful in your previous projects. What is wrong with what you were doing until now?"

A few seconds went by.

"That's not where the action is," André finally said. Françoise waited for him to say more. "Twenty years from now, people will remember whoever worked on string theory – no one else. It's that groundbreaking. I've got to take my chance."

Françoise got up and placed her empty cup in the sink. She sat down again, stared at her husband. "I don't think you should grieve your father by changing research areas." The voice barely sounded like hers.

André looked up from his bowl. "That's not what I'm doing," he said in a cold voice.

"You chose not to go back to France years ago. Not being there for your parents as they aged was part of that decision. You knew that from day one." Françoise leaned over the table and clutched André's hand. "There's no point in beating yourself up for it now."

"I don't see what you're talking about." André withdrew his hand. Françoise leaned back in her chair.

"It's not Pete's fault we didn't return to France. We would've had a good life in Lyon, but you didn't want it. Don't take it out on him now." André clenched his jaws. "It can't be easy for him to get started on a whole new topic."

"Pete's a smart kid. He'll figure it out."

André's mother died in 2004; she fell asleep and did not wake up. André had received the High Energy and Particle Physics prize from the European Physical Society the year before, in no small part thanks to Pete's new work. People now whispered his name as a contender for the Nobel Prize – maybe not as an imminent winner, but someone who made the short list. After the M.I.T. donors' magazine printed a lengthy article about him and his most recent award, complete with a large color picture, André ripped the page out and sent it to Solange. He added his own translation to make sure his mother would understand every word, especially every word of praise, of which there were many. André found the article in Solange's nightstand when he packed her belongings after her funeral. It had been folded and unfolded so many times that the paper was tearing at the creases.

24.

Footsteps clattered down the hallway. Susanna frowned, cup of tea in hand, as Olivia raced past her, stopped in front of Professor Greenawalt's office and knocked vigorously on the door although the lights were off and it was getting late. No one answered. Olivia knocked again.

"I think he's gone for the day."

"When did he leave?" Olivia was out of breath. "Maybe I can catch him in the parking lot."

Susanna shrugged. "The light has been off for an hour."

Olivia pursed her lips. She raised her hand but lowered it without knocking again. Her umbrella dripped on her feet. "I guess I could send him an email."

She did not move.

"Or you could talk to him tomorrow." Susanna unlocked her own door. She glanced at Olivia before stepping in. "What's so important anyway?"

"Nothing." Olivia's eyes twinkled with excitement.

"Then you don't even need to email him."

Olivia broke into a grin. "I was right!" She giggled like a twelve-year old. "Nobody wanted to believe me, but I was right!"

Susanna threw her tea bag into the wastebasket and, leaning against the doorframe, took a sip of her drink. The harsh light of the halogen lamp accentuated the wrinkles around her eyes and the streaks of grey by her temples. She had worked very hard for many years to get where she was now.

"Who didn't want to believe you?"

"André." Other students called their advisors by their first name; in front of faculty members, Olivia liked to pretend she enjoyed the same familiarity with her supervisor.

Susanna raised an eyebrow and pointed at Thomas Greenawalt's door. "What does he have to do with this?"

Olivia shifted her weight from left to right, and then left again. "He said maybe we could write a paper together, you know, to help me graduate. No big deal. I'll talk to him tomorrow." She took a step back.

A door closed. "Olivia. I thought that was you." Evelyn was standing in the corridor, coat thrown over her arm, gloves and hat in hand. "How did your meeting with Françoise go?"

"It went fine. It wasn't really a meeting. She left me alone most of the time." Olivia answered quickly. Susanna's eyes narrowed.

Looming in Evelyn's back, André's office – dark, quiet – reminded everyone walking by of the professor's absence. Another faculty member had been dispatched to write the final exam, hold review sessions for the course he had been teaching. Evelyn collected old quizzes and assignments because no one could access the computer files where André had recorded the grades. Students had been slow in returning marked materials, leaving holes in her spreadsheet, complicating the matter. People disagreed on the appropriate course of action. Should everyone be given an A under the circumstances? Should only the lectures up to André's stroke count?

Sergey had moved his books to a room down the hallway, which he shared with Thomas Greenawalt's students – if he used the north stairwell to come and go, he could avoid the sight of his advisor's office altogether. Hyong Mo pretended he did not care. He had been struggling with his coursework and welcomed the break from research, although he did work on his topic every so often to show his supervisor some progress once he returned to work. People unfamiliar with André's situation assumed that he would spend three months in a nursing home and reappear once his health had improved. Medicine progressed so fast. Boston counted some of the best hospitals in the country. Evelyn kept his mail neatly stacked in a box on her desk, ready to hand it over when he came back; she also watered his plants every week – he would not enjoy staring at dead orchids upon his return, especially since they were gifts from former students after graduation. She took good care of them. How pleased he would be when he returned.

"Did you tell Françoise how outraged I am? It's just ridiculous. That journalist has no shame." Evelyn buttoned her coat and lifted her hair from under the collar of her coat. "How's she holding up?"

"She's doing alright. As well as you could expect, given the circumstances."

Olivia dug her hands into her pockets, inched toward the exit.

Evelyn smiled. "I'm glad. See you tomorrow."

She turned around and headed for the stairwell. The sound of her high heels clicking down the steps did not fade until she had reached the next floor.

"You saw André's wife?"

"She invited me over."

"What for?"

Olivia shrugged. "She needed company."

Susanna raised her cup of tea to her lips but did not drink from it. "You mean you found out you were right in your research somehow, and that has nothing to do with spending time at your advisor's home?"

Her glare made Olivia look down. She was not fond of Susanna, who showed no interest in taking female students under her wing, and worked sixteen-hour days before going back to what everyone assumed was an empty house, but the woman asked good questions.

"I only spent a few hours. And I was right, I've been right all along. I figured everything out by myself months ago." Olivia clutched the strap of her bag.

"Good for you." Susanna snickered. A door opened and closed at the end of the corridor.

"I found the mistake on my own. I don't know how to fix it, because I stopped working on that when André said I was wrong, but I'll find a way."

"That doesn't explain how Tom got involved."

Olivia made a vague gesture with her hand. "He's just trying to help. He heard that André called me when he got off the plane, the morning he had the stroke, and he wants to give me a hand, you know, so that the years I spent working in the lab aren't lost."

Susanna rolled her eyes and dropped her paper cup into the trash. "Come on in for a second." Olivia did not move. "Come on in. It won't take long."

Olivia trudged inside. Susanna closed the door and took a seat behind her desk. A framed picture of her receiving the Lilienfield Prize was propped up on the table, next to a wall calendar showing New York City landmarks, which she had abundantly scribbled over. Every day was packed with activities – students to meet, reviews to write, submissions to revise. The shelves were lined with back issues of *Physical Review Letters,* volumes on quantum mechanics and various textbooks she used in her classes. A photograph of a cat playing with a ball of wool was taped to the computer monitor. Over it hung her diploma and an award from the American Physical Society.

Olivia sat down on the edge of a chair. Susanna looked at her.

"Why would you give André's notes to Tom? That's not his work. André wouldn't want him to get involved."

"I told André everything months ago and he didn't believe me. I can do whatever I want with my results now. I was right all along. He should've believed me back in August when I first told him."

Susanna looked unimpressed. "That doesn't make it okay to bring Tom in the picture."

"André almost fired me over this. He said I'm unreliable and I make mistakes and he got angry when I tried to protest."

"Why do you think he called you that morning when he got off the plane?"

Olivia folded her arms across her chest. "I have no idea."

"Maybe he wanted to apologize."

The suggestion was met with complete silence.

"It's easy to say that now," Olivia said after a while.

"That'd make sense, though. He realized he'd been wrong and called you the first chance he got."

Olivia blinked. Her eyes had lit up, almost in spite of herself.

"He's a good man," Susanna insisted. "When I came up for tenure and half the faculty was on the fence about my case – Tom included – he's the one who fought for me the day of the vote and turned things around. And he never said a word about it. I would never have known if another faculty member who was at the meeting hadn't told me." She paused. "Now, is what you found really important?" Olivia nodded. "Is it critical?"

"There's a mistake in one of his proofs. That makes the whole theory collapse." Susanna pressed her hands against the desk. Olivia sat a bit taller in her chair. "He leaves a lot of the calculations to the reader, so it was hard to realize something was off. I guess that's why nobody figured it out before. People just assumed they'd made an error along the way, if they even bothered to retrace his steps." She pressed her bag against her chest. "They thought it was their own fault."

"Which paper are you talking about?"

Olivia pinched her lips. "I'd rather discuss things with Tom first." Thomas Greenawalt had instructed her to call him Tom when they had chatted in the hallway – not 'Professor', not even 'Thomas'. 'Tom.' Wasn't that nice? He treated her as an equal. Claire had shrugged: of course he was. He wanted André's notes and would flatter Olivia until he got them. Olivia had brushed her roommate's comment aside.

Susanna leaned back in her chair. "It has to be in his recent work. The result can't have been in print for long. Otherwise, someone would've found the error by now." Olivia did not react. She did not contradict the woman either. "I bet it's in a proof buried in appendix. André has this way of writing arguments in fifteen parts that make everyone pray he knows what he's doing." Olivia smiled faintly. Susanna eyed her over the desk. "It's not his breakthrough paper, now, is it? He made this huge contribution to science. He can't be wrong on that."

The connection André has established between anti-deSitter space and conformal field theory – although it sounded very technical and not particularly interesting – was considered a landmark achievement because it related string theories, which incorporated gravity, to gauge theories, which did not. His findings had given researchers hope that they would soon be able to unify gravity with the other three forces and obtain that Holy Grail of theoretical physics: a Theory of Everything.

Olivia squirmed.

Susanna opened her eyes wide and covered her mouth with her hand.

Outside, the rain had turned into a drizzle. The temperatures were warmer than average for December, but another cold wave – with sleet and maybe snow – was expected to reach Boston by the end of the week. Someone hummed a tune in the hallway while strolling by the closed office door.

"Maybe I can fix it," Olivia finally said. "Maybe a similar result will hold."

"I'd never expected Matt to make such a mistake. He would've been the last person to slip up like that." Olivia's eyelids fluttered but there was no point in pretending the conversation was not about Matthew Johnson's final paper – published in *Science* to high acclaim and responsible, in large part, for André's receiving the High Energy and Particle Physics Prize from the European Physical Society a few years back. "I sat on his dissertation committee. He was a very conscientious student. He had some hard time wrapping things up, sent us the draft of his thesis at the last minute, but he gave one of the best dissertation defenses I've seen in my career. He would've been an outstanding professor." Susanna pushed her swivel chair away from her desk. "At the defense he did look like he hadn't slept in weeks. I bet he'd be mortified if he knew what was going on."

"Anyway, no one will care about the mistake once I've corrected it. That'll be a breakthrough all the same." Olivia sounded defiant, very sure of herself. "André thought I was doing something wrong so I gave up, but with Tom's help, I'll figure out what to do."

Susanna shook her head. "If you want to discuss André's work, I can think of someone who'll give you far better advice than Tom."

25

The bar filled with cheers when the Bruins scored the first goal of the evening.

"It didn't take long," Kurt said.

Jim waved to the bartender. "That round's on me." George looked surprised. They all went out for beers every Thursday night, and Jim rarely showed more than a passing interest in hockey. Jim made a big grin. "I got a feature in last Sunday's paper. Sixteen hundred words. It'd been a while."

George tapped his glass against his friend's.

"You didn't know?" Kurt chuckled.

"I don't read the *Globe* much."

"Your mistake," Jim said.

The bartender aligned the beers on the counter – Guinness for Jim, Budweiser for the other two. Kurt reached for his glass and took a gulp. He worked as a cameraman for the New England Cable News; George was a sound technician for the local PBS station. Jim did not socialize with co-workers at the *Globe*, never had – he had stayed away at age twenty-three when he competed against every other college graduate in town and he certainly would not mingle now, when reporters ten years younger than him broke stories about procurement scandals on Beacon Hill while he was left with the crumbs. At least the feature about the M.I.T. professor had reminded everyone of what he was capable of. People had congratulated him – in the elevator, by the water cooler, in the *Globe*'s lobby. Some had not been aware of the article, but they had all shaken his hand or slapped his shoulder or nodded their head vigorously when he had told them the details. Congratulations, that's great. Congratulations. It sounds fascinating. Say hi to Carol for me. How are the girls? I'll certainly read it. Good job. You must be thrilled. Congratulations. That man does seem awful. And those poor students. It boggles the mind. I gotta go. Congratulations. You're right. He's a jerk. He had it coming. Well done. I need to run. Congratulations, congratulations. I really have to go.

"I got lucky on that one. If Diane hadn't told me about the guy, I wouldn't even have known he existed."

"How did she hear about him?"

"He had a stroke, ended up at M.G.H."

"You get your breaks where you can," George said.

The Bruins were racing around the Senators, rushing forward to intercept the puck, slamming rival players against the fence.

"It's a good article. I'm proud of it. Diane was very excited that her idea paid off." Jim spoke forcefully, although he talked to no one in particular. George grabbed a handful of peanuts and stuffed them into his mouth. "It made a splash, let me tell you that." Patrons streamed into the bar after a long workday. Jim raised his voice above the laughter and chitchat around him, the squeak of chairs being pulled out, the clink of beer mugs against the tables. "Ethics scandal at M.I.T.? That thing gets you in the headlines every time." Jim elbowed Kurt. "How come you guys didn't do a piece on him?"

He never missed an opportunity to point out gaps in NECN's news coverage.

"Didn't see the need, I guess."

"The story went out on the wire. It got picked up by the *Hartford Courant,* and whatever paper they have up in Maine."

"*Portland Press Herald.*"

"I knew that." Jim shrugged. "The *New York Times* might run the story too, although someone over there will probably rewrite it first and put his name on it."

"It's the *Times.* That's what they do. They write their own stuff."

Jim shook his head. "I write as well as those folks." He took a gulp of Guinness.

"So what's the story about?"

"There's a physics professor at M.I.T. who had a stroke about two weeks ago."

"It's more of a profile than an article," Kurt said helpfully in Kurt's direction.

Jim cut him off. "There's some tension too. The guy's students say he made some kind of discovery right before he had the stroke. They suspect that triggered the whole thing. He treated them like dirt for years, so they're not exactly heartbroken."

"What did he find out?"

"No one knows for sure."

"Maybe he didn't find out anything." George shrugged. "What goes around comes around," he quickly added when Jim gave him a dark look.

"You're right about that." Kurt kept his eyes on the screen above the bartender's head. A large man with a New York Jets sweatshirt pushed his way to the bar and wedged himself between college-aged youngsters to bark for a whisky. "Do you remember that aide to the mayor, Robert something, the one who always told us what to do? I heard he's no longer on the staff. I'm sure his little outburst when he thought the camera wasn't rolling played a role in that."

"I've got a ton of stories on open mikes," George said. "Funny how people forget those things have an 'on' button."

Jim scowled. "You can't compare André Darrieux with some obscure staffer at City Hall." He waved his beer in George's face. "Darrieux's a professor at M.I.T. He's a contender for the Nobel Prize. He abused his students and took advantage of them. That's completely different."

"Don't get so upset."

"He wasn't beating them up, now, was he?" Kurt laughed.

"He pressured them to cut corners." Jim's voice was rising steadily. "Held them under his thumb. Refused to sign their thesis if they didn't get the results he wanted."

Kurt drank his Budweiser. "Everybody's under pressure. I am, you are. That's not the problem. It's how people react to pressure that's the problem."

"But his students didn't have a choice. They had to do as they were told, or they wouldn't graduate. Years of their lives wasted. They couldn't get any jobs without their diploma. Darrieux exploited them over and over again." Jim's mouth twisted with disgust. "That guy's despicable."

"Jimmy, man, come down your high horse."

A player for the Senators pushed one of the Bruins to the ground. The crowd in the lounge booed – the man with the New York Jets sweatshirt louder than most – while people on the rink yelled at each other. The Bruins' right wingman threw a punch, but a referee quickly broke the fight. The game resumed.

"It's a question of integrity. He took advantage of his students."

"Did they ever tell someone? Tried to get help?" Kurt asked.

"They were afraid."

Kurt raised his glass and eyed his friend above the rim. "They waited till his brain fried to accuse him." The television screen displayed statistics on the Bruins goalie, which George read with fascination, as if he had never seen them before. "It's too bad you couldn't include the guy's viewpoint. I wonder what he would've said."

Kurt finished his drink, motioned to the bartender that he wanted another beer.

"I'm aware of the story's weaknesses," Jim snapped. "I wish I'd been able to interview Darrieux too. You might not believe it, but I did consider both sides and weighed all the arguments before I wrote the piece. I'm a professional." His voice swelled with anger. "I talked to his wife. That's the best I could do. Even if I'd waited a year, it doesn't look like I would've been able to interview the guy. But I was fair and even-handed. It's not my fault he's a slave-driver – and that's his student's word, not mine. They had no choice. They were at the complete mercy of the guy."

Kurt waved his hands in surprise. "Alright, man. Alright. Let's not argue over this."

"I'm tired of everybody complaining that this poor guy can't protect his name, that it's easy for his students to accuse him when he doesn't even know which city he lives in."

"What do you mean, everybody? I made one comment."

Jim clenched his jaws.

THE BREAKTHROUGH

The bartender placed another Budweiser in front of Kurt while George emptied his glass. The Senators neared the Bruins' net; a player took a shot and missed. The bar heaved a collective sigh.

George turned toward Jim. "I liked reading about the rumor. I thought that was a good angle. It makes a lot of sense, even if no one can prove anything."

The crowd applauded an action by the Bruins. Kurt wolfed down a fistful of peanuts.

Jim let the silence stretch, but could not resist talking about André. "I'd have a stroke too if whatever I staked my reputation on crumbled in front of my eyes."

"No wonder your guy was driving his students hard." George grabbed the peanuts before Kurt had a chance to finish the dish. "So what's your take on this? Do you think his reputation can be salvaged?"

Jim scoffed. "No way. He's a fraud. The only reason he won't be forgotten next month is because I've exposed him and his name's all over the Internet." He paused. "Did I tell you his son refused to let me interview him? I reached him on the phone in San Diego and he shouted: 'I will not talk to the press about my father.' Then he hung up on me."

George shrugged. "If the man spent all his time in lab chasing the next breakthrough, I can see why his kid ended up with nothing to say about his dad."

Jim's cell phone buzzed in his pocket. He read the caller's name on the display, hesitated for a second before answering.

Kurt leaned toward George, his mouth covered with his hand so that Jim would not hear. "He would've gotten along grand with that professor guy."

George chuckled. Jim, of course, would never draw a link between André's workaholism and his own, André's tense relationship with his son and the breakdown of his own marriage to Carol.

"Who was it?" George asked while Jim put his phone back into his pocket.

"Someone at the paper. I'm working on a new project now – the safety of the water reservoirs in Boston, and how technology can help us detect a bacteria outbreak."

"Didn't you talk about this a while back?"

"I sure did. My editor finally gave me the green light."

George raised an eyebrow. "I thought you didn't want to do it."

"No, not at all. My problem was that Daniel wouldn't leave me enough time to research the issues. But he liked the piece about Darrieux and figured, maybe I'll nail two winners in a row."

26.

That student would fix it. She had to. She would rise to the challenge, one way or the other – André had seen something in her, after all, when he had let her into his research group. She would be keen to prove her worth; at least, she seemed eager to give it a try. In Belmont, she had pored over André's papers, browsed through his notebooks, and the more time she had spent in his office, the more excited she had become. Françoise could hear her giggle when she walked past the door. Olivia had made no promises, though. She had explained she needed to consult additional preprints and study André's notes in detail before she could be sure of what he had discovered. This would take a week, maybe more because of her exams. Françoise had appreciated her candor – such a nice, honest student.

"Buddy!" Françoise tapped her hand against her thigh. The dog slowed down, glanced behind him, and then resumed sniffing at the bushes as if he had not heard. "Come back here!"

André and Françoise brought their dog to Fresh Pond Park in Cambridge every Saturday and strolled with him around the water reservoir. Françoise did not usually come by herself, but it looked like it would not rain and she did not want to stay in the empty house all day long, staring at André's things. Other dog owners strode along the path, their pet yapping and bounding around them – a Yorkshire with a tiny knitted coat, a Dalmatian by a jogger in a tracksuit. Françoise smiled at the dogs.

Olivia's hand had lingered on the door handle when she had been about to step out of the car. Françoise had thanked her for her time, again. Olivia nodded and opened her mouth to speak, but – after a second of puzzling silence – only added that she would be in touch and headed for the Alewife T station. Françoise watched her until she disappeared inside. Perhaps Olivia wondered what

Françoise would do with her newly found knowledge of theoretical physics – a legitimate question Françoise could not answer. She clung to the belief that learning the reason for André's behavior, that morning before the stroke, would help her figure out the next step. Because if it did not, what would she do?

"Buddy! Where do you think you're going?" The dog, who followed a scent nose on the ground, had strayed about twenty yards from the trail and was paying Françoise no attention. "I'm not kidding, Buddy!" Françoise hurried behind him, grabbed his collar and put his leash back on. "You will not get into any kind of trouble until André comes home. What if you get lost and I can't find you?" The dog opened big, surprised eyes and wagged his tail. "I'm serious. Let's go."

Uncovering what had bothered André might not solve a thing. Maybe no one would care. People who read the *Globe* would remain outraged that he treated his naïve, well-meaning research assistants with such callousness. They would not remember that some students became disgruntled and some journalists liked to embellish stories; they would not give André the benefit of the doubt. To change people's view of her husband, Françoise needed to give the media a new reason to write about him – something big enough to push Jim Calloway's article into the oblivion it deserved. She leaned toward the tale of an unlikely friendship: that between a disabled genius and the student he had once shown the door, who would now help her mentor regain his standing in the research community.

But maybe it would not be enough. Maybe it would not work.

Françoise sighed at her dog. "Don't tug on the leash. You're going to hurt your neck."

An elderly couple hobbled toward her, preceded by a bull terrier. Françoise did not remember the name of the couple but the dog was called Nugget. The man had worked for a biopharmaceutical company before his retirement. André often chatted with him about whatever physics program had been broadcast during the week on PBS or the Discovery channel.

Françoise smiled. "How are you? It's such a beautiful day."

The woman nodded and stroked the dog under his snout. "Hi, Buddy."

THE BREAKTHROUGH

A bicyclist in full gear and helmet pedaled past them on a dirt bike, and then past a family with a toddler and a little girl with pigtails. Françoise's gaze lingered over the girl. She had stopped feeling envious a long time ago, stopped asking why them and not me, but the occasional tinge of regret still surprised her. It had become more frequent now that Bernard had moved away.

"Your husband didn't come?" the man asked. "That's the first time I see you by yourself."

Françoise's eyelids fluttered. Did the question have a hidden meaning? Was he trying to discuss André's stroke? It was hard to believe he had not read the article in the *Globe*.

"He's sick."

"I'm sorry to hear that."

On Sundays, the circulation of the *Boston Globe* exceeded half a million copies – Françoise had checked the numbers. The population of the metro area stood at about four million. That meant one in eight residents could have come across the article. Françoise had bought groceries at Whole Foods, dropped by the nursing home after lunch, braved traffic to get to the pond – one in eight customers, visitors, motorists could have read that piece of garbage, and her calculations did not even include the people who had typed André's name into a search engine while they looked for his papers and had stumbled upon the *Globe*'s website by mistake.

"This weather's treacherous. Cold one day, mild the next." The elderly woman shook her head. "Especially when you work with students. My sister used to be a teacher. The kids catch a lot of things. Did one of his students give him a bug?"

"It's possible." Françoise felt her cheeks redden.

She glanced at the man, silent by his spouse, and imagined his reaction when he had opened the Sunday edition – someone he knew, in the *Boston Globe*! And that Frenchman seemed so nice. The stranger would whisper to his wife while they walked away in a slow, unsteady gait behind their dog: I read about him in the paper. Didn't I tell you?

Don't believe what's written, Françoise wanted to implore them. There will be a better story soon. In the *New York Times*, no less, if I have my way.

She would enlist Olivia's help – the girl owed André, after all he had done for her: giving her a chance, assigning her to a cutting-edge project. Olivia would be the first one to admit so. She would say good things about André and no one would suggest again that he had mistreated his students. Readers would take pity on him – he sat in a nursing home, barely aware of his surroundings, incapable of uttering a full sentence. Olivia had no reason to distort the truth. She would have more credibility than Françoise. The public would trust her. She would recount the hours André spent poring over his students' work, teaching them the ropes, editing their preprints. His commitment to train the next generation of scientists would take readers aback.

It would be a story of friendship, perseverance and loyalty. With a bit of luck, the *Times* would print it.

"Tell your husband we hope he gets well soon," the man said.

Françoise nodded. "I will."

She avoided his gaze. He knew. She was sure he knew. How could he not know? Everyone did. And she had a nagging feeling that she would need a lot more to interest the *New York Times,* the *Washington Post,* or any newspaper that could salvage André's reputation, than a few quotes by a student trying to help him.

She yanked Buddy away from the scent he had smelled in the grass and hurried toward the end of the trail, her car on the parking lot. "Thirty-five years of dealing with the real life while André imagined discoveries on his little cloud," she hissed between her teeth, "and I've got this mess now to thank me for my trouble. None of this would've happened if we'd gone back to France."

Her mouth twisted in anger for the first time since the stroke – for the first time since she could remember, in fact. How long had it been – years? Then she shook her head, collected herself and made a warm smile to every single stranger she crossed on the path.

27

"How's André doing?"

The question took Olivia by surprise. "He's doing alright given what happened, I guess. It's going to be a long road."

She dropped her bag at her feet and sat down. Hans-Hermann Walzenberger trudged to the other side of the desk and lowered himself into his armchair.

"Is it as bad as people say?"

Olivia fidgeted on her seat. She tried to pick the right words. "I don't think he's aware of what's going on, so it's a lot worse for the people around him." The professor nodded, taking in the news. "You haven't visited him yet?"

Hans looked outside the window, although a tree was blocking most of his view. He stared at the leaves. "Not yet, no." He paused. "I want to. It'd be a bit awkward, though. We haven't talked in years. I mean, we exchange platitudes at the faculty meetings, but that's about it. And even then, we don't go much beyond 'hi'."

The black-and-white poster of a jazz pianist stretched across the wall, above a bulky computer monitor that showed its age. Old issues of the *National Geographic* were stacked by the loudspeakers. A small fridge hummed under the desk. The room contained its fair share of scientific journals and monographs, crammed on the top shelves, but the only physics material that lay nearby was the solution of a homework assignment, left on the table.

Olivia reached for the sheets of paper in her bag. She had forgotten her scarf in her apartment and missed the #1 bus by seconds; her cheeks were pink from the long walk to the physics building in the cold.

Hans turned toward her.

"As André might've told you, we've had our disagreements."

"He never said anything about it." Not once, in the three years and a half Olivia had spent at M.I.T., had her research advisor pronounced Hans's name in front of her. She had not known who had supervised André's dissertation until she had found the thesis in the library's stacks, noticed the signature on the cover page – "H.H. Walzenberger," in narrow letters stretching upward. It came as no surprise to her that the two men were not on speaking terms.

"He could've been much more successful if he'd stuck to QCD." By that, Hans meant quantum chromodynamics – the quantum field theory for the strong force, which kept protons and neutrons inside atomic nuclei. "I told him so. He didn't want to listen. I guess string theory was too glamorous for him to pass on." Olivia retrieved a pencil and placed it across her notes. "I always thought he'd have an extraordinary career. He was so talented."

Olivia nodded. "He's very smart." She glanced at the pictures on the desk – two studio portraits, one of a couple with a baby and one of another couple with two young kids, which obviously showed the professor's grown children with their own family. His wife did not appear anywhere, although he wore a wedding band.

"When we worked together, back in the seventies, we used to convince ourselves a breakthrough was just around the corner. That kept us going for months on end." Hans coughed. "Look at us now. So little panned out."

"The conjecture might still hold. It makes so much sense – there must be another way to prove it. Let me show you." Olivia picked up the paper and flipped it open.

Hans adjusted the glasses on his nose. "That's the paper André got the EPS prize for."

"What prize?"

"The European Physical Society Prize, on High Energy and Particle Physics. He's got the certificate framed on the wall. You can't miss it."

"Oh, right. Of course."

Olivia had stared at the document many times while André searched through his books for a theorem he had just told her about – work that could help their project, or insights already obtained by a competing team. He had received the award when she was finishing her first year in the PhD program. It now hung by his desk, near the visitors' chairs, in the most expensive frame sold at the campus bookstore. Guests sat close enough to admire every curve of the calligraphic writing, whether they wanted to or not. André beamed with pride whenever he caught them deciphering the inscription. *Awarded to André Jacques Darrieux, for his contributions to theoretical physics…* He did not care nearly as much about his honorary degrees, dismissed them with a shrug when people inquired about the other frames on the wall – hadn't all faculty members in the department received a few of those, at some point in their career? But the certificate for the High Energy and Particle Physics Prize of the European Physical Society, he dusted off himself.

Hans leaned in his chair. "That paper brought him that close," he held his thumb and index finger half an inch apart, "from unifying gravity with the other forces and finding a 'theory of everything.' It generated a lot of excitement, back in the days."

"It glosses over a few steps, though." Olivia pointed at the notes she had taken from André's study. "This is what André was looking at before he had his stroke. He must've written most of the pages on the plane and the rest at home, because he changed pens toward the end – right after he got to the result I couldn't prove last August." Hans's eyes narrowed. Indeed, the last few pages were written in a different ink. Olivia pointed at an equation that stretched over multiple lines. "He crossed stuff, started over. You can see he's getting upset. He couldn't find what he wanted, what Matthew Johnson had told him it all came down to." Hans followed the movement of her hand. From that distance, he probably struggled to read the notes, but he could not miss the handwriting becoming hurried and the lines being crossed vigorously. Olivia shook her head. "I told him over the summer, but he refused to listen. He wanted the proof to hold so badly."

Hans nodded in silence. Olivia waited for him to say a word, but he seemed lost in thought. Two, five, ten seconds went by before he placed his elbows on the armrests and pressed the tips of his fingers against each other. "So what can I do for you?"

"I was hoping you'd take a look, tell me what you think. I have some ideas on how to fix the proof, but I'd love to hear your suggestions first."

"I'm not an expert on string theory."

Olivia looked surprised. "Susanna said you'd give me good advice."

Hans grimaced. "I don't think she meant helping you fix the paper. I haven't done research in a while." He paused. "She must've felt that, since I supervised André's research when he was in graduate school, I might have his interests more at heart than other members of the department. She's right on that one."

Olivia pursed her lips. "Will you at least take a look?"

Hans plucked the sheet of paper from her hand. "The sad thing is, once the right people hear about this, André's prize is going to get withdrawn."

"The EPS prize? Are you sure?"

"The result doesn't hold. There's no breakthrough. What do you expect people to do? They can't pretend it's no big deal." A door closed. Almost immediately, a pair of high heels clicked down the hallway. Evelyn was going to lunch. "André must have known his prize was in trouble. Every single one of us makes blunders in our work, at one point or another. Nobody's proud of it, but it happens. We find the mistake and publish an erratum. Now, losing one of the most prestigious prizes in the field, that's a whole other story."

"He won't lose his prize if we fix the paper fast enough."

"We?" Hans raised an eyebrow. "André should've stayed away from all that junk. String theory has wrecked many scientists' careers, and now it's ruined his. It's a siren song, I tell you. He was quite successful before. I never understood why he switched topics so abruptly. Which year was it, 1995, 1996? It happened almost overnight. He gave me no warning."

"A lot of people switched topics back then. They wanted to give string theory a try. I don't blame them."

"Gold-diggers." Hans smirked. "Somebody unifies a couple of models, and then people call it a second revolution." He paused. "But André was smarter than that. He wouldn't have followed the crowd just because it was fashionable." He paused again. Olivia stared at her notes. "If he'd stuck to QCD, he would've made major contributions to the field, and he'd be remembered for them. He would've received the Nobel Prize."

"He's a contender now."

Hans shrugged. "That's only a rumor he likes to circulate. He's not above that. Or should I say 'wasn't'? This is going to take some time getting used to." Voices echoed by the door – students were heading for the food trucks on Vassar Street. Olivia's stomach growled. Hans leaned back in his chair. "André made a strategic mistake when he changed research areas. The field's crowded. The math's gruesome. All the low-hanging fruit's been plucked. The odds of finding anything groundbreaking now are close to zero."

"Matt's paper has a lot of potential."

"And it's wrong." Olivia winced. "People spend their time tinkering with each other's models and make up theories they can't verify, because the equipment to prove or disprove them hasn't yet been invented. André wasted his talent."

In the years Olivia had spent working with her advisor, André had never expressed any second thoughts about his choice of topics, any qualms about the long-term impact of his findings. Instead, he hurried his students along, burdened them with extensive to-do lists, lectured them with a sense of urgency: a breakthrough was imminent, but another group might find the result first – they would be set back by months if that happened. Students toiled away in fear that a rival would come up with the same idea and submit it for publication before they had ironed out the kinks in their own theorems; their labor would become meaningless overnight. They had to put up with such risks in order to do cutting-edge research – having no competition whatsoever would have boded ill for the relevance of the work. André had always appeared to thrive in that environment. If he had wasted his talent, he had seemed curiously unaware of the fact.

Olivia had heard the rumors, though, on how he had treated Peter Neumann and Matthew Johnson. Only desperate people behaved like that.

But if he had wasted his talent, then Olivia had wasted hers, too, and she was not ready to accept that.

The young woman slid to the edge of her chair and glanced at the books lined on the top shelves. The dark, dusty covers would not have been out of place at the library, among the rows of volumes students no longer checked out because more recent monographs had rendered them obsolete. Teaching awards hung on the wall – Teacher of the Year three years in a row, back in the nineties – but Hans boasted no honorary degree, no research prize for all to see in his office. What did he know about string theory anyway?

"If I were you, I'd switch to something else, like ultra-cold matter, or quantum fluids. They're just as cutting-edge and you've got a much greater chance of making an impact."

Olivia laughed – she had never studied either and did not intend to start. "I'd rather try to salvage the paper first." She tucked a strand of hair behind her ear. "So what do we do now?"

"We can contact the journal's editor-in-chief and let him know about the mistake. Or we can get in touch with Matthew Johnson and ask him to withdraw the paper."

"There's got to be something we can do to correct the proof – change a few things, tweak some hypotheses. The setting might be too simplistic. We should add more parameters. Maybe duality will hold in a space of higher dimension."

"You could spend a long time looking for a magic formula, and it's far from clear you'll ever find it. Do you want to still be here, five or six years from now, with no publication, no degree, and a career in shambles before it even started?" Hans made a sweeping gesture with his hand. "You're better off burying the matter and finding a new research topic."

A raindrop splattered on the windowpane, and then a second, third ones, until the drops fell so quickly it was no longer possible to count them.

"Susanna said you'd help," Olivia insisted.

"I'm helping. I'm telling you to move on. I'm also telling you that going to Tom Greenawalt and giving him André's notes won't solve anything." Olivia's face turned crimson. Susanna had had a chat with him. "You wouldn't find a single professor willing to write you a recommendation letter after that." Olivia opened her mouth to protest, but Hans did not let her speak. "Anyway, if you want to have a future in this field, you shouldn't spend your time correcting other people's mistakes. You didn't come here to play second fiddle. That won't make a dissertation."

"Tom works on similar topics. He could advise me."

Hans clasped his hands behind his head. "Quite frankly, I've known Tom for many years, and I'd stay away from him if I were you. He doesn't treat people well."

"Because André does, maybe?" Olivia scoffed. "He's a slave-driver."

"Don't believe what you read in the paper."

"I didn't read it in the paper." The words tumbled out of Olivia's mouth. She pinched her lips almost immediately, swallowed hard.

Hans rotated in his swivel chair and eyed her over the desk. "I see," he said after a while. By then, the raindrops were falling in a steady downpour.

"He's a slave-driver. He really is. I worked day and night on the project he gave me, and I almost got fired when I said things he didn't want to hear. And I was right." Olivia raised her voice. Her hands were shaking.

Hans opened the door of the mini-fridge and retrieved a plastic container with what looked like pasta with chicken. "You should get in touch with Matthew Johnson. It's better if the retraction comes from him. Eventually you'll be glad you moved on to something else."

He stood up with his container, clearly intending to go and warm it up in the lounge, which had a small microwave.

Olivia gathered her belongings and stuffed them into her bag, grabbed the pencil she was about to forget. "Thank you for your time." She got up and hurried to the door, glanced behind her shoulder before she stepped outside. "Maybe you should go and visit André at the clinic when you get a chance. I never see anyone there, besides his wife."

28

The Miracle of Science was packed. Olivia and Claire would have to wait for a table.

"We could go to Austin Grill."

Olivia shrugged. "This is fine."

Her roommate squinted at the menu, which was written in color chalk on a blackboard in the back of the room. "Graduate school hasn't done me any good. I can barely see a thing from here. What are you going to get?"

Olivia turned her head toward the board. "The cheeseburger, I think."

"Sounds yummy."

Olivia folded her arms across her chest and stared at the patrons – those who were already seated and enjoying their meal – with a sullen look on her face. Outside, it had stopped raining but the pavement was still wet. Cars sent sprays of water into the air when they barreled through the puddles on Massachusetts Avenue.

"Everything alright?"

Olivia sighed. "I spoke with Hans Walzenberger today. I thought he'd help me with André's paper, but it turns out he's not interested." Claire raised an eyebrow, waited for Olivia to say more. "He's out of his depth. I guess that when you've fallen off the research bandwagon, you can't hop back on and pretend you're a good scientist again all of a sudden." The waitress finally ushered them to a table by the bay window. Claire sat down with her back to the street; Olivia plopped onto the other chair. "He said I should get out of the field, if you can believe it."

"Out of physics?"

"No, out of string theory. He finds that the area is too crowded, and there's no way to test any of the models going around."

Claire unfolded the paper napkin on her lap. "That sounds like good advice."

Olivia scoffed. "He also said I should study ultra-cold matter instead." Claire, who studied economics, did not know what ultra-cold matter was, but did not ask for details. "He's a dinosaur that M.I.T. lets hang around because he teaches a class or two."

The waitress came to take their orders and then disappeared into the kitchen.

Claire smiled. "Did I tell you I scheduled my committee meeting? It took me a while to find a time that worked for everybody."

"I'm glad that things are moving along for you." Olivia grimaced. "No one's telling you to drop everything you've worked on since you came here and switch to a topic you know nothing about."

"Don't do it if it bothers you so much."

Claire's gaze drifted to the patrons on her left, two college girls in their early twenties who were also waiting for their food. Both had stopped talking after Claire and Olivia had sat down – the girl facing the window, who glanced at Olivia every so often, seemed to be listening in to the conversation.

"He doesn't want to admit he should've gotten into string theory. It annoys the heck out of him that he never found anything big, while André had a breakthrough that made his career." On Claire's right, the man was finishing a hamburger and the woman was cutting her chicken quesadillas into tiny little pieces. "Now he's jealous of his own former student. How pathetic is that?" Olivia scoffed. "He even hopes André will lose an award the European Physical Society gave him. He can't stand the fact that he's been left behind."

"Why did he refuse to write a paper with you, then?"

Olivia shrugged. "Don't ask me. The only thing that matters to him is that I shouldn't show André's notes to another professor in the department, as if that was any of his business."

The women on Claire's left pushed their glasses to the side when the waitress brought them their orders, placed sodas on Claire's and Olivia's table. Olivia took a sip of Diet Coke.

"He said that I shouldn't try to salvage André's results because it might take me years to figure out I can't fix them, and anyway I shouldn't play second fiddle to those other graduate students who came before me if I want to make a name for myself."

"He's got a point."

"Don't take his side. He said that the professor who offered to help me doesn't treat his students well but the truth is, they're all feeling threatened: Hans, Susanna, all of them. They never had a breakthrough in their life so they don't want anybody to have one either."

On Claire's left, one of the women mentioned a movie she wanted to see before winter break. Her friend showed less enthusiasm. The critics had found many flaws with that movie and she did not like thrillers.

Claire dipped a potato chip in the salsa. "I'm sure you can ask some of his former students how that helpful professor is really like and judge for yourself."

"Even if he treats them like dirt, why should I care? I'll fix the paper by myself if I have to." Olivia eyed Claire defiantly and, after a few seconds, reached for her drink. "I found the mistake on my own, I can find the solution on my own too."

Claire ate more potato chips. "I don't understand why this paper means so much to you," she finally said. "You didn't write it."

"It's an important work. It is, it really is. It's much more than a paper. It's a whole new approach," Olivia made a sweeping gesture with her hand, "that could completely change the way people approach string theory and unify the four forces and do all those things hundreds of physicists have been after for decades." The waitress brought them their food at last. "I should've watched what I said when I talked to that reporter. I made stupid comments."

"You've beaten yourself up enough already."

Olivia had woken her up on that Sunday morning to show her the *Globe*. Someone had sent her an email to let her know she was in the paper and she had run out to the newsstand to buy a copy. The quotes attached to her name sounded innocuous enough, but the journalist had given a prominent place to the slave-driver remark she had made off-the-record – it was attributed to an anonymous source, in the passive voice reporters sometimes used to obscure the number of people who had expressed the same view. In spite of this precaution, Olivia had sensed right away she was in trouble.

"I didn't realize he'd print it. I got carried away."

The conversation with Jim Calloway had drifted to New Mexico and places to visit if the journalist ever headed to Albuquerque – until then, Olivia had answered his questions with monosyllables, nursing her headache and keeping her voice down, but the mention of her home state had made her talk more excitedly. There were so many tips she could share, restaurants to try, vistas not to be missed! After a few minutes, Jim had asked about André again. Olivia had shrugged and made the comment, offhand, to take a load off her chest. She would not have given it a second thought if she had not caught a twinkle in the journalist's eyes. It's off the record, she had added as quickly as she could, remembering those detective movies she used to watch with her father when she was in junior high. Jim had smiled and told her not to worry. He had kept his word: he had not named her.

"Journalists always want to sell copies."

"We spoke for so long. The guy could've quoted me on something else."

Claire shrugged. "I would've done the same if it'd been me. That good of a quote is not easy to pass up." Olivia glared at her. "Anyway, I'm sure people have already forgotten about it."

Olivia looked at her as if she had lost her mind. "The whole department's been gossiping about those words. They're all trying to figure out who told what to the reporter. It's become the big game in town." A group of young professionals stepped inside, eager for a beer after a long day spent in ties and business suits. They left the front door slightly open behind them. Olivia shivered in the draft. "I should've kept my mouth shut. I really feel bad for André's wife."

"Having her husband called a slave-driver seems like the least of her problems at the moment."

One of the young women on Claire's left winced, and chewed her food a little faster.

"You haven't met her. Françoise cares a lot about what people think of her husband. I'm glad I'm done helping her. That was getting awkward." Olivia shook her head. "I didn't mean to backstab him or put him in trouble. It was just a stupid thing I said."

Claire nodded. "Those things happen."

"I don't even think he's a slave-driver. I don't like him and we don't have the best relationship, that's all. 'Slave-driver' sounded like a good way to summarize the situation – a good one-liner, nothing else. I was tired and upset and I wanted to look witty. I didn't expect that journalist to take it at face value."

"It's behind you anyway," Claire said, a little sharply. She had heard the story before.

There was a moment of silence.

"I said it again this afternoon in front of Hans." Claire blinked. Olivia talked faster. "He doesn't like the professor who wants to help me and thinks I shouldn't show him André's notes. I wanted to defend myself. I just blurted it out again. I felt like I should stand my ground, which doesn't make sense, because I don't think André is a slave-driver to begin with, but sure enough, that's exactly what I said. I was trying to explain he's no better than that other professor who wants to take me on into his research group."

Claire took a gulp of soda. "At least you're consistent in what you tell people," she deadpanned. One of the college girls suppressed a giggle. The conversations were becoming louder while the bartender poured drink after drink to the new arrivals. Someone cranked up the stereo.

"So I did some thinking this afternoon," Olivia tucked a strand of hair behind her ear, twice, "and I decided that I really should try to salvage André's paper, you know, show I'm not going to jump ship simply because it's convenient for me." She sat a little taller now and spoke more assuredly. "I've created enough trouble. It's time I fixed that mess."

"What if it doesn't pan out and you end up back where you started, with nothing to show for your efforts? Doesn't that worry you?"

Olivia shrugged. "Understanding that paper is the only thing I've accomplished since I've come to Cambridge. I'm not going to give up on it. I'm going to fix the results all by myself – I even have some ideas on where to start. People will have to take me seriously then."

Claire gave her a quizzical look.

Hans raised his hand again but lowered it without knocking on the open door. André, seated in front of the *New York Times*, had yet to turn a page. He stared at the columns of text as if they could be read without his eyes moving from left to right.

"Hans. What a surprise." Françoise stood in the hallway, clutching her bag.

"I thought I'd drop by, see how André was doing."

Françoise stepped into the room with a big grin on her face. "Sweetheart, look who's here."

André turned his head toward the voice. Françoise pointed above her shoulder – not a muscle in André's face twitched when his eyes stopped on his old mentor. He stared at the newcomer, though, instead of letting his gaze drift by.

Hans swallowed hard. "Hi."

There was no reaction.

"We're so happy to see you," Françoise said. She picked up the card – prominently displayed on the desk – that Evelyn had sent on behalf of the department, and showed it to Hans. "Look at all the wonderful things people wrote. This one over there is my favorite." The sentence read: Get well soon, we need you to teach in the spring semester. Françoise chuckled and beamed at her husband.

Hans shifted his weight from side to side. "Even if he doesn't teach in the spring, maybe he can come back in the fall. We're all looking forward to that."

Françoise brushed the comment off. "He'll be ready to teach in the spring."

Hans's face reddened. "I mean, if he wants to give himself more time to recover, he could stay on leave for a few extra months. I'm sure no one in the department would object. His health's more important."

THE BREAKTHROUGH

Françoise placed the card back on the table, next to the picture of André carrying little Bernard on his shoulders, the summer they had gone to Disneyland. "Anyway, he doesn't have to decide on the spot when he'll be back at work."

Hans nodded.

The room was sparsely furnished – a bed, a table, a chest of drawers – but cushions and a comforter added a welcoming touch. On the table, by the newspaper, a bookmark held André's place in the biography he had started before leaving for the conference. Françoise had expected her husband to continue reading it after the move to the nursing home but he had not opened the book again. The therapist had said that the process would take time. She had not used the word 'recovery'.

Hans dug his hands into his pockets. "I wish we'd talk under better circumstances."

"It's not your fault. I keep telling André that we should invite you and Brigit over, but something always comes up. Of course, we can't compete with the dinner parties at your house. I remember the ones you used to have when André was in graduate school. We both enjoyed them very much." Hans chuckled wistfully. Françoise leaned against the table and clasped André's fingers. "How is Brigit doing, by the way?"

Hans blinked. "She's doing alright. She sends her best wishes."

"I haven't seen her in the longest time."

"She doesn't attend faculty events anymore. You can imagine what it's like, having to make small talk with my colleagues."

"But she loves the department functions. She's always been the life of the party."

Hans shook his head. "I don't want her to break any more glasses, knock over yet another vase. We agreed it was better if she didn't come."

"She never did it on purpose. She just tends to lose her balance a lot when it gets late." Hans gave Françoise a long look. "I hope she can come some other time," she said.

"She definitely will. It's just that," Hans kept his eyes on the bedside rug, "she wasn't in any state to get out of the house this morning. I'll make sure to bring her along when she feels better."

Wheels squeaked in the hallway. Françoise's eyelids fluttered for a second, as if she had forgotten that this was not her own house. A middle-aged woman pushed a wheelchair by the open door with a man and teenager in tow. Françoise could only see their backs while they strolled out of earshot – their thick winter jackets and a hunting cap on top of the elderly man who sat in the wheelchair.

"We'll be here throughout winter break, so the two of you are welcome to drop by any time," Françoise said. "We had tickets to fly back to France, but after what's happened, the doctors say it's not safe for André to fly and I don't want to leave him here all by himself."

André brought his eyes back on the visitor. He seemed to wonder why this man was standing in his room, talking to Françoise as if they were old friends. But maybe he did not remember his wife either. Maybe he did not understand why he had two guests today.

Hans glanced at him. "Do you think he's upset I came?"

"No, of course not. What a silly question."

"We haven't talked in a while. On campus he barely acknowledges me when we run into each other. I wasn't sure if he wanted me here."

Françoise shrugged the comment aside. "He makes little time for people who don't work in his research area, that's all."

Hans's laugh sounded like a sneer.

"What's so funny?"

"Nothing. You're right. He's a busy man." He stared down and rubbed his forehead.

"What?"

"It's stuffy in here, don't you think?"

Françoise gave him a puzzled look – she had yet to remove her coat and wore a turtleneck sweater underneath. "I'm fine, but we can get some fresh air in the courtyard, if you'd like. You'll have to help me put André in his wheelchair, though."

Hans opened his eyes wide and frantically waved his arms no. "Maybe he'd rather have someone else touch him. He's ten years younger than me, for God's sake. I should be the one sitting there."

"It's either you or a nurse. I can't lift him by myself."

"I don't want to embarrass him."

"He's fifty-six, Hans. Look at him now. He's got plenty of reasons to be embarrassed already, whether you help him into a wheelchair or not."

There was a moment of silence. André's gaze flickered over the *New York Times*, hovered above a picture.

"You're right. I apologize."

Françoise grabbed a coat, slid André's arms into the sleeves, tied a scarf around his neck. Then she positioned herself by his side and counted for Hans. "One. Two. Three."

They pushed up with a grunt.

Hans lost his balance, stumbled forward under the weight, but he caught himself while Françoise struggled to do her part. The two of them lifted André into the wheelchair at last. Françoise placed her husband's feet on the footrests and got up. Her hands quivered – for a second she seemed about to cry. But she swallowed back her tears and quickly rolled the chair into the hallway, head up, chin high, as if she dared anyone catching a glimpse of her husband to feel anything but awe at this sighting of the famous scientist.

Outside, the air was crisp and the sun shone through the branches of the leafless trees. The middle-aged man and the teenage boy who had trudged past André's room minutes earlier now sat awkwardly at the edge of the stone bench, one gazing at his feet, the other at the cloudless sky. A woman in her mid-forties wiped saliva from the mouth of an elderly man who might have been her father, bundled up in a parka. His face disappeared under a hunting cap pulled over his ears and forehead. A nurse on break leaned against the wall while she drank a cup of coffee.

"You're right. It's much nicer outside." Françoise dragged a metal chair next to André and made a comment in French with a sweet smile. Hans lingered at a distance, not wanting to interrupt. Françoise gestured for him to join them. "Don't stand over there by yourself."

Hans took a seat opposite André. After a couple of seconds, he sighed and rubbed his forehead again.

"Aren't you feeling better?" Françoise asked, more concerned now.

Hans leaned forward, his elbows resting on his thighs, and pointed at André. "How much does he understand of what we say?"

"Most of it, I think." Hans raised an eyebrow. Françoise grimaced. "Part of it. According to his therapist, he's lost a big part of his ability to process language. She says it's called aphasia. It'll come back, though." She pronounced that last sentence with unusual authority, discouraging any dissent. There was no point in arguing with her. "He's doing better already."

"I'm glad to hear that." Hans pushed a pebble away with the tip of his shoe. "I didn't only come to see how André was doing. I've got bad news about his research."

He looked up at Françoise, then André, who was staring at the garbage can. Françoise blinked but André did not move.

"How bad?"

Hans mouthed: "Very bad." Françoise became pale. "Do you want me to tell him? Or I'll tell you, and you can decide what to do."

"That'd be better, yes." Françoise got up. "We'll be right back, sweetheart." She stepped to the side, far enough that André would not overhear the conversation, but close enough to keep an eye on him. Slouching on the bench, the teenage boy stared at the three of them with interest.

"You might remember that the European Physical Society awarded André a prize a few years back."

Françoise nodded. "That prize means a lot to him."

"As it should. It's one of the most prestigious prizes in our field." A wind gust swept across the courtyard. The nurse threw her Styrofoam cup into the trash and headed back inside. "André received the prize for research he did with a student named Matthew Johnson." Françoise nodded a second time. "Their accomplishments were remarkable. Thanks to their insights, we hoped that a 'theory of everything' was within reach at last – that has been the Holy Grail of theoretical physics for decades." Françoise nodded again, tentatively, because André had not discussed the specifics of his discovery with her. Hans continued: "His paper was extremely significant for the scientific community."

Françoise gave her husband in his wheelchair a faint but proud smile.

"Unfortunately," Hans said with unease, "it appears that he made a mistake." Françoise turned her head toward him, her mouth wide open. "It's a small mistake buried in a proof at the end of the paper, but it causes the theory to collapse. The result doesn't hold." He paused slightly before delivering the final blow. "There is no breakthrough."

Françoise covered her mouth with her hand, the sudden whiteness of her cheeks all the more glaring because the crisp air should have tinged them pink.

Hans softened his voice. "I wanted to tell you, because the Society will almost certainly withdraw its prize once the situation becomes known. I thought you should be prepared."

The middle-aged woman on the other side of the courtyard had stopped talking to her father and sat down next to him, looking dejected. There was not a single noise to be heard. On other days, the silence was often punctured by the distant wail of sirens when ambulances raced to nearby M.G.H. At that very moment, though, no car drove by the clinic, no one honked nor hit the brakes – the most complete silence reigned while Françoise tried to comprehend what Hans had just said.

"Are you sure?" she asked.

She barely knew Hans. Could she trust his judgment? André had been suspicious of him when he had first joined his research group – he had judged him too young and inexperienced to give thoughtful advice. She remembered the conversation along Massachusetts Avenue, while she walked to Central Square with André to buy furniture for their studio in the last days of August 1971, as if it had happened the week before. Indeed, the facts had proved André right: Hans had turned into a failed scientist, he had also acknowledged that his former student now cared little about him. Even if he meant well, why should Françoise believe what he had told her?

"Are you absolutely certain there's a mistake?"

Hans nodded.

Françoise could not put her doubts to rest. "How did you find out?"

"Someone showed me."

Françoise clutched her purse against her stomach and pressed her lips tightly together. Her knees trembled.

Hans touched her elbow. "Do you want to sit down?" He continued, when she did not reply: "I doubt the mistake is André's, to be honest. I assume Matthew Johnson did most of the calculations." At this, Françoise finally made eye contact with him. She seemed about to cry. "The steps weren't spelled out in full, so it took a while for people to realize there was a problem. Now that they have, though, I expect them to move swiftly."

Françoise contemplated that prospect for a second. "Maybe they'll give us time if we ask them, some kind of grace period to fix the paper before they withdraw the award."

"I wouldn't count on it. They might wait until their next meeting after the New Year to make an announcement, but that's the only respite we're going to get. It won't be long enough."

Françoise bit her bottom lip. Her gaze drifted to the patio, the building, the trees, while she absorbed the news. Then she turned again to Hans. "Do you have any idea," she asked in a low voice, "what this prize means to my husband?"

He hesitated only briefly. "I know what it'd have meant to me."

"It made all our sacrifices worthwhile. It gave them meaning – some long overdue meaning, both for him and for me. Why did we stay here all this time if we end up with nothing to show for our trouble? Why did we uproot ourselves and spend thirty-five years away from our families? Why did we leave our country and so many of our friends behind?"

Hans shifted his weight from side to side. "I often ask myself the same thing."

The teenage boy, and now his father seated next to him, watched intently while Françoise moved her lips and shook her head several times. Even André had been jolted from his daydreaming and blinked in the direction of the two people who had wheeled him into the courtyard.

"It's not André's fault no one noticed the error," Françoise said. "People should've paid more attention when they were deciding whether to give him the prize. They have no right to take it back now."

"They can't pretend the mistake doesn't matter."

A few feet away, André began to rock back and forth in his chair, unable to understand the conversation but agitated nonetheless – doctors insisted he could still process the expression on people's faces, a right-hemisphere skill, and Françoise looked highly concerned.

"We'll be right there, sweetheart!" Françoise shouted. And, to Hans: "So, that's it? It was a mistake and the model is wrong and it's all over? We should just resign ourselves to André losing his award and his reputation being ruined?"

"There isn't much we can do."

"What about Olivia? Maybe she could fix the paper."

Hans grimaced. "I'd leave Olivia out of this if I were you."

"Give her a chance." Françoise sounded hopeful all of a sudden. "She knows what André's been working on and she's eager to help."

Hans scoffed. "Her," he paused, "eagerness might be getting in her way sometimes."

Françoise glanced at André, fidgeting in his chair, before turning back to his colleague. "What do you mean?"

She liked Olivia. André had thought highly enough of her to take her into his research group. Besides, she listened patiently to Françoise's stories about her husband and shared her own. She had even sounded receptive when Françoise had shared some words of wisdom with her, during the car ride to Belmont. Maybe she would invite her for coffee again.

Hans cleared his throat. "She's the one who badmouthed André to that journalist." Françoise blinked. "It's not that big of a deal. People will forget about the article – André has bigger problems to worry about anyway. But asking her for help is not a good idea." He looked at Françoise. "You should sit down. You're very pale."

Françoise tucked a strand of hair behind her ear. She was not wearing gloves and her hands had turned a reddish pink. "What makes you think the comment came from her?"

"She owned up to it."

The teenage boy and his father, at the other end of the court-yard, followed the scene with attention. Both looked genuinely disappointed when their mother and wife stood up and, pushing the wheelchair of the elderly man in the hunting cap, headed toward the glass doors – it was time to bring the family patriarch back to his room. The boy's gaze lingered on André, younger than his grandfather by at least two decades, before he strode away. The prospect of leaving the nursing home had put a spring in his step.

"I feel like running home and disinfecting everything," Françoise said.

Hans nodded. "I don't blame you." And then: "You really should sit down. You look like you're going to faint."

Françoise pointed at André. "I don't want him to find out about any of this."

André was no longer rocking back and forth, but the scowl remained tightly screwed on the half of his face that he still had control over.

A nurse hurried across the courtyard, a winter jacket thrown over her shoulders, and disappeared into a building.

Hans sighed. "I think he already knows. Not about Olivia, but about the mistake." Françoise shook her head, twice. "I think he found out at the conference," Hans continued, "and he understood right away that he would not get to keep his prize. One of my colleagues saw him with a competitor's student after he gave his talk. They spoke for a long time. André seemed agitated afterward." Hans dug his hands into his pockets. "It's only a matter of days before the news breaks out."

Françoise did not reply right away, and did not try to argue when she did. "Life is funny, isn't it? I was so annoyed at the jour-nalist. Then it turns out, his article is the least of André's problems." Her chuckle turned into a wave of uncontrollable, nervous laughter. Hans squirmed. "If the prize is withdrawn, the media will print more articles in the same vein. Journalists like Jim Calloway will convince everyone that my husband got awards he didn't deserve and his research didn't amount to much." Françoise, calmer now, glanced at André and clenched her jaws. "That Matthew Johnson," she hissed out his name, "ruined my husband's reputation, when André only tried to help him do good work. That's not fair."

"Matt made a mistake. That happens."

"Don't you find it odd that of all the mistakes he could've made, he picked the only one that worked to his advantage?"

Hans shrugged. "When you make an error in a proof, you don't know what will come out."

"Maybe he simply wrote the results he was trying to get."

"Matt put a lot of time and effort into his thesis. He did the best he could. This was supposed to be the crowning achievement of his scientific career – he works on Wall Street now. I'm sure he'll be devastated when I tell him to withdraw the paper."

"He should've left science before. He shouldn't even have entered graduate school. That would've saved André a lot of trouble." Françoise remained quiet for a second. "Do you know how to get in touch with him? I'd love to hear what excuse he'll come up with."

"Evelyn tracked him down. He was hard to find – he didn't update his contact information after he graduated – but she got hold of another former student on the department's soccer team, someone he stayed in touch with."

"He didn't want to be found," Françoise said. "His conscience is gnawing at him."

"He lives in Brooklyn now. Evelyn has his phone number, if you decide to give him a call. She even found his home address, but I doubt you'll need it."

30

Rex barked in the hallway. Françoise wiped her hands off her apron and paused the *Rosenkavalier* CD that had been playing in the small boom box by the microwave.

"What's wrong, big boy?" The dog barked again and lunged at the front door. Françoise hurried out of the kitchen. "Let Daddy work. There's no point in bringing the house down." André was preparing the talk he would give at the University of California at Santa Barbara the following week and she did not want him to interrupt his work, step out of his study to inquire what was going on.

Françoise pulled the dog back and glanced outside through the windowpane. A Volkswagen Jetta with a dent on the rear bumper was parked in the driveway; Bernard was making his way toward the house. He carried a brown paper bag, narrow but very tall, of the kind that was only used in liquor stores to hold customers' purchases. His laptop case was slung over his shoulder. He looked tired – his second semester at Harvard Business School was keeping him busy – but he made a big grin when he saw his mother.

Françoise unlocked the door. Rex darted outside.

"You're early." Françoise kissed her son on both cheeks. "I haven't finished preparing lunch. We won't eat for another hour or so."

"That's alright. We'll chat." Bernard stroked Rex on the back. "Hi buddy, how are you doing?"

Françoise chuckled. "You're going to confuse that poor dog if you keep calling him buddy."

They returned to the house. Rex, trotting alongside them, sniffed the paper bag but realized quickly it contained nothing of interest to him.

THE BREAKTHROUGH

"What sort of wine did you bring?" Françoise closed the door behind them. "André really enjoyed the Cabernet Sauvignon you gave us last time."

"It's not wine. I thought maybe we could enjoy a drink beforehand." Bernard, without taking his jacket off, pulled a bottle of champagne from the paper bag. Françoise gaped. "I've got news. Where's Dad?"

"In his office, working. André! André!"

André emerged from the study and opened his eyes wide when Bernard brandished the bottle of champagne in his direction.

"I'm starting my own company."

"I've got to sit down," Françoise said, and leaned against the wall. André laughed. He looked very proud. Françoise smiled. "You've wanted to become an entrepreneur since you were a kid. I still have the booklet you made in fourth grade, when you asked shopkeepers for stories about their business and sold it at five dollars a piece. That was such a good way to promote the local community."

"It raised money for the school orchestra," Bernard said.

André nodded. "That wasn't a company, though. The tutoring service he started in junior high was his first real business venture. Tutoring in math and science. You had a knack for explaining difficult concepts to others."

"But I liked the marketing part better. Especially advertising the video I made to help kids with their science experiments."

"I have a copy of that somewhere too." Françoise laughed. "It's a collector's item now. That video sold out."

She fetched a box of crackers and three champagne flutes while Bernard hung his jacket in the hallway. The family gathered in the living room, around the coffee table that André cleared hurriedly from his books.

"So what's your company about?" Françoise asked.

"I told you at Christmas – it's the idea I had with friends from HBS. Timeshare for personal jets."

Françoise nodded pensively: she remembered.

"It sounded interesting," André said. "Ambitious, but interesting."

"We decided to take the plunge. With the economy in recovery, it's as good a time as any to enter the market. We talked it over with one of our professors and he agrees with us. Our business plan really impressed him."

André uncorked the bottle. The popping sound startled the dog, who hurried toward the safety of the kitchen.

"So far we've only been able to work on our project between classes, but we're going to give it a big push over the summer. It'll be fun to be our own bosses."

André poured champagne into the flutes, raised his glass to Bernard's company. "Neither of us likes hierarchy much. We have that in common. Although you do like to surround yourself with people a lot more than I do, and you're more of a risk-taker."

"But you work in a team too. We're both," Bernard chuckled, "creative types looking to break new ground. Free-thinkers who value flexibility and the opportunity to be our own bosses." It sounded a little pompous, as if he had rehearsed his speech beforehand.

"Give us more details," André said. "Who are the people on the team? How much money have you raised?"

Rex, drawn by the memory of the food, proceeded cautiously back into the room. Bernard sat down on the couch next to his mother, facing André in the armchair across the table. His gaze drifted over the pictures taken on his father's birthday six months earlier – André and Bernard smiling together for the camera, Françoise cutting the cake she had pulled out of the oven – on display in silver frames on the chimney mantel. Rex stared at the plates on the coffee table. He would have already snatched a mouthful of cheese crackers if Françoise had not grabbed him by his collar and pulled him against her leg.

"John's the CEO. You know about him – he's the one whose father owns a chain of department stores in the Midwest. In fact, his father is lending us most of the money to rent our first plane. It's not free money, but it's a pretty good rate. That definitely helps, given the sums involved."

"You're renting a plane?" Françoise repeated with a bewildered look on her face.

Bernard chuckled. "It sounds incredible, doesn't it? But yes, we are, although the correct term is 'leasing'. You have to dream big in life, otherwise you'll never achieve anything. But we also have the contacts to make our dreams happen." He munched on a cracker. "The idea is to have complete control over our aircraft, so that we can schedule trips in the most economical manner. Later, we'll buy a couple of pre-owned planes, but there's no rush. First we need to establish a track record and secure funding from venture capitalists."

His announcement was met with stunned silence. Pre-owned planes? Venture capitalists?

"You've got big plans," André said. "I thought most startups these days were about creating a website or providing a service on the Internet."

Bernard let out a nervous laugh. "Tech startups are overrated. There are too many of them, and the barriers to entry are so low. We could spend years perfecting our product and have our market share wiped out by a new entrant within months. Besides, the margins are too small." He swallowed a gulp of champagne and pushed his eyeglasses up his nose. "We wanted a niche area that required a substantial upfront investment to scare off copycats."

"This deserves more than crackers from a box. Let me see what I have." Françoise got up and dragged Rex into the kitchen with her, to make sure that he would not steal any food while she was gone.

André looked at his son. "Who else will be working with you?"

"Vijay will be our Chief Operating Officer. Igor will handle the software and the website."

"Is that the same Vijay who was taking flying lessons last semester?"

Bernard nodded. "He's the one who got the idea to begin with. Without him, we wouldn't stand a chance. He knows the business in and out. We tasked him with hiring the crew and dealing with all the logistics." He paused. "Igor will code the program to make reservations online. We're targeting wealthy executives – the least we can do is to offer them customized software. Besides, that'll cost us less money than paying a license for some off-the-shelf product."

"Fair enough," André said.

Bernard adjusted the glasses on his nose again and leaned against the armrest of the sofa. "You should see all the apartments Igor's father has. He owns condos in New York City, Aspen, the Florida Keys, and some other place I forget. He's lending us some money too and putting us in contact with potential customers. Business associates of his. Those people don't bother flying commercial when they travel, even in first class."

"You've got well-connected friends."

"That's the magic of the HBS network, I suppose, although not every student comes from those sorts of families. I know that first-hand." Bernard laughed at his own self-deprecating remark.

"You must be very good at what you do, for them to take you on their team."

Bernard's cheeks reddened. He sat a little taller. "I'll be in charge of marketing and communications. It's an important job. We can have the best product in the world but nobody will buy it if our target clients don't know it exists. I wish I could do more, though." He pushed his glasses on his nose one more time.

Françoise returned with a platter of cold meat. André plucked a toast from the tray and clicked his glass against Bernard's. "To a future millionaire. I'm very proud of you."

Bernard smiled gingerly.

Rex settled down in front of the cured meats. He refused to move until Françoise had given him a slice of ham, which he wolfed down so fast he seemed determined to claim he had not received a thing, and then beg for more. Françoise laughed.

"I hope we'll recoup our investment within two years," Bernard said a little quickly. "We plan to go public at some point, which would give the VCs a handsome reward and help us repay our initial investors." He reached for a bit of turkey but did not eat it. "When the IPO market rebounds – and it will, sooner or later – people who supported us from day one will see two- or threefold returns on their investment." Neither André nor Françoise seemed to appreciate the magnitude of these numbers. "It's the safest way to make money without breaking a sweat." Bernard gave his parents a long look. "Let me show you the slides I've prepared for our investors."

THE BREAKTHROUGH

He unzipped the laptop case and turned his computer on.

"I don't know if we need to see the slides," André said.

"Initially, we'll focus on business executives in the Northeast. We expect most of our clients to fly between two and eight hundred miles, and value convenience and comfort when they travel. They're not interested in big airports or long security lines. We'll build a customer base by giving deep discounts our first year, and then we'll move to our steady-state subscription model." Bernard, pushing the computer toward his parents, pointed at the projected sales, which were showcased in a colorful chart with a sharp upward trend. "We'll charge a membership fee to pay for the staff year round and smooth out our revenue – make it less volatile from month to month. We'll also have a usage fee, which will depend on the distance traveled and the number of days a plane is unavailable for our other clients." André, who loved numbers, nodded at the screen. "Our biggest challenge will be to achieve critical mass. We need to create a reliable, polished service that will attract customers before we actually make money from operations. In particular, we have to get another plane soon. That's why we need venture capital." Bernard cleared his throat. "We sure need all the money we can get."

André and Françoise stared at the presentation, looking impressed.

"It's an exciting time," Bernard continued. "We wouldn't embark on this if we weren't convinced we'll be successful. Hugely successful. We put together the best possible team. We know what we're doing."

Françoise smiled.

"It sounds like you're off to a great start," André said.

"We are, but we need to make sure we keep the momentum going. That costs money. That's why everyone's pitching in. John and Igor got their fathers to secure loans, Vijay's taking a second mortgage on his house." Bernard fidgeted on his seat. "I want to contribute too. I bring the least to the table – I have to make up for that somehow. Otherwise the others will feel I'm not pulling my weight. I can't let that happen." He took a deep breath. "I maxed out my credit cards, but I didn't have a high limit to begin with. I wouldn't be able to attend HBS if you guys didn't help pay for it.

Except my car, which is showing its age, I don't have any asset to put up as collateral. I'm kind of the odd man out on the team."

"You want money." André was not smiling any more, but he did not sound angry – disconcerted, but not angry.

"We're investing as much of our own cash as we can, and asking friends and relatives to pitch in. The VCs won't lend us capital if we don't have the support of people who know us. We'd lack credibility. I'll pay you back with our first or second round of funding."

"How much money are we talking about?"

"Whatever you can contribute." Bernard made a helpful smile.

"But how much money do you need so that you won't feel like the odd man out?"

Bernard grimaced.

A car idled in front of the Connors' home across the street; the elder of the two boys – twelve years old maybe, thirteen at most – hurried out the door and hopped inside.

"John and Igor understand I'm not as well-off as they are. They're already covering a large chunk of the startup costs, which are not small. They just want to see I'm committed to the project."

"How much?"

Bernard adjusted the glasses on his nose. "I don't need the money in one chunk. Installments would be fine. Maybe the VCs will give us funding early." André waited for a straight answer. "We could start with forty thousand dollars."

Françoise pursed her lips.

"What's the total amount you're looking for?" André's voice sounded cold. He did not like to play games. "Give me a number."

"It depends on how the fundraising goes. I can't give you an exact number. Eighty thousand dollars would probably do the trick, although one hundred thousand would put us more on the safe side."

Françoise covered her mouth with her hand.

"A hundred thousand dollars," André repeated.

"Just think about all that's involved: planes, fancy amenities on the planes, but also flight crews, maintenance crews, baggage handlers, and as much advertising as we can handle."

THE BREAKTHROUGH

André placed his champagne flute on the table. He had not finished drinking.

"You know I don't have that kind of money lying around."

"It's just a safety cushion before revenues come in." André glared at his son. "I wouldn't ask if there was a risk I wouldn't pay you back. This is an incredible opportunity. I'm just trying to do my part to make the company a success."

"You're letting your friends' wealth impress you. We raised you better than that."

Françoise, on the couch, did not say a word. Even Rex sensed something was wrong: he had stopped ogling the food and crawled under the coffee table, flattening himself on the carpet to fit in the narrow space.

"It's the American culture of entrepreneurship. You launch a company and your relatives help you get started. The attitude toward debt is a lot more laid-back than in France. I'll return the money with interest. You've got nothing to worry about."

"We still have to pay for your second year at HBS. I'm not going to pull forty thousand dollars out of a hat."

"If we invest less upfront, we'll have less to lease the equipment, run operations, market our services. That would hurt us down the road. That would jeopardize the company."

André scoffed. "You're in over your head."

"I think I can do it," Bernard insisted. "I've got no interest in spending the next ten years working for a big multinational hoping that someone, someday, will notice I'm there. I just need one break to prove myself."

André shook his head. "I don't like this."

Françoise reached across the table and placed her hand on his arm.

31

Diane stepped out of the Copley Square T-Station and headed for Dartmouth Street. Jim grabbed her by the elbow before she had time to stroll too far ahead. She recoiled when he touched her.

Jim pointed in the opposite direction: "This way. The lecture hall is in the Johnson wing."

Diane folded her arms across her chest and gave him a dark look, but she walked behind him, reluctantly, when he entered the Boston Public Library through the doors on Boylston Street. They strode past the metal detectors, paused in the lobby to admire the black-and-white photographs in a temporary exhibit. The two of them stood so far apart that anyone who had not seen them outside would have assumed they did not know each other. Diane in particular was careful not to let Jim come close and ambled away whenever he took a step toward her. Her eyes twinkled with excitement, though, as she admired her surroundings: the high-ceilinged lobby, the marble floors. She was looking forward to the event.

Jim headed downstairs to the Rabb lecture hall, from which drifted a growing murmur of conversations.

"I hope we get good seats," a voice said in his back. Until then, Diane had not spoken a word since they had left the apartment. "That's a prestigious assignment you drew, covering Andrew McNeill and his take on health care reform. Hasn't he sold hundreds of thousands of books since he left the *New York Times*?"

Jim nodded. "I've got a pretty tight word limit, though. But that's better than nothing."

Outside the auditorium, seated at a long table, a young woman in a red cardigan watched over the writer's literary output: his latest release in hardcover, displayed prominently in tall piles that looked like monuments, and his previous books in paperback, gathered to the side. An elderly couple waited patiently while the volunteer computed their sales tax on a hand-held calculator. Jim glanced at their purchase on the counter.

"I have those books already."

Diane shrugged. "You have most of his books anyway."

"I bought them years ago, when I realized I wouldn't succeed as a biology major and pondered my next move. He showed me there were important stories to be told in science and technology, even if the field wasn't nearly as popular then as it is today."

Diane pulled a paperback from the display and let out a shriek. "That's the book I know him for. I didn't realize it was still in print." She shoved her gloves into her pocket to browse through the table of contents.

Jim grimaced. "That was a commercial success, but he has written better books."

"He made an important critique of the health care system."

"Indicted the usual suspects and proposed very little. No, I'm most impressed by his book on Nautalin, and how that drug went from miracle drug that treated morning sickness to culprit for many birth defects. The way he covered the behavior of management made that book a bestseller – that's what gave him an edge. That book is his masterpiece."

Diane closed the paperback critiquing the health care system and glanced at the back cover. "I read this in high school, after my father was diagnosed with diabetes. A bit over my head – I was so young – but a real page-turner. I didn't understand how much truth there was in it until after I had started working." She hesitated for a second before waving the book at the young woman behind the desk. "I'll take it. I want to read that again." She smiled at the volunteer. "We can all use some inspiration once in a while, can't we?"

She paid and hurried with Jim into the auditorium.

Jim motioned toward a rare cluster of empty seats in the back. Diane shook her head. "I'm going to sit closer to the stage." Jim grimaced but followed her to the front. He knew before she did that the long unoccupied row she had spotted by the lectern was reserved to the press and although he could sit there, Diane was not supposed to.

A woman with long hair and dark-rimmed glasses stood in the aisle and smiled firmly. "This section is for the media."

Diane bit her bottom lip.

Jim flashed his press card and pushed Diane forward. "Boston Globe," he said. The woman stared at Diane while she stumbled past her but did not attempt to hold her back.

Diane grinned. "Don't tell me you didn't want to do that."

Jim chuckled.

They took off their coats with a laugh and sat down in front of everybody. For a moment, all was well again – Jim could feel proud and Diane could feel impressed. Jim retrieved a notepad from his satchel, wrote the date on top of the first page. Diane placed McNeill's paperback on her lap and glanced at the back cover. She wore her one cashmere top with a necklace Jim had never seen before, earrings that jingled softly when she moved her head. She had even put pink nail polish on and blow-dried her hair, all that to listen to a famous author.

A man jogged past the lady with the dark-rimmed glasses and pumped the organizer's hand up and down next to the podium. They exchanged a few words while members of the audience elbowed each other, pointed at the newcomer with knowing smiles. His hair had grayed and his forehead was barred with wrinkles but one could not fail to recognize Andrew McNeill, who had given the country so many first-rate works after a brief stint as a newspaperman. According to the legend, the rookie reporter had felt he would never write the books he had in him if he kept a day job. His decision had paid off.

Diane clutched her book. "How well do you know him?"

Jim shrugged. "He's given me a couple of quotes over the years." He fished another pencil out of his bag, in case the lead of the first one broke.

"Do you think you could introduce us? His book has meant so much to me."

A bald, large man with a paunchy stomach made the whole row shake when he sat down. Jim gave him a nod. "Boston Herald," he said between his teeth.

"Maybe we can talk to him afterward." Diane pointed at McNeill.

Jim did not even pause to consider the request. "If I talk to him, it'll be for an interview to the *Globe*. You'll have no business being there. He has a hefty reputation as a science journalist. He won't have time for chit-chat."

"So what are you going to ask him?"

Jim frowned.

"What are you going to ask him?" Diane repeated, ignoring the earlier slight. "If you're going to interview him, you must've prepared questions already."

"I've got a couple of things in mind." Jim flipped through his notes, to a list of bullet points he had composed the night before after he had leafed through McNeill's new book. Diane waited for him to elaborate but he simply underlined a word, drew a small arrow in the margin while the silence between them stretched uncomfortably, all the more conspicuous because of the chatter elsewhere in the room.

Diane cracked open her paperback, glanced at the table of contents, returned to the title page. Jim dropped his pencil and leaned forward to pick it up. When he looked up again, Diane had left her seat and approached McNeill, book in hand, under the quizzical eye of the organizer who did not have time to stop her.

"Nurse" and "M.G.H.," Jim heard her say before she showed McNeill his own book. "High school." McNeill beamed at her as if he had run into an old friend. Diane nodded vigorously at his reply. Snatches of their conversation drifted to the first rows: father… diabetes… insurance… Medicare… McNeill shared an anecdote – Jim could tell it was an anecdote by the way he moved his arms and spoke without interruption. Diane nodded her head again, her blow-dried curls and large earrings bobbing around her face.

The man who had organized the reading glanced at his watch and sized up the crowd.

"We're going to get started," he finally said. His voice lacked authority but McNeill did not argue with him. The auditorium was almost full; latecomers struggled to find a good spot. Soon attendees would begin to sigh and fidget on their seats, wondering about the delay.

Diane held out her paperback open to the title page. McNeill grinned. He retrieved a pen from his shirt pocket and autographed the page in one long stroke.

The organizer cleared his throat. "Let's not keep people waiting."

Diane, clutching her book, sauntered back to her seat under Jim's angry glare. "You're such a groupie," he scoffed. Diane did not acknowledge him when she sat down, but her smile faded quickly. "You're sitting in the press section. People assume you're a journalist. What kind of impression does it give, to see you flirt and beg for an autograph like a teenager?"

"I was not flirting." Diane stared straight ahead.

McNeill stepped behind the lectern, opened his book – the hardcover – at the chapter he was planning to read. He asked something to the organizer. "About forty minutes," the man answered, "and then we'll open the floor to questions."

"Your behavior was completely inappropriate," Jim insisted. "I won't take you along again if you embarrass me like that."

Diane pinched her lips. "McNeill is a good writer. You should read his work sometime."

"I've read his work," Jim said, so forcefully that heads turned in his direction. "I started reading his books long before you had even heard of him."

"Well, re-read them," Diane said matter-of-factly. "You might learn a thing or two."

The organizer unfolded a piece of paper – McNeill laughed at something he saw on it. "You can leave that part out. I don't mind if you keep the introduction short."

"You should follow his advice more. He would never have written the kind of article you wrote about André Darrieux."

"You don't know that."

"He would've come up with something more fair-minded, and an awful lot more quotes of people willing to speak on the record." This time, Diane looked Jim in the eye. "He would've asked how Darrieux could not have known there was a mistake for so long but also remembered that he couldn't defend himself. He would've tried to understand why research meant so much to him. He wouldn't have published his piece before he understood what happened at the conference."

"Maybe you should've told McNeill about Darrieux instead of me."

The organizer tapped on the microphone. Conversations quieted down. "Ladies and gentlemen, thank you for joining us for the latest event in our reading series. We are honored to have with us today…"

Diane leaned toward Jim. "You're right. I should have. What a difference it would have made."

Then she leaned away from him, as far away as she could while staying in her seat.

32.

A key turned into the lock. Kate Johnson looked up from her book just as her husband opened the door and dropped his bag by the shoe rack.

"How did it go?"

Matt shrugged and hung his windbreaker in the closet. He was very tall, perhaps a bit too thin, with brown hair neither long nor short and enormous dark circles under his eyes.

"What did Darrieux say?" Kate wanted to know.

Matt trudged into the living-room – past his books on string theory and Kate's on chemical engineering, past the poster of John F. Kennedy conferring with Bobby in a hotel room and the reproduction of the Flatiron Building in New York City photographed by Berenice Abbott, past the bicycle helmet, the blooming orchid, the child-rearing magazines – and sank into the futon. "He said I need that result to graduate."

"Did you tell him you don't think you can do it?"

"I tried, but he insisted I'm selling myself short, I'm almost there, everyone gets tired at the end."

Kate closed her book. "We planned for this. We rehearsed all evening yesterday."

Matt took off his glasses. His eyes were blood-shot from the lack of sleep. He rubbed the bridge of his nose. "I'm sorry. He can be so convincing, you know? He has an absolute faith I can make it happen. He finds counterarguments to every objection I come up with." Kate joined him on the couch, wrapped her arms around his shoulders. Matt placed his hand on top of hers. "Of course, he won't let me give up. It's not in his interest. If I pull this off, we'll both be famous. Not famous-famous, but famous enough on academia's standards. Who can say no to that?"

"But you don't think you can do it."

Matt groaned and rested his forehead on his arms, folded across his knees.

Kate stroked his back. "I'll heat some lasagna. You need to eat something."

Matt searched for the remote to turn the TV on, spotted it across the room, let it stay there. Getting up would have required too much effort.

"Darrieux often says we're alike," he mused aloud, "but I doubt we're as alike as he thinks. He doesn't get along with his son, that's all."

Kate slid a pan in the oven and adjusted the temperature. "I don't mind him viewing you as his adoptive child if that makes him sign your dissertation faster."

Matt chuckled. "Be careful what you wish for. He had a pretty bad falling-out with his son, although I don't know the details. I prefer not to ask." He stifled a yawn, wrapped himself in the throw on the couch as if it were a blanket. "How's Vicki?"

"She fussed a lot earlier, but she's asleep now. Not sure how long that's going to last." Kate leaned against the counter that separated the kitchen area from the living room. "Did you tell Darrieux about Goldman Sachs?"

Matt shook his head. "He thinks I'm taking the post-doc in Wisconsin." Kate folded her arms across her chest and gave her husband a long look. "There's no point in breaking the news now. He'll complain I'm going to the dark side, worry that I won't have time to revise our papers after I've left. Nothing good can come out of that – he'll simply make it harder for me to graduate. I'm having enough trouble already." Matt clasped his hands behind his head and closed his eyes.

"But he doesn't understand you're supposed to start in July, then. We have to find a place to live in New York, pack, move." Kate walked to the futon and, when she got no response, tugged at Matt's sleeve. "I have to get another job and interview nannies."

Matt opened his eyes. "We said you could stay home if you wanted."

"I like my job. That's what I trained for. Anyway, it doesn't look like I'll be able to stop working any time soon, now, does it?"

Matt's gaze hardened. Kate sighed. "I don't care if we stay in Cambridge. I'll return to Merck after my maternity leave – that's not a problem. But I'm worried about Goldman Sachs." She sat down on the edge of the couch. "I don't want them to have second thoughts and withdraw your offer. That kind of opportunity won't present itself again. And the money! My mom didn't believe me when I told her how much you'll be making." Kate reached for her husband's hand. "We'll be able to pay off our college loans, and send Vicki to private school if we think it's better for her, and once you're promoted we'll buy a nice retirement home for my parents, and send yours around the world like they've always wanted to. But it all rides on you taking that job."

"I'll see if I can push my start date to early fall. Maybe two more months is all I need." Matt covered his eyes with his palms. "I wish I could prove that last result. I just don't have any clue how. And sometimes I stop and ask myself, why am I doing all this? My work is neither going to cure cancer nor end global warming. What's the big deal if we never find a way to unify the four forces? Why did I get so sucked into this? I've spent six years of my life obsessed with a miniscule part of theoretical physics, trying to prove something that will have no impact on the world whatsoever." He pressed his fingers against his temples, hard. "I feel I've woken up from a spell and I can't figure out what the craze was all about."

Kate shrugged. "Now is not the moment for philosophical musings."

Matt dumped his book bag by the closet and kicked off his shoes.

Kate muted the TV. "Hi, hon." She folded her legs under her, tugged on the sleeves of her sweatshirt, eyed her husband as he made his way to the kitchen. She did not ask him about his day – his body language had already told her what she needed to know. Kate braced herself for the evening ahead.

Matt placed his keys on the counter, opened the fridge without a glance at the many photographs displayed on its door – his and Kate's wedding picture, photographs of Vicki as a newborn, his parents, Kate's parents, old pictures of trips they had taken years earlier. He refused to look at any of that. Instead, he retrieved a bottle of soda, plucked a glass from the shelf, poured the soft drink so quickly that the foam built up and up and overflew.

Kate pinched her lips.

"I'm not graduating in June. Or in the foreseeable future, for that matter."

Matt stared at the puddle on the countertop but did not move. Kate, on her feet now, grabbed a paper towel and wiped the liquid away for him. "What happened?"

Matt shrugged. "Darrieux says I'm on the right track, but he's not willing to schedule the defense until I'm done. He found a paper describing a new technique that might help us. It's going to take me a while to get up to speed and figure out whether we can use this or not. His take is that I should make the work as good as I can – that in the grand scheme of things, no one will remember whether I graduated this semester or next." Matt took a big gulp of soda. "Whenever he starts a sentence with 'in the grand scheme of things', I feel like banging my head against the desk. I always know what he's going to add." Kate gave him a hug. "I guess it's my fault," Matt said. "I kept telling him that our current approach isn't working. He finally decided to believe me, but I don't have any energy left to try another way."

He sprawled onto the couch. Kate had been watching one of the late-night comic shows and Matt looked at the images, without the sound, for about five seconds before deciding he was not interested. He flipped the channels to TCM, made a faint smile when he recognized a Clint Eastwood movie. Eastwood fought hard and dirty and he always knew what he was doing. Matt raised the volume, although not by much, because Vicki was sleeping in the bedroom a few steps away.

"There's about forty-five minutes left," he said. "I might as well watch."

Kate pushed the latest issue of *Metropolitan Home* magazine with her foot under the couch, where it was joined by the Crate & Barrel catalog. She had garnered its pages of Post-it notes next to the items she planned to buy for their future apartment. Matt did not need to see that. "Maybe I'll watch with you."

The bank robber played by Eastwood in *Escape from Alcatraz* was discussing his escape plan with the two brothers about to help him and a third acolyte who, Matt explained, would not get out of his cell in time to participate in the attempt.

"How's Vicki?" he asked during a lull in the movie.

Kate made a vague gesture with her hand. "She's fine. Eating and sleeping. I wish life could be that simple for the rest of us."

Matt laughed. Kate rested her head on his shoulder. "Do they succeed?" she asked, pointing at the screen.

"Nobody knows. Their bodies have never been found. I like to think they did, although the odds were against them. They probably drowned in the San Francisco Bay." Kate's interest in the movie grew as the preparations for the escape intensified. The images of the Alcatraz prison were bleak – no wonder it had been closed shortly after the escape, the inmates transferred to other jails. "I don't want to push my start date back a second time," Matt said after a while. "I doubt Goldman Sachs would let me. They were very accommodating the first time around, but it's a lot more serious this time. Now Darrieux is saying I should take as long as I need to finish and there's no way to know how long that's going to be."

Kate clasped his hand in hers, intertwining their fingers. "You'll figure something out. We need that job. We could do so much with that money." Matt chuckled wryly but did not comment. "Can't Darrieux ask some other student to finish your work after you're gone?"

"He didn't pay me all these years to quit before the end. He won't let me, at least not if I want a doctorate. Nobody in his position would. It'd set a precedent." He gulped down his soda and took his attention back to the screen. "Without the last result, there is no thesis."

"Who cares!" Kate, surprised by her own outburst, covered her mouth with her hand and listened for infant cries that did not come. Vicki remained sound asleep. "You don't have time to try another approach," she added in a whisper. "It's either the one you've been working on for the past year or nothing. You know that. Get Darrieux to sign the paperwork and let's be done with it."

"What if I can't make it work? What do I do then?"

"There's no point in thinking about that now. You're tired. Get some sleep. You'll feel better tomorrow morning and think more clearly."

Matt scoffed. "You talk exactly like him. Like Darrieux. You hope sleep and pep talks will solve every problem. That'd be so convenient, wouldn't it? But things are more complicated than that."

In June, Matt rented a car and drove to Cape Cod with Vicki and Kate for a four-day weekend. That was not any long weekend – it was the first weekend in June, when M.I.T.'s new doctors received their academic hood during a ceremony at the Johnson Athletics Center, and then took part in the Commencement exercises the following day. The campus would swarm with two thousand happy graduates and their family members, taking photographs and waving their degrees. One could not avoid them, at least as long as one stayed in Cambridge.

Matt headed a hundred miles away to Nauset Beach, where he helped Vicki build sand castles and Kate sunned herself. He admired the view, enjoyed the food, and tossed around in bed every night: that last result, the result that would make the pieces of the puzzle fit together and bring fame to both André Darrieux and himself, the result that would allow him to move on with his life, continued to elude him.

Maybe there would be no dissertation after all. Six years of his life, spent on nothing.

The phone rang. Kate left the half-folded shirt on her ironing board and picked up the handset. At the other end of the line, Matt spoke so excitedly that she could not make sense at first of what he was trying to say.

"I did it!" Matt yelled. "I proved the result! I'm done!"

Kate, squealing, jumped up and down like a teenage girl.

The elevator doors opened and closed. Someone sauntered along the corridor toward the Johnsons' apartment. Kate checked her hairdo, smoothed her black dress – too tight around the hips because of the baby pounds – while Matt fumbled through his pockets. His wife opened the door before he had time to insert his keys into the lock.

"Surprise!" She brandished a bottle of wine.

Matt laughed and lifted Kate up in the air. "We're moving to New York! I thought this day would never come."

Vicki cooed in her playpen. "Hi baby," Matt said, "your dad's getting his degree."

"Daddy did it! Daddy did it!" Kate chanted to their bemused daughter.

Matt sat down at the table, opened the bottle of Merlot. Kate waved him to stop when her glass was halfway full; she could not drink much because she was still nursing, but she wanted to celebrate Matt's accomplishment with him. Matt poured himself a full glass. He had earned it.

"I'm going to be a doctor," he said. "No one can take that away from me now." Kate clicked her glass against his. "I told Darrieux already – he was ecstatic. I've never seen him that relieved. For one second he looked about to cry, if you can believe it. I knew this work meant a lot to him, but I didn't expect him to become so emotional over a thesis." Matt tasted the wine, made an appreciative nod. Kate pushed a plate of antipasti toward him – cured meats, olives, artichoke hearts and mozzarella. She had not found time to run to the store for anchovies and provolone, but Matt did not seem to care. This was feisty enough. "I'll type everything tonight, give him the draft tomorrow. This way, he can make his final comments while I schedule the defense. Let's be done with it – this has been dragging on for too long." He took another sip of Merlot and grinned. "I've done it. I've made us famous."

Kate woke up in the middle of the night to feed Vicki who was crying. She found Matt's side of the bed empty, stumbled into the hallway and poked her head into the living room.

"Doctor Johnson! Are you going to stay up all night?"

Matt, sitting in pajamas in front of his laptop, cast a side glance at her. "Just a few more minutes. I've got one last detail to check and I'll be done." He forced himself to smile.

THE BREAKTHROUGH

Because it was so late and she struggled to keep her eyes open, Kate did not notice how pale, how drained her husband looked after the euphoria of the previous evening. She did not suspect a thing.

33

"He called you?" André said. "He called you to tell you the news?" He locked the car door and walked straight toward the house, satchel in hand, in spite of Rex bounding around him as if he had not seen André in years.

Françoise nodded.

André let out a scoff. "That boy has no spine," he hissed when he entered their home.

"He sounded very distraught. He probably doesn't want to see anybody." Françoise closed the front door behind them.

"He's a coward." André took off his coat. "He should've come here and told us in person. In my family, when we lose tens of thousands of dollars of other people's money, we go and say it to their face. Of course, in my family, we don't lose tens of thousands of dollars of other people's money to begin with."

Bernard had called his mother, earlier that afternoon, to tell her the company had run out of cash. Françoise had not known what that meant. It means we filed for bankruptcy, Bernard had yelled over the phone, upset that she had made him spell it out. We lost all of our investors' money. I lost your and Dad's savings. But I'll make it up to you – I promise.

"He said he'll pay us back, even if it takes years."

"This is not about the money," André said. Bernard had not called him – he had spent uneventful hours at work, in committee meetings, meetings with his students, never suspecting that this day was about to take a much different turn. Françoise had met him in the driveway when he had returned home. He had known right away that something had happened from looking at her face. "I won't retire for a while. We've got a steady source of income. I'm not thrilled, but we'll handle it. No, what angers me is that he doesn't even have the spine to tell us face-to-face. And that idea of his!

Timeshare for personal jets! Can you get more grandiose than that? Why would he and his friends, of all people, make that sort of venture work? I thought, his plan makes no sense, but he's my son and he wouldn't put his own parents' savings at risk." He shook his head. "How dumb I was."

André reached for the phone and dialed a number. "I'm going to give him a piece of my mind." He remained silent for a second. "He's not picking up – he's not stupid. It's going straight to voice mail." He took a deep breath. "Bernard, your mother and I are expecting you tonight at seven o'clock at our home so that you can share your big news with us in person. We're counting on you not to be late."

"I really thought he would succeed. He talked so excitedly about his company. And the strategy terms he explained for us! Porter's five forces, the BCG Growth-Share Matrix."

"Buzzwords," André said.

"It sounded like he knew what he was talking about. And you never contradicted him."

"I'm not the one finishing Harvard Business School."

André strode into the living room after hanging up, grabbed a photograph on the chimney that showed his son with Françoise during a recent Thanksgiving dinner. "You can keep that if you'd like, but I don't want to see it again. Eighty thousand dollars went up in smoke, and he can't even spare a moment to break the news in person."

Françoise took the frame from his hands and pressed it against her chest. "He's embarrassed. He wanted so badly for the company to be a success. He knew the lengths we went to, to find him the money."

"We refused to see the signs. The fact that he started to skip our regular lunch, for instance. His pretense of being too busy because the company needed to raise more money – too busy for spending two hours every other Sunday with his parents. And the fact that he kept eluding all the questions we had about his business. We should've known better."

André picked another photograph, this one of the three of them by the Christmas tree, behind a row of just-opened presents.

"Go and hide that thing too," he told his wife. "Make sure I don't find it."

Later that spring, Bernard announced he had accepted an offer with a San Diego-based company. He would start as soon as he graduated. The firm had bought the scheduling software that Bernard's startup had developed and wanted Bernard to help market it to doctors' offices, hair salons, spas, yoga studios, any place where people would care to schedule an appointment on the web.

"It is going to take a lot of yoga lessons for him to pay me back," André said. "Not quite the high-end product he had imagined."

Françoise shrugged. "You know very well what he's doing. He's running away from you, moving as far away from Boston as he can while staying in the States. He'll only come back after he has made the software a success. He wants to prove himself."

André scoffed. "I thought he'd had his chance already."

Bernard's pictures remained off the chimney mantel.

34.

Françoise lay on her bed, stared at the ceiling in the dark. She reflected on what Hans had said, about Olivia but mostly about André's prize. Buddy sat by her nightstand at first, very straight, to keep an eye on her; after a while, he curled up on her slippers and fell asleep. Françoise knew he was asleep because he snored. Her thoughts drifted to Matthew Johnson, whom she had never met, and then back to the prize, which had meant so much to her husband – and her. It had vindicated them. André liked to say he could not have achieved his breakthrough anywhere else than in the States.

Françoise adjusted the pillow behind her head. She, who for years had introduced herself as a psychiatrist by training, imagined the practice she would never open, with its plaque by the door, the plants in the waiting room, and the comfortable chairs in her office for clients to sink in. She would have helped families in need. She would have been good at her job. Her teachers had told her as much: they had praised her listening skills, her empathy, her talent for sensing hidden conflicts, her ability to make people take action. She still remembered those compliments, thirty-five years later.

When the tears came, her sobs shook her shoulders so hard they woke Buddy up. The dog leaned forward on the bed, poked Françoise with his snout. She hesitated for a second before wiping her eyes.

"I've got to handle it."

35

Kate picked up a teddy bear, kicked a plastic toy out of the way, arranged the cushions on the sofa.

"I don't understand why she has to come. Can't the two of you talk over the phone?"

Matt shrugged. "She wants to meet face to face. For some reason, that's important to her." Kate rolled her eyes. "Look, Darrieux had a stroke. I can indulge his wife for two hours and tell her stories about him if that makes her happy. She won't pay attention to the mess."

"She'd better not, or she'll run away screaming."

"You're the one who wanted to get back to work. Both times."

Vicki tugged at her mother's sleeve and showed her a drawing of a little girl with blue hair and green arms, standing on one leg in the middle of a circle, and a pink bundle by the side.

"That's beautiful, sweetie. Is that your little brother with you at Rockefeller Center?" Vicki nodded. "Maybe we'll go ice-skating again next week." Kate gathered loose papers around the couch and hid them in the cupboard. "Why didn't she ask you to write your memories about Darrieux and email them to her? It would've saved her a lot of time, instead of driving down from Boston."

"She said she's visiting friends in the area."

Kate shook her head. "I didn't even have time to vacuum. You could've told me earlier."

"I thought you were taking the kids to the museum."

Kate stopped. "You meant you wouldn't have said a thing if I hadn't changed my plans?" Matt stood in front of the poster of Jack and Bobby Kennedy discussing strategy in a hotel room in Los Angeles, during the 1960 Democratic National Convention, and adjusted the frame so it would hang perfectly straight. Kate pinched her lips but she did not press the matter further. She did not have time – their guest would arrive any minute now and the house was in complete disarray. "You could've met her at a coffeehouse, a restaurant, wherever. This is embarrassing." Kate stacked a dozen DVDs on the shelves and crumpled an old receipt in her hand.

"I offered to, but she insisted on coming here."

Kate frowned. "That's odd." Matt pushed the chairs under the table of the living room. Kate eyed him suspiciously. "Is there something I should be aware of?" Matt did not look at her. Kate raised her voice. "Matthew Alan Johnson, what in the world is going on here?"

Matt smiled at Vicki, who stood by the armchair with a bored look on her face – the girl did not like it when her parents stopped paying attention to her, which they had been doing frequently since her little brother had been born. Matt pointed at her pencil box on the floor. "Why don't you do another drawing? Maybe you can draw Mom and Dad this time."

Kate waited for an answer. It did not come. "I'm serious, Matt. This makes no sense. Why is this woman coming to our house, all the way from Boston?"

Matt stared at his feet. "I assume she wants to see what kind of lifestyle we're able to afford thanks to the doctorate I don't deserve." Kate raised an eyebrow. "She probably also wants to ask me in person how I could've made such a mistake when I was well aware of the importance of the paper and should've triple-checked all my proofs."

"What mistake?"

Matt dug his hands into his pockets. "Do you remember I had to prove one last result in order to graduate, and for months I couldn't figure out how to do it?"

Kate nodded. "Of course. You only nailed it at the very end."

"It turns out I didn't nail it after all."

Kate, in her surprise, plopped onto the faux-suede couch she had bought at West Elm. Vicki watched her mother, then her father, then her mother again.

"When did you hear?" Kate asked.

"A colleague of Darrieux's emailed me a few days ago." Matt shifted his weight from one leg to the other. "He said that the paper's being withdrawn, and Darrieux's going to lose the prize he got for it – the one from the European Physical Society. All that because the result I'd told him I'd proved doesn't hold."

Vicki, pencils in hand, climbed onto the couch and cuddled on her mother's lap.

Kate blinked furiously in search of something to say. "You did the best you could. Don't beat yourself up about it. It doesn't mean you didn't have any talent." Her voice lacked conviction. "You opted out of that race. That's very different." Matt scoffed. "Did someone tell you what's wrong with your work?"

"I know what's wrong with it. I've known for a while." Matt looked out the window, at the driveway he had salted the previous evening but would have to salt again, the knee-high mounds of snow lining the street and fencing off the cars parked along the curb. On the other side of the hedge, his neighbor – the tort lawyer with a corner office overlooking Manhattan – watched while his gardener shoveled snow out of the way. "As a matter of fact, I knew even before I handed in my dissertation."

"You're kidding me."

"I made a mistake one afternoon when I thought I'd found a way to prove the result, but I didn't realize it was a mistake until later that same night when I went over my calculations again. By then I'd already announced to anyone who would listen that I was graduating, and I was so psyched up about getting out of there that I couldn't bring myself to admit it'd been a false alert." Matt sighed in the middle of his spacious, airy living room, in the house he had bought in a coveted neighborhood of Brooklyn, with good schools and a great safety record, thanks to his comfortable salary. "I was so tired, so sick of it all. I thought, if I can make Darrieux believe the proof for just a few weeks, I'll pack and leave for New York and be done with it. Who cares what happens once I'm gone? I was convinced Darrieux would catch the mistake before sending the paper out for review, and if not, the reviewers would find it themselves. He would be upset but that'd be the end of it. I never expected things to spiral out of control the way they did."

Kate pinched her lips. "You could've told me."

Matt looked down. "I didn't want to disappoint you. I was supposed to earn that doctorate. I didn't set out to be a liar."

Kate raised her eyebrows and lowered them almost immediately, in a quick little movement Matt did not even notice, which meant: too late for that.

A station wagon drove by the house at slow speed.

"That might be her," Kate said.

Matt shrugged. "That could be anybody."

Kate's gaze drifted across the living room, over the toys and the magazines and the smudges on the windowpanes. The task ahead overwhelmed her. She stayed in her seat, her left hand on Vicki's shoulder, her right elbow on the armrest. The little girl – her head on her mother's lap – sucked her thumb while keeping an eye on her father, who rarely talked that much. Kate stroked Vicki's hair. "Why didn't Darrieux check the proof more carefully if he knew it was giving you trouble?"

"I told him my main issue had been with a lemma I knew I'd done right, and I steered him away from the part with the mistake. So he went over the lemma line-by-line and barely glanced at the rest before he signed off on my thesis. He trusted me." Matt shook his head. "I was convinced I'd be found out before the paper got published. I never thought Darrieux would become a contender for the Nobel Prize. That was surreal."

"You knew all this time."

"I meant well. I didn't plan to fake the proof. I tried to prove the result – I tried really hard. It's just the way things worked out. Later, I kept hoping someone would discover the mistake and put an end to that farce, but it took years before it happened."

Kate twisted her mouth in disgust. "You let Darrieux embarrass himself in front of his colleagues, let him believe he had hit it big, let him become famous based on castles in the air. He didn't deserve any of this. His reputation will never recover."

"Don't you think I feel guilty enough?" Kate started – she had not expected Matt to yell. Vicki buried her face into her mother's sweatshirt. "A post-doc from Stanford got in touch with me recently. He said he couldn't duplicate my proof and asked for details. I knew right away he'd found my mistake. I ignored his emails – he contacted me three times – but he wrote he would get in touch with Darrieux after his plenary talk in San Francisco. I guess I wasn't sure whether Darrieux would give him the time of day. In hindsight, of course, I could bet some serious amount of money they had a long talk. That's the guy who dropped the bombshell: some stranger in a fancy hotel far away from home."

"It should've been you." Kate pressed her lips together. "Maybe Darrieux wouldn't have had a stroke if you'd prepared him to the news."

"That's easy for you to say now. You were ordering all these catalogs from Crate & Barrel and West Elm and Williams-Sonoma. You pressured me to finish so you could go apartment-hunting."

Kate gaped. "I never pressured you for anything." Matt scoffed. "Don't you dare putting the blame on me. I paid every single bill while you were in graduate school and gave you all the time you needed. You're the one who had the choice. You decided to lie. I've got nothing to do with your lack of ethics." Kate waved a finger at him. "And you're more than happy to have a well-decorated house and buy your suits at Brooks Brothers."

The same station wagon drove past the house again. This time, Kate jumped to her feet. She scooped up an armful of books, prospectus, newspapers, pieces of mail she did not care for, added baby toys to the pile and hurried down the hallway.

"I'm sorry!" Matt shouted at her as she dumped her load into the laundry room, nearly tripped over Barbie's pink Jeep Wrangler when she closed the door over the mess. She jogged back to the living area and began to dust the television with her sleeve. "I never meant for this to happen! I'm sorry! I'm sorry! How many times do I have to say it!"

The shouts startled Vicki, who began to cry. A baby wailed in the bedroom.

"You've woken Noel up," Kate said matter-of-factly. She disappeared for a moment and returned with the six-month-old infant in her arms, bouncing him on her hip, speaking baby talk. She glanced at Matt. "I don't know how you're going to look at that woman in the eye."

36

Françoise locked the doors of the car. Buddy barked behind the windowpane, scratched the upholstery.

"Quiet."

Françoise checked that she had put enough coins in the meter – now was not a time to get the Volvo towed – and wound the strap of her purse tightly around her wrist. There were thieves in Brooklyn. New York City was a dangerous place. She had read about the crime wave in the early nineties, and who knew whether things had really changed?

She leaned toward the dog. "I'll be back in two hours. You be nice and don't draw attention to yourself."

Françoise buttoned her coat, tied her scarf around her neck and giggled softly. She'd done it! She had made the trip to New York all by herself, dropping on the car floor pages of instructions she had printed from Mapquest.com, one after the other, while the trip progressed, and also keeping an eye on the screen of the GPS. She had not missed one exit nor misread one sign – André would have been proud. Françoise had used his computer to prepare for the trip the previous evening, decide in advance where she would stop for a cup of coffee and refill the gas tank, right after calling Matthew Johnson. She had told him little white lies to meet with him. Of course, she was not visiting any friend in the area – she did not even know anyone in a two-hundred-mile radius.

She drove past the Johnsons' house several times in her search for a parking spot, but in the end left the car farther away – she did not have a choice. All the spots nearby were taken or blocked by mounds of snow. Françoise looked around and headed east after hesitating on which direction to go. Buddy barked again. She hurried out of his sight and stifled a yawn. It was not quite ten yet; for many people, the day had barely started, but she had been up since four o'clock and the long drive down I-95 had exhausted her. The cold air woke her up, somewhat.

A family – two parents in winter jackets, two children with woolen hats pulled over their ears – ambled down the sidewalk. The husband carried the younger child in his arms; the wife held the elder one by the hand. Françoise smiled when they strolled by and waved at the kids. The toddler beamed back, showing off his milk teeth. Down the street, an elderly man in an oversized parka trudged to his mailbox to pick up the newspaper. The quiet, peaceful neighborhood reminded Françoise of Belmont. She understood why Matthew Johnson had chosen to live there.

She had found André's inbox flooded with good wishes when she had checked his emails the night before. Many of the names she did not recognize. She had been taken aback that André would know tens of people she had never even heard of, but he was famous in his field and she should not have been surprised. The fact that casual acquaintances prayed for his recovery had filled her with joy and, for reasons she could not fully explain, motivated her to go through with the trip. It would not erase André's stroke, would not allow him to keep his prize. But these strangers stood on André's side and if the stroke was to any extent Matthew Johnson's fault, Françoise wanted to meet in person the man who had wreaked havoc on her husband's life.

Besides, she had nothing else to do.

She rounded a corner, found herself on the Johnsons' street. A man shoveled snow out of a driveway. At first, Françoise thought she had chanced upon "him" – Matthew Johnson, in the flesh – but she quickly realized the number on the mailbox was off and headed for the next house. It looked like it had received a fresh coat of paint during the summer, and like the porch had been rebuilt not too long ago. The thick snow that covered the lawn had already been pierced by tiny children's steps. Françoise stopped on the doormat and pressed on the bell.

Footsteps drew near. A woman in her early thirties – a bit disheveled, in a Purdue sweatshirt and without any makeup – unlocked the door. "You must be Mrs. Darrieux. It's a pleasure to meet you." She stretched her arm out. "I'm Kate. This is Noel." She pointed at the baby she carried on her hip.

"Hi Noel." Françoise smiled.

Kate invited her in. Françoise kicked the tips of her shoes against the doormat, to make the snow fall before she entered the house. Kate shoved a Fisher-Price doll aside with her foot.

"I'm sorry for the mess. I recently got back to work after my maternity leave and it's been hard to keep everything under control. The living room is sparkling clean, though. I did that this morning."

Françoise kept smiling. "It looks like a house that's lived in, that's all. It certainly beats the place being empty."

Kate ushered her into the living room. "I'm sorry about your husband. I couldn't believe it when Matt told me. That's awful."

A man in his thirties lunged forward and pumped Françoise's hand up and down. "How are you? It's nice to meet you after all these years. I wish it was under other circumstances, though."

Françoise nodded. Matthew Johnson towered above her, with a large neck, puffy cheeks, strands of grey hair, and wrinkles that appeared around his eyes when he spoke. His stomach bulged slightly over his belt. He was better dressed than his wife, with a buttoned-down shirt and creased pants – he did not look like a graduate student anymore, certainly not the student he had been in Cambridge: thin, lanky even, slightly underweight. There were pictures of him from that time on the bookshelves. André himself may not have recognized him.

Françoise stared at the stranger.

"Please, sit down. Would you like something to drink – coffee, tea, orange juice?"

"Coffee would be nice."

Kate headed for the kitchen.

The sofa was positioned against the window, in front of a flat-screen television. Two armchairs bracketed the coffee table. Françoise picked the armchair on the right, which offered the best view of the room, while Matt sat on the sofa. There was an awkward moment of silence.

"I'm sorry about what happened. It's incredible. He's way too young to have a stroke." Matt shook his head. "He was always so full of energy. In fact, he had more energy than me or any student in the lab, and we were thirty years his juniors."

Françoise did not reply. She admired the large photograph of the Flatiron Building on the wall, which she felt she had seen elsewhere – in an exhibition perhaps, or a museum catalog – and then she examined the poster of Jack and Bobby Kennedy, with its stunning use of natural light. The other items in the room (trinkets on the chimney, wedding pictures on the shelves, a small clock, scented candles) lacked originality, but whoever had selected the black-and-white photographs was not afraid of showing their taste. Françoise hoped it was Kate. She balked at granting Matt any redeeming qualities.

"So you'd like to discuss my memories of your husband."

"The doctor thinks André doesn't remember much of anything, but there's a chance his memories will come back if we prod him. From what I've been told, that part of his brain only suffered," she hesitated on the correct wording, "moderate damage from the stroke. This could help André recover faster." She paused again. "I don't know if 'recover' is the right word. Maybe it would undo a small part of the damage." She looked at Matt, hoping to catch a glimpse of his embarrassment, but he only listened with a kind gaze. If he was troubled, he hid it well. Investment bankers, Françoise thought. "He spent a lot of time at work, though, and I know so little about that part of his life. I'd be grateful for whatever you can share."

Matt nodded.

Kate returned to the room with empty cups on a tray – the coffee would be ready in a minute. She had applied some lip-gloss and traded her sweatshirt for a more sophisticated top and cardigan. Someone tugged at her sweatpants, which she had not found time to change. Kate chuckled. "Look who's here."

A little girl appeared behind her mother's leg and made a shy smile to the guest.

"Hello, sweetheart," Françoise said. "How old are you?"

Vicki held up four fingers.

"You're a big girl."

Vicki grinned.

THE BREAKTHROUGH

Noel, snuggling in Kate's arms, pointed at Françoise and warbled unintelligible but happy noises. Kate grabbed Vicki by the hand. "Let's go back to the playroom while Daddy talks with the visitor."

Matt waited until his wife and children had stepped out of earshot. "How bad is it?" he finally asked.

"He has a long road ahead of him."

"I remember him so full of energy, so enthusiastic about research. Even when things didn't pan out, he was fascinated by what the setback meant and how we could use that information to move forward. And he was a good person. He wasn't the warm-and-fuzzy type, but he had a big heart." Matt rested his elbows on his thighs, kept his eyes on the floor.

"Tell me more."

"There was this one time, I must've been a fourth-year student, where we both attended a workshop in Italy and I had my wallet stolen on our first day. Luckily, my passport was in my hotel room, but my credit cards and my money were gone. André stuck with me for the whole trip, paying for all my expenses, giving me cash for the cab rides and the meals. He didn't keep the receipts, so I knew he wouldn't get reimbursed – he was using his own money. I tried to pay him back later but he refused to let me. I got him the binary clock just after that trip. My way to say thanks."

Françoise forced herself to smile. "He still has it on his desk, in his study – he loves that thing. He assures me he knows how to read time with it. I'm not sure I believe him."

"It's not that complicated. You have six columns of dots, two for the hours, two for the minutes, and two for the seconds." Françoise's bored glance stopped Matt. "Maybe I'll explain some other day." He came up with another anecdote. "Sometimes we talked about sports. We joked about how Europeans only cared about men's soccer and Americans loved women's soccer instead. Apparently, women's soccer doesn't have much of a following in Europe. When the United States won the World Cup in 1999, André teased me that perhaps the American women had been the only team enrolled in the competition."

Françoise chuckled. "That sounds like him."

"He gave me a lot of advice. He always made me rehearse my talk with him before I left for conferences. It wasn't completely altruistic, because I was going to present our work and he wanted our research to impress the competition. But you don't find too many professors who take the time to coach their students so that they won't look like fools in front of a crowd." Matt grimaced. "He was very disappointed when I decided to leave academia. I can't blame him – he'd invested so much in me. I did feel that at some level I'd betrayed him." Matt glanced at Françoise. For one second he looked like a student again, directionless, worried, in need of encouragement. "Do you think he felt betrayed?"

Françoise raised an eyebrow. "I doubt it'd be enough for André to feel betrayed. Upset, certainly, but betrayed?" She dismissed her own question with a wave of her hand. "The worst I've ever seen him in three decades of marriage was on the morning of the stroke, but since he wouldn't talk to me, it's hard for me to tell you what he was feeling."

Matthew stared at his feet.

Kate returned, alone, with the coffee pot. A pair of denim had replaced the sweatpants and she had applied mascara on her eyelashes. "Sorry the coffee took so long." Her good cheer sounded forced. "Cream and sugar?"

Françoise nodded, her eyes on Matt.

"I heard about the article in the *Boston Globe*," he said. "A friend of mine forwarded it to me. That was a terrible piece, with a ton of speculation and little to back it up. The journalist clearly had an agenda."

"Maybe he had, but that's the least of André's problems now, isn't it?" The smile on Françoise's face hardened while Kate filled her cup. "I talked with one of his colleagues the other day. He told me that a paper you wrote with my husband is going to be withdrawn, and the prize he got from the European Physical Society is going to be withdrawn too."

She had never seen anyone's face turn crimson so fast.

"You mean Hans Walzenberger? He emailed me a few days ago with the news. I didn't want to believe it at first, but I looked over the calculations and indeed, there's a mistake toward the end of my last paper with André."

"You still remember how to do these calculations, years later?"

Matt blinked. "Absolutely. I've done them thousands of times. They're hard-wired in my brain now. It's like riding a bicycle – you don't forget that kind of things."

Kate poured him a cup of coffee, her back turned to Françoise. She must have been mouthing to her husband something that he did not want to hear, because he glared at her and then turned his head away.

"We're devastated," Kate said. "Matt put so much time and effort into this."

Françoise bit the inside of her cheeks and looked at Matt. "It's too bad you remember the calculations so well now but couldn't do them correctly the first time."

Matt winced. "It's not unusual to make mistakes when you're trying to graduate – you're so sleep-deprived. It's unfortunate, but not unusual." Kate gave him a long look. "Of course, I wish it hadn't happened."

Françoise took a sip of coffee and waited.

"I do feel like I've let him down." Matt sighed. "He trusted me, and I've turned his life into such a mess." He avoided looking at Françoise.

"I guess you didn't mean to," she said, coldly.

She noticed Matt blinking again, although he kept his head down.

"Bye!" Vicki, clutching her teddy bear, waved her tiny hand while she ran after the guest in the driveway.

Françoise stopped at the gate and stroked the hair of the little girl. "Goodbye, sweetie. Don't step on the road." Kate and Matt stood on the front porch, Kate with Noel in her arms, Matt ready to intervene if the child ventured any farther.

Vicki gazed at Françoise, brought her thumb to her mouth and removed it almost immediately.

"Daddy's sorry," she blurted out. "Daddy's really sorry about what happened."

Françoise gave her a faint smile. "I hope so, sweetie."

"Daddy didn't mean to, but he kept trying and he couldn't do it, and then it was time and so he made it up." Françoise frowned. "He thought," Vicki took a breath, frowned while she tried to remember the exact words she had overheard, "people would find the mistake before the paper got published. He didn't think things would spiral out of control the way they did." She repeated the words as if they belonged to a foreign language – she had no clue of their meaning, but she guessed Françoise would understand. The little girl squeezed her teddy bear against her chest and looked at Françoise with big, sad eyes.

A car drove by in the street. Snow fell from the roof of a house and landed on the ground with a soft thud.

Françoise kneeled down. She had become very pale. "You listen to your parents' conversations a lot, don't you, little girl?"

"Daddy's sorry. He keeps telling Mommy he's sorry. She's very upset. She didn't know. But Daddy's sorry."

"I'm sure he is." Françoise's whisper sounded like a hiss. Vicki seemed about to cry. "But it's not your fault, sweetie. Thanks for telling me. You're a good girl. It's not your fault." She patted the little girl on the head. Vicki tried to smile.

Françoise got up, slapped a smile on her face, waved at the Johnsons. "Goodbye now! It was nice meeting you!"

She stepped onto the sidewalk but could not resist leaning toward the girl one last time. "Tell your daddy I'll be in touch."

37

Françoise's cell phone rang after she had passed a tractor-trailer, jaws clenched, hands gripping the steering wheel. She dreaded passing trucks, but that one – laboring along at forty-five miles an hour on a slope – had not given her a choice. She felt a surge of exhilaration when she spotted the cab in her rearview mirror. Then her phone rang.

At first, she thought it was André – the only person who bothered calling her on her cell. She would tell him she had passed a truck and he would chuckle and say bravo; he knew how much she disliked driving by tractor-trailers. It took her a second to remember the stroke, the nursing home, and conclude it was a wrong number. The call went to voice mail but her phone beeped almost immediately: the stranger had left a message. Françoise put more distance between the truck and her car before reaching for her phone. She glanced at the Caller ID.

Bernard.

She must have sounded like a madwoman on his answering machine, while she babbled about prizes and reputation and so many things her son did not care about. Françoise would listen to his message when she got home.

Her phone rang again twenty minutes later. Françoise hesitated but did not pick up.

"That was Bernard," she yelled at the dog curled up in the cargo area. She never called her son Bernie, the way his friends did, obeying the American custom to shorten names, which irritated her. Her son was not Bernie and she was not Fran. André was not Andy either, although she liked that one – Andy Darrieux sounded like the name of a thirty-five-year-old Canadian adventurer, talented and fit, with countless victories under his belt and many more ahead of him.

A racecar driver perhaps, or a mountaineer. A three-time Winter Games gold medalist.

Françoise turned the radio on. NPR, of course. In Boston she also listened to 99.5 FM, Classical New England, but that station would remain out of range until she reached Rhode Island.

Her phone rang a third time when she was about to cross state lines into Connecticut. Bernard's message was short – call me when you get this. Françoise exited the highway, parked in front of a gas station and dialed her son's number while Buddy sniffed around.

"That article was published two weeks ago!" Bernard yelled. "Why didn't you tell me?"

His mother cupped one ear with her hand and pressed the phone against the other, muffling the sounds of traffic. "I didn't want to bother you. You're so busy with your job and your new responsibilities."

Bernard cursed at the end of the line. "Mom, the whole passive-aggressive routine is getting old." Françoise winced, but Bernard had a point. "That journalist's a jerk. His article's a piece of garbage. You should've told me right away."

A pickup truck zoomed by the gas pumps, stereo blaring behind the closed windows, bass notes thumping from the speakers. Françoise rubbed her nose, which had turned red in the cold.

"As I said in my message, your father has worse problems to deal with right now." She meant it. Jim Calloway's article had lost its importance. Only the prize mattered.

"I should've talked with the guy when he contacted me. Maybe I would've changed his mind."

Buddy was rummaging in the bushes. Françoise dragged the dog away – who knew what motorists had thrown in there.

"You should steel yourself for more articles in that vein. Your father's about to lose the prize he got from the European Physical Society a few years back and when that happens, I doubt the media coverage is going to be friendly."

Bernard remained very quiet for a moment at the other end of the line. Françoise wondered whether her words traveled snail-like from cell phone tower to cell phone tower until they reached California, or whether Bernard had only marked a pause to come to terms with the news.

"What do you mean by 'Dad's going to lose his prize?'"

"One of his students made a mistake in his calculations. The model André got the prize for – his big breakthrough – doesn't hold. It's," Françoise searched for the right word, "junk, I guess. Complete junk."

"You've got to be kidding. How long have you known?"

"A little less than a week. Hans Walzenberger told me. Do you remember him? He was your father's advisor, back in the days."

Françoise opened the hatch, cell phone pressed against her ear. Buddy hopped inside.

"Mom, you should've called as soon as you heard. You've got to tell me that kind of things." Bernard hesitated. "Do you think Dad found out? Is that why he had the stroke?"

"I hope not." Françoise snuggled inside the Volvo and cranked up the heat. "It's so hard to pinpoint the reasons for a stroke. Each one's different."

"You think Dad found out."

She sighed. "I've never seen him more upset than when he returned from the conference. Only he could tell us for sure, though."

"So Dad found out." Françoise did not protest. "But he's been doing research for decades. He has other accomplishments. He deserves that prize."

"He received the award for that specific work. If the result no longer holds, then there's no reason for the society to let him keep it. It'd set a bad precedent."

Buddy poked his head between the headrests. Whenever the car was in motion, he flattened himself against the floor and barely moved until the Volvo came to a halt, but here, because the station wagon was parked, he climbed over the back seat and sniffed Françoise, wagged his tail. She stroked him under his snout. When she returned to Boston, she would buy a cage for the dog to travel more safely with her. What if she had to brake hard? What if that threw him against the seat, the door, and he hurt himself? She had been telling André to buy a cage for years, but they usually did not travel long distances with the dog, and André kept telling her she was overreacting.

She would buy a cage as soon as she was back in Boston.

"Besides, your father supervised the student. People will say he should've caught the mistake." Françoise shook her head. "Your father can be so gullible when he's decided he was going to trust someone."

Buddy slithered between the front seats, apparently targeting the space under the glove compartment. He was too big to complete that maneuver, though, and Françoise slapped him gently. She did not need him to get stuck over the handbrake and the gearbox.

"It's not a question of Dad being gullible. I'm sure the student didn't do it on purpose. Not that it solves our problem."

Françoise scoffed. "Matthew Johnson knew exactly what he was doing."

"Mom. Come on."

"He was leaving academia. He couldn't have cared less. I talked to him this morning."

"And he said that?"

Françoise shrugged. "Not in so many words, but he was well aware he was deceiving André before he left. His daughter told me."

A steady line of cars proceeded onto the entrance ramp of the interstate. A lot of people seemed intent to use the weekend for their Christmas shopping. Françoise suspected it would take her an hour just to cover the last few miles near Boston. She did not mind – as long as everyone crawled along, no one could go very fast, which limited the potential damage in an accident. That always made her feel safer.

"Mom?" Françoise started. "There has to be something we can do."

"I've been telling myself the same thing, but I don't see what."

Bernard did not answer right away. Françoise's mind drifted back to Christmas – she had yet to take the tree and garlands out of the attic. That had been André's job for thirty-five years: he would perch on his stepladder and hang ornaments throughout the house, while Françoise placed figurines on the tree and set up the nativity scene – baby Jesus, the Magi, a shepherd with his left arm glued back into place.

Françoise leaned against the car seat. She did not want to celebrate Christmas this year.

"We can't let Dad's reputation be destroyed," Bernard insisted over the phone. "He's given decades of his life to physics. That has to count for something."

Françoise rubbed her forehead with her free hand, blocked Buddy from sneaking forward with her elbow. "I agree, but his theory doesn't work and the two of us aren't going to fix it. His prize is going to get withdrawn. The media is going to write about it. That's just the way it is."

Bernard considered the situation for a second. "Are you home?" he asked. "There's a lot of noise in the background."

"I'm running errands."

"Call me when you're done. I've got an idea."

"I might not get home for a few more hours." Bernard did not find anything wrong with that. "I'm at a gas station in Connecticut," Françoise admitted. "I drove down to New York City to talk with that former student of André's, the one who made the mistake."

"You did what?"

"I wanted to talk to him face to face."

"You drove to New York City by yourself? You?"

"I would've taken the train but I couldn't leave Buddy alone for so long," Françoise said modestly. "Besides, I'm glad I made the trip – now I can tell for sure Matthew Johnson made the mistake on purpose." Her mouth twisted with disgust. "That prize mattered enormously to André – it was the one thing that justified leaving our families behind and coming to this country. And now it's lost."

Françoise bit the inside of her cheeks.

"Look, Mom. Don't worry about it. I know what we're going to do. I'll give you a call later this afternoon, alright? Consider the whole thing taken care of."

38

"I saw a flyer in the Infinite Corridor. I figured I could use some advice."

The counselor nodded. Olivia sat in the armchair near the window, the stranger in the one near the shelves. A coffee table separated them, with tiny scented candles arranged in a circle in the middle and a box of handkerchiefs near the visitor's seat. On the desk, away from the computer, a miniature water fountain made soft bubbling noises.

"People have given me plenty of advice already, but I wanted an outside perspective." The woman nodded. "My roommate has an opinion, and the professors in my department, and just about everyone I've talked to." Olivia made a wry smile. "Of course, they don't agree with each other. That'd be too easy. But even if they did, I'm not sure I'd trust them."

She paused, tugged on the sleeve of her University of New Mexico sweatshirt, kicked her bag with her foot.

"Why is that?" the woman asked. She was in her early fifties, with grey-and-pepper hair and a warm smile. Olivia did not remember her name. The flyer in the Infinite Corridor mentioned 'walk-ins welcome', so she had stepped into the Office of Student Support Services on a whim and asked the assistant if anyone was available. It had turned out that woman was – the assistant had called her by her name but Olivia, who had been busy examining her surroundings, had not paid attention to it. She browsed through a magazine until the woman came to greet her and walked her back to her office.

"They all have an agenda," she continued, "or at least very strong views. For instance, my roommate is the upbeat type. She believes all challenges can be overcome if people are persistent enough, and the fact that it might set me back by five or ten more years doesn't bother her at all." This time, Olivia kicked her bag so hard it slumped to its side. "According to her, I should find a new advisor for my doctorate, start from scratch and not let any of this discourage me, because I'll be proud I've survived it all when I'm done and this will make me savor the victory even more."

"That's one way to look at it," the woman said. She sat there with perfect calm, nodding her head, encouraging her visitor to go on. High-definition pictures of orchids and snapdragons hung on the wall behind her.

Olivia kept tugging on her New Mexico sweatshirt, covered her hands with the sleeves. She rarely wore the sweatshirt in Cambridge, where the students she knew preferred to showcase affiliations with M.I.T. or the Ivy League, but when she did, she did so with an air of defiance that dared any passer-by to lack her respect. The idea of being an underdog gave her strength.

"I've already spent three years and a half developing expertise on a topic, but faculty members in my department feel that, no matter what else I decide, I shouldn't work with another professor on the same problems."

The woman frowned. "What do you mean by 'same problems'?"

"Issues I uncovered about my advisor's research. They think it should all stay with him, although he can't do a thing to correct them, now that he's had a stroke. Besides, I shared my concerns with him back in August and he didn't want to listen." Olivia made a grimace. "When I insisted there was a mistake, he flew into a rage and threatened to fire me."

The woman raised an eyebrow, but it was not clear that she believed Olivia or was simply practicing her listening skills.

"Even if he hadn't had a stroke and was still able to do research, I wouldn't be interested in working under him anymore. For months after our meeting, I thought I'd made a fool of myself, because I'd been so sure something was wrong but I couldn't get him to agree, and who was I to contradict him? When I got my hands on his notes from the morning he had the stroke, though, I realized I'd been right all along." Olivia raised her chin with pride. "I know he tried to reach me by phone when he got off the plane but honestly, I don't care about earning back his respect or receiving an apology at this point. It's too late. I'm never going to forget how he treated me last summer."

"You sound angry," the woman said.

"I am angry," Olivia replied with a nod. "And the sad part is, he has no clue I am, because he's in a nursing home now and doesn't understand what's going on."

"So what's the point of holding on to all that anger, then?" the woman asked. Olivia shrugged. "Maybe you could try putting it down for five minutes and see what happens. Maybe you'd feel better." The woman smiled encouragingly.

Olivia leaned back in her chair, folded her arms across her chest. "I don't think the whole 'forgive and move on' thing is going to work for me."

"Why not?"

"Because the other professors in the department aren't going to forgive me for what I told the *Boston Globe*. Forgiveness should go both ways, or no way at all." Olivia bit the inside of her cheeks. "I didn't even mean what I said. I was tired and angry and I blurted out something that made a great quote for the journalist." She tucked a strand of hair behind her ear. "People found out it was me. Now I worry I'm always going to be the girl who called her advisor a slave-driver in the *Globe*." The woman blinked. "This represents such a minuscule part of who I am. I want to graduate, get a post-doc at a top research lab, become a faculty member, have my own group, make important discoveries, mentor female students, make a difference in the world." Olivia caught her breath. "Whatever I said to the *Globe* shouldn't matter. It's so unimportant."

"Your relationship with your advisor might need some repair, but that can be done with time, if you work hard on it." The woman did not sound quite as cheerful as when she had greeted Olivia.

Olivia rolled her eyes. "That's beside the point. He's not going to come back to work any time soon. It's the other faculty members I'm worried about." She grimaced. "I'm trying to decide whether I should continue working on my project with another advisor or whether I should give up and start something completely different, and if so, who in the world will be willing to advise me."

THE BREAKTHROUGH

"There might be some issues of intellectual property involved, if you work with someone else on the project your supervisor gave you." The woman's voice had become noticeably cooler.

"But his paper was wrong. I uncovered the mistake. He didn't want to listen. It's about my intellectual property too now." Olivia pulled on her sleeves again. "The thing is, I'm not sure if I can make it right. You always hear about the determination of successful people, how they didn't quit when the going got tough and how that's what sets them apart from the crowds. Refusing to give up – that's the key thing. You're supposed to hang in there no matter what. But I do research in theoretical physics – if you fail to prove a theorem, you're never sure whether you weren't capable of pulling it off or whether the theorem really is wrong." Olivia seemed disoriented all of a sudden. "Successful people aren't supposed to relent until they've achieved their goal, but when do you admit it's not going to work out and you're just hitting your head against a wall?"

The woman thought about Olivia's question for a moment. "It depends what your goal is," she finally said. "Is it to complete this project? To obtain your doctorate? Or to make an impact in the lives of young girls? You said you wanted to become a mentor. You don't need a doctorate for that." Olivia scowled. That was clearly not what she wanted to hear. "I'm just saying, there are different ways for you to achieve your long-term objectives. What you write your dissertation on – if you do decide to go down that route – is only one part of the big picture." Olivia did not react. "Now, since you do plan to stay in the program, have you considered other projects, asked professors if they have openings in their research groups?"

Olivia shook her head.

"Maybe that'd be worth looking into."

"I don't find it realistic to start another project at this point."

"It's not ideal, but it happens. I know students who've done just that. They lost a few years but graduated eventually. I'm sure you can do it too."

Olivia took a deep breath and reached for the strap of her bag. "It's good that I came. Talking about this really helped me organize my thoughts." The woman waited for her to say more. "I guess,"

Olivia continued, "I haven't looked into other projects because deep down I know exactly what I want to do." She raised her head at last. Her gaze did not flinch when her eyes met the woman's. "I'm not a quitter. I'm going to finish what I started, even if it's by myself."

39.

"I don't think it's a good idea," Françoise said.

"I think it's a great idea." Bernard cut a piece of bagel with his fingers, lowered his open hand toward Buddy. The dog snatched the food from his palm.

"Foundations are for dead people. André's not dead." That sounded simple enough.

"Plenty of living people have foundations too."

"Wealthy people. Not us."

Bernard rubbed his eyes. It was seven a.m. Pacific Time and he had just emerged from his childhood bedroom, in pajamas and slippers; Françoise, by then, had prepared coffee, walked the dog, picked up the mail, made grocery lists, resisted the temptation of vacuuming the carpets while her son was asleep, tidied up the living-room, and added Christmas decorations to the kitchen – one more garland running on top of the cabinets, a small tree on the counter, an Advent calendar taped to the wall – using the boxes of ornaments Bernard had hauled from the attic. The house needs decorations, he had protested as soon as he had crossed the threshold. We've always celebrated Christmas. This year will be no different.

Buddy scratched Bernard's leg with his paw.

Bernard smiled. "Bud, you're going to look like a little barrel on legs if you keep eating like that." The dog stared at him with big, loving eyes. Bernard chuckled and gave him a small second serving. "All kinds of folks set up scholarships, Mom."

Françoise shook her head. "The very rich and people who want to honor the memory of their loved ones. We don't have a lot of money." She did not point out that they had even less money now than they used to, since Bernard had wasted the tens of thousands of dollars his parents had invested in his business venture.

"We can't launch a memorial fund either – André's alive and well, and getting better every day."

There was a moment of silence. Bernard raised the cup to his face and took a gulp. "You prepare coffee better than a professional barista."

His mother beamed. "They don't make it like that in San Diego, I'm sure."

Buddy sniffed at the table and scratched Bernard's leg again.

Bernard leaned to the side, stroked the dog under his snout. "You want some coffee, Bud?" He laughed at his own joke.

Françoise rolled her eyes, a faint smile on her lips, while Bernard gave the dog another tiny bite of bagel.

"I wonder how I'll manage when André comes home," she said. "He's not supposed to have caffeine. It's bad for his arteries." She poured herself a cup, although she had already eaten breakfast. "I can't have him smell coffee every morning and not be able to taste it, but I need coffee to start my day."

Bernard shrugged. "I doubt one cup of coffee a day will make much of a difference, given the state he's in."

Françoise glared at her son. "He's improved already. You might not notice the change, but I do. He's made tremendous progress."

Bernard drank his coffee without a word. He sat with his back to the window, keeping the same spot at the table that he had occupied for the past twenty-five years. Françoise sat to his right – the closest to the stove. André usually faced her, but the placemat on Bernard's left, where Françoise would have set her husband's silverware if he had been home with them, disappeared under a stack of magazines along with unopened mail. Those items did not belong on the table – Françoise usually kept the mail in an inbox tray by the phone and the magazines piled in the living room. But there was nothing she could do about the empty placemat in her kitchen, except trying to hide it.

"He won't be teaching again anytime soon, Mom. He won't be doing research in the near future either." Bernard made a broad gesture with his hand. "He devoted his whole life to science, and for what? His legacy's going up in smoke."

"Don't be so negative. No one objects to the rest of his work. His career isn't limited to that one paper with Matthew Johnson." Françoise's voice lacked conviction, in spite of her pronouncing all the right words.

"That was his ticket to fame. It wasn't just a paper. It was a brand new theory that was going to make every physics undergraduate in the country learn his name." Bernard paused. "His main accomplishment has vanished, Mom. We've got to give him something else."

Françoise took a sip of coffee, and then another one. "What if he gets better in three months, and he doesn't like the idea when he finds out? The foundation will bear his name. He never talked about philanthropy – he contributed to the greater good by teaching and mentoring students. He was happy with that."

Bernard shrugged. "He'll help talented kids afford school. What's not to like?" He had already written the mission statement of the Darrieux Foundation, at the airport in San Diego while he waited to board his plane. The statement would appear on the main page of the website – he had not decided on a design yet, but he had browsed through the sites of other nonprofits for ideas, compiled a list of web developers he could ask for advice. "People will say, his last paper was flawed but he's a good man, he has a good heart. We'll get good PR from it, you know, if we play our cards right."

Buddy, who smelled the remaining bits of toasted bagel on the table, sat up straight, his pink tongue sticking out, and stared at Bernard.

Françoise did not look convinced. "That is not a good reason to set up a foundation."

"There are tax benefits too," Bernard said matter-of-factly.

"We don't have a lot of money."

"You will once I finish paying you back. I've already given you some of your money back, you have to grant me that."

Françoise rolled her eyes. "You don't have that money now. That's why you still owe it to us, and now is when we'd need it, if we wanted to go ahead with that odd plan of yours."

"I'll find a way."

Françoise shook her head and looked outside. Her neighbor's roof was covered with an inch of snow. Grey clouds crowded the sky. The weatherman on New England Cable News had predicted another snowstorm before the end of the week but he maintained the accumulations would not last.

"We don't need as much money as you think. If we set up a scholarship at my old high school, we'll get much more recognition for the same dollar amount than if we donate to a college or university."

"But André has no ties to Danbury Latin."

"It's one of the best schools in the nation. Those students will go places, and when they do, they'll remember most the first people who helped them along the way. By the time they reach college, they'll already have cobbled together scholarships and fellowships and loans and whatever other sources of financial aid they could find. We won't stand out so much in their mind anymore." Françoise listened with an indifferent expression on her face. "The school will be happy with a multi-year commitment. We don't have to give all the money right away. Trust me, I'll make it work." Bernard paused. "I've got a good salary now. A degree from Harvard Business School does open a lot of doors." He smirked. "I guess the diploma isn't worthless after all."

Françoise got up, placed her cup into the sink. "You know André didn't mean it that way. He was upset about what happened with the startup. We're very proud of you."

Buddy wagged his tail, hopeful that Françoise's standing up boded good news for him, especially if she stepped closer to the cupboard that contained the dog food. Bernard split the last bit of bagel. The dog swallowed his part at once. "I want to help. It's only fair. You and Dad gave me a hand before. It's my turn."

"André would never let you." Françoise placed the bottle of milk back into the fridge and wiped the crumbs off the tablecloth.

"Dad can't decide for himself anymore. Besides, he'd agree it's more important to save his reputation than to hide behind his pride."

Françoise scoffed. "Don't talk to me about pride. André isn't the one who moved to the other end of the country because he couldn't deal with his business failure."

Bernard leaned back in his chair, folded his arms over his chest. "I wanted to take a fresh start." He hesitated, and then made a little smile. "It took me a while to realize that Dad, for all his rants about what I should've done differently, would probably have failed miserably in the real world. He's too much of a dreamer. I had a rocky start, but now I'm two rungs away from the CEO, in a high-tech company listed on NASDAQ. I have responsibilities. If my ad campaign fails, people get laid off. We're not talking about a little mistake buried in a paper that stays undiscovered for years." Françoise stared at him. "Anyway, we've been hiring like crazy, and it's my turn to help."

He finished his coffee, showed his empty hands to the dog, who turned toward Françoise. She showed him her empty hands too. Buddy, resigned, ambled under the table and curled up into a ball.

"I don't understand why you're so sure money will solve everything." Françoise sighed.

Bernard let out a chuckle. "Welcome to America, Mom."

"Can't you find a journalist who'll write a friendly article in, say, *The New York Times*?"

"That's not the way reporters work. Besides, what do you expect the Times to say? Dad's theory is wrong – no journalist will pretend otherwise. We have to focus on the legacy he's going to leave. If it can't be research, then it should be philanthropy."

Françoise grimaced. "I still hope it can be research."

Bernard shook his head, pushed back his chair. "It doesn't look like that's going to happen."

Françoise grabbed her latex gloves and turned the faucet on. "I don't want to decide now." She doused the dirty plates with dish liquid. "I'm not ready for this. There's no rush, anyway."

40

Françoise wheeled André into the house. A "Welcome home!" banner hung from the banister. Buddy, who had been asleep in the kitchen, bounded toward the newcomers. The dog lowered himself to the ground as soon as he caught sight of the wheelchair, crawled forward, sniffed the leg of the person sitting inside.

Françoise smiled at her husband. "He recognizes you."

André raised his left hand toward the dog. He had not regained the full use of his right hand – his writing hand – although he did squeeze a rubber ball when the therapist asked him to and uncurled his fingers, one at a time, while the doctor counted up to five. Françoise grabbed the dog by his collar and dragged him to the other side of the chair. André cradled his small head with the palm of his hand. Buddy, sitting straight while his owner stroked him, furiously wiped the floor with his tail.

Françoise leaned toward the dog. "It's been a while, hasn't it? Daddy's finally home." She smiled and plucked the gloves off André's hands, the knit hat off his head. His coat gave her more trouble – one sleeve got stuck around his elbow. She struggled to free André's arm, succeeded at last, stood up with a shrug.

"In a few weeks, you won't even need me anymore. You're improving so fast." She hung the coat in the closet, wheeled André into the kitchen. "I prepared your favorite desserts. I couldn't decide whether you'd prefer *tarte tatin* or *chocolate mousse* after all that hospital food, so I did both. I figured you wouldn't mind." She grinned.

Not a muscle moved on the right side of André's face, but his eyes twinkled when he heard *chocolate mousse*. The left corner of his mouth turned up.

Françoise pushed the chair André usually sat on out of the way and wheeled her husband by the table. "Not much has changed while you were gone. You weren't in the hospital that long." She grabbed two plates, plucked forks and knives from a drawer, reached into the fridge. The *chocolate mousse* could have easily fed six people. "The Hartwell kid got offers from Rochester and Olin College. I think he's leaning toward Olin – he likes hands-on projects – but his father graduated from Rochester and speaks highly of it. He's in a bit of a dilemma." She gave André a generous portion of *mousse*, cut his slice of pie into tiny squares because he could not use his knife – that would have been right-hand work.

Buddy sat down by the wheelchair but did not move, did not bark, did not scratch André's leg with his paw. He just waited with the absolute certainty that André would give him a piece. Françoise helped herself to the *tarte tatin*. "The Dempseys put their house up for sale. They haven't had any taker yet. Bernard thinks their asking price is too high – that house needs a lot of repairs." She paused. "I brought your car in for an oil change. The mechanic said the injection pump and the thermostat will need to be replaced soon. Given the age of the car, we'd probably be better off getting a new one. I told him there was no rush. We'll buy another car when something breaks down."

André did not react. He wore a checkered shirt with his favorite cardigan – the one that had extra padding at the elbows – ate at his usual place in the kitchen and, although he had lost weight, had the same round eyes, the same large forehead, the same thick glasses as in mid-November, before he had boarded the flight to San Francisco. They could have shared a late lunch one weekend afternoon. Within minutes, André would retreat to his study and finish editing the paper he had been working on. Françoise would clear the table. They would resume their routines. Their lives had never been so normal.

André raised the spoon to his mouth. His hand quivered, threatening to dump the content of his spoon back onto the plate. Françoise looked away. She searched for something to say that would distract both of them from that trembling hand and pointed at the magazines on the table. They no longer covered the placemat but were stacked in a neat little pile on her husband's right. "We received those while you were in the hospital. I thought you had enough to read already, so I kept them here, waiting for you to come back."

She realized with dismay while she spoke that she had pushed them to the wrong side – the side of André's limp hand – when she had tidied up the kitchen before heading to the nursing home. Without missing a beat, she scooped up the magazines, walked around the wheelchair and dropped them on André's left, as if it was the most natural thing to do. "They will keep you busy for a while." Françoise smiled, arranged the ends of her scarf across her blouse. She had overdressed for the day – silk scarf, pencil skirt, expensive jewelry, and brand-new leather ankle boots, to step across the last mounds of snow for the season. The occasion deserved that much. "How does it feel to be home?"

André lowered the spoon onto his plate. His left shoulder twitched. It might have been a shrug, though. He scooped another bite of *chocolate mousse* and raised his spoon again. Françoise tensed up at the sight of that quivering hand. Her instinct was to grab it, steady it, but she clenched her jaws and kept her arms by her side. The doctor had told her to let André eat at his own pace.

"I think you'll enjoy the documentaries on the History Channel later this week. They sound interesting. I circled them up in *TV Guide.*"

André looked at her, closed his eyelids, opened them again.

"Am I talking too fast? I'm sorry." Françoise rubbed her forehead. "I'm just happy you're back. Maybe I should start again from the beginning and speak more slowly."

André shook his head, lifted a piece of *tarte tatin* from his plate and tossed it to the left. Buddy galloped around the wheelchair and dove for the crumb, licked his chops several times after eating the treat. Françoise watched him with amusement – it had been a rather small piece of pie, unworthy of such displays. André extended his arm and stroked Buddy under his snout. The dog, forgetting the rest of the pie that awaited him on the table and the *chocolate mousse* in the glass bowl, half-closed his eyes with delight.

Françoise smiled.

"What do you plan to do while you recuperate? It might take a few months for the doctor to give you the go-ahead to return to work. Then it'll be summer already and you won't have to teach before Labor Day." She munched on her pie. "You don't want to do research until you've completely recovered. Otherwise you might do mistake after mistake and it'd just be a waste of your time." André did not protest – he did not agree either. He simply looked at her with a frown, as if he did not understand her words. The speech therapist had warned Françoise that her husband needed to relearn the meaning of basic expressions people used around him, and that it would take a lot of patience on her part.

Françoise leaned forward and raised her fork up in the air. "Bernard had an odd idea some weeks ago." She paused for effect. "He thought you should start your own nonprofit foundation, if you can believe it. It'd give scholarships to needy high school students with an interest in physics." She chuckled. André's eyes were set on her – he understood 'physics' somehow, although the meaning he attached to the word remained unclear. "Bernard always comes up with grandiose plans. I wonder where he finds them. Not that I'm against helping youngsters achieve their dreams, mind you, but we don't have that kind of money – especially to spend on other people's kids." She shook her head. "You've got better things to do. You've got to rest, recover. Soon enough you'll resume working. You don't have time for philanthropy. Who cares that it'd show you in a good light?" Françoise pinched her lips – she had said too much already – but André did not seem curious to learn why it mattered, all of a sudden, for him to put his best foot forward.

"I'll call Bernard and tell him no."

41

"I don't want to go home after I've walked the dog. I find excuses to stay out longer. Sometimes I reach our street and then I turn around. Of course, Buddy doesn't understand. He recognizes our house. He knows we should be heading the other way." Françoise entered the museum, closed her umbrella, unbuttoned her coat. "I followed your advice, though. I went to the *Alliance Française* and registered for a conversation group. Our first meeting is next week."

"Let me know how that goes." Diane's short, black curls bounced around her face when she turned to Françoise and smiled. Françoise had noticed the new haircut as soon as she had stepped out of the Green Line train on Huntington Avenue; her compliments had pleased Diane. She had not asked why Diane had felt the need to change her hairstyle, which was a good thing, because Diane would not have known what to answer. She had never told her about Jim and it seemed a little late, now that the relationship was over, to mention she had lived with the *Boston Globe* journalist who had written about Françoise's husband.

"Thanks for suggesting this. I haven't come in years. I kept telling André we should go, but he never found the time."

Diane nodded. The outing had been her idea. She had called earlier that week to check on her friend and offered they get together. They viewed each other as friends now, ever since Diane had sent Françoise a Christmas card – she had interacted with enough spouses turned caregivers to know the Frenchwoman would appreciate her reaching out, and they had chatted so many times at the hospital that the card would not seem inappropriate to Françoise at all. Indeed, she had given Diane a call the day she had received her note, happy to share André's progress, discuss Bernard's plans for a foundation (which Diane heartily approved of), chat with someone, anyone, who would contact her. They had met at Faneuil Hall for lunch and stayed in touch.

The two women headed for the admissions desk. It was Wednesday afternoon and admission at the Museum of Fine Arts had been free since four o'clock – Diane kept track of those things – but they still needed a ticket to enter. The line moved quickly.

"I see that man on the left, and I think, why are you healthy? What did you do to deserve being healthy while André isn't?" Françoise shook her head. "That's so unfair." Diane followed her gaze – the object of Françoise's wrath, an elderly gentleman in a raincoat, walked away from the counter with a ticket in hand. "He doesn't even limp," Françoise said.

Soon it was her and Diane's turn to hold tickets.

Françoise motioned toward the American wing. "I want to see that Sargent painting with the four little girls."

"*The Daughters of Edward Darley Boit*?"

Diane blinked, surprised by the coincidence. That canvas had fascinated Jim's younger daughter – Tricia had even tried to touch the girl in the foreground once, before Diane had dragged her away under the disapproving glare of a security guard. A smile fleeted on her lips; it all seemed amusing now. She missed the girls.

The Daughters of Edward Darley Boit still hung on the spot where Diane had seen it, framed in the gallery by the same two large vases depicted in the picture, with three of the girls facing the painter and the last one turning away – the elder daughters almost swallowed by the shadows while the younger two remained firmly in the light.

"It's comforting to come back here and find the same paintings hanging on the walls," Françoise commented. "That's one thing that hasn't changed." Both women stared in silence at Sargent's masterpiece. Françoise folded her arms across her chest. "I know André's had a good life. I'm grateful for the years we've had together. And yet I feel so angry." Diane waited for her to say more. Françoise stepped away from the canvas and admired the overall effect. Then she moved back closer to examine the artist's brushstrokes. "I keep thinking there has to be a silver lining, but even if something good comes out of this, it won't make up for what happened. André has yet to read a book. He browses through magazines when they have lots of pictures, but he doesn't understand abstract terms." Françoise sighed. "His whole line of work is theoretical. I have no clue what we're going to do."

A tourist clicked his camera at the artwork.

Diane pointed at Sargent's painting. "Did you know none of the girls married?" Françoise shook her head. "The two in the background suffered from some kind of mental illness as adults, I think, although Sargent couldn't have guessed any of that when he painted them."

She had researched the painting on the Internet to assuage Tricia's interest, but in the end she had shared little of what she had found, emphasizing instead ideas that the five-year-old could understand – the oddity of the painting's size, the space separating the daughters from each other, the contrast between the light and shadow, the loveliness of the child holding her doll on the rug.

Tricia identified with that one the most.

Footsteps echoed on the hardwood floors of the gallery. A woman in high-heeled boots glanced at the painting, adjusted her glasses. Her expression softened when she read the artist's name. She moved about for a better view, and examined the *Daughters of Edgar Boit* for all of five seconds before ambling away to another canvas.

"I like to believe the daughters donated the painting to the museum so that others would remember the promise they held in their youth, before they had become isolated and lonely and life's disappointments had come in the way. It wasn't just about offering the community a famous canvas." Diane searched for words. "They knew it wouldn't change what had happened afterward – it wouldn't turn back the clock, wouldn't solve the elder sisters' emotional problems, wouldn't make any of the four find husbands and start families of their own – but it'd shine a light on that blessed time in their life when a painter had decided to immortalize them, of all the people he could've chosen. I think they felt that was good enough. They took their victories where they could."

She glanced at Françoise, her cheeks bright red, and then looked down, tucked a strand of hair behind her ear.

Françoise nodded. She understood.

She called Bernard on his cell phone afterward and, when he did not pick up, dialed his number at work.

"We should talk about the foundation again."

"What about it?" Bernard said in that absent-minded voice that revealed he was trying to do several things at once – eat a late lunch at his desk, check his email, sift through his papers, talk on the phone with his mother.

Françoise took a breath. "I think we should go ahead. It's time. Let's give your father the legacy he deserves."

42.

The European Physical Society announced a few weeks into the New Year that it was withdrawing the Prize for High Energy and Particle Physics awarded in 2003 to Dr. André Darrieux of the Massachusetts Institute of Technology. The one-paragraph statement, which was picked up by the Associated Press, referred to inaccuracies recently uncovered in one of his papers, but elaborated neither on the findings that had come under scrutiny nor on the events that had triggered the probe.

The science reporters at the *New York Times* went to work.

43.

Jim beamed at the intern who had brought him the wire. The boy's thankless job was to read the news coming from the AP and Reuters and figure out who in the building would benefit from that information. Jim had drilled into his head that every statement about science belonged with him.

"Have you seen Dan?"

"He's at his desk, I think."

Jim unzipped the winter jacket he had put on only moments earlier and strode through the newsroom in search of his assigning editor. Journalists hunched in front of their computer monitors, typing relentlessly. One scribbled notes while he grunted follow-up questions into his phone. Dirty Styrofoam cups filled the trash bins. Two lone donuts were left in a very large box. Jim looked around for the thirty-three-year-old who had written about the procurement scandal on Beacon Hill but the man was nowhere to be found. Jim wondered which leads he was out chasing. The main stories for the day revolved around the bankruptcy filing of a local business that employed two hundred people, an early-morning fire that had displaced a dozen of Quincy residents, and – Jim guessed this one had aroused the curiosity of his fellow journalist – the surprise announcement by a Boston councilman that he would not seek reelection. Reporters hurried in and out, determined to interview one more witness, add one more detail to their copy before the deadline.

By comparison, the science and technology writers seemed almost serene. One of Jim's colleagues chewed gum as he sifted through pages of information he had gathered over the previous week, on what this year's flu strain meant for the vaccine's effectiveness. Someone had been tasked with writing about a robot that recognized people's facial expressions and reacted to them with gestures of its own. A car manufacturer was testing software that would help drivers parallel-park and navigate busy streets; of course, it would take many years before that innovation became widely available in the marketplace. Few readers would notice if the managing editor delayed publication by a day or two. These articles were not urgent. Jim's new idea was.

He glanced at the reporters, bent over their keyboards, and smiled at no one in particular while he strode toward the editors' table – a scandal had just rocked M.I.T and only one person at the *Globe* knew about it, but he would make sure it did not stay that way.

He slapped the piece of paper next to Daniel Radinowski's mouse pad. "Did you read this?"

"I thought you were taking off."

"I'm on my way out. Got to go and meet my ex-girlfriend. She's finally getting her stuff from my apartment. Did you read this?"

Dan stretched his arm and glanced at the AP wire. "What about it?" He looked tired, with dark pockets bulging under his eyes, and not particularly interested in the European Physical Society.

"That's the man I wrote about in November. André Darrieux." Jim suppressed a chuckle. "My article did this."

Dan read the statement again. "It doesn't say."

"It's obvious. How else would they know? No one else has spent a line on him. They must've heard about my article."

The editor rubbed his forehead. "As much as I'd like the rest of the world to read the *Globe*, I doubt it's the newspaper of choice for the," Radinowski paused for effect, "European Physical Society."

Jim's smile narrowed. "Dan, my article did this. I'm sure those guys started looking into him after I outed him. We should run a follow-up."

"That man had a stroke. He's a vegetable. He's lost the most important prize of his career. I think you can move on to attacking people who can defend themselves now."

Jim clenched his jaws. "You approved the article."

"No need to remind me." Dan leaned back in his armchair and clasped his hands behind his head. "I'd like to believe we don't ruin people's reputation just because they work at a famous place and it makes us sell papers."

"Why are you telling me this now?" Jim scoffed. "Did readers complain? I've received some nasty emails myself. I know the piece is controversial. But all the good articles are." A handful of readers had taken offense at the way André Darrieux had been portrayed, but that did not mean a thing. They did not know any better. They could not see beyond Darrieux's inability to defend himself. Olivia Reynolds had not minced her words, though – he was a slave-driver and she was glad he had a stroke. Jim believed her.

"The wife didn't write. She would have, if she had disagreed."

She wrote to Giesenhalt." He meant Arnold Giesenhalt, who had been named Globe's publisher by the New York Times Co., the Globe's parent, only a few months earlier. "From what I understand, she asked him how his relatives would react if he had a stroke, and the *Herald* printed he was a megalomaniac whackjob who deserved every bit of misery heaped on him, as if the stroke was some kind of divine punishment for his misdeeds."

The young copy editor seated by Dan pinched her lips and made a quick change to the document on her screen. Although she seemed engrossed in her task, Jim had a clear sense she was listening to the conversation.

"You know that's not what I wrote."

"I can see how what you did write could be interpreted in that way, though."

"Is she suing us? Because she doesn't stand a chance in court, let me tell you that."

"It's not about a lawsuit." Dan paused. "I heard she's starting a foundation in her husband's name."

Jim frowned. "That doesn't sound like her. I talked to her for hours – she's not the type to launch nonprofits, or any kind of business, for that matter. She'd have people stepping all over her before she even filed the paperwork."

"Her foundation will give scholarships to local high school students with an interest in physics. She asked Giesenhalt for money."

Jim chuckled. "Good luck with that."

"Actually, he invited her to lunch. He calls this," Dan raised one hand in the air, "a unique opportunity to demonstrate the Globe's commitment to education."

The copy editor glanced at Jim and then looked away. She was twenty-three, twenty-four at most, fresh out of school – the new generation of Globe employees. Jim remembered chatting with her once by the vending machines. What was her name again? Sara, Lynn? He had no idea. But he thought he had impressed her – he had a long track record at the company. His byline had appeared on numerous articles.

She did not look so impressed anymore.

"He's taking her side?" Jim asked – whispered, really.

"Be glad he didn't donate your entire salary."

Jim shrugged. "He doesn't have that much money lying around." Dan gave him a long stare. Jim tried to scoff, but only managed a little cough. "That's ridiculous. I'm well-respected here."

He thought he saw Sara repress a chuckle.

"Ridiculous or not, you might want to keep a low profile. Although I've heard there might be an opening at the *Worcester Telegram & Gazette*, if you feel like getting some fresh air."

Sara tapped nervously on her mouse, eyes on the screen.

Jim swallowed hard. "How come I'm only hearing about this now?"

"He didn't read your article until he got her letter." Dan browsed through the wire again, crumpled the piece of paper and threw it into the wastebasket. "If you had a stroke tomorrow, what would your kids say about you?" Jim rolled his eyes. "'Dad spent all his time working, hoping he'd stumble on something no one else had found before'? Isn't that the reason why Carol filed for divorce – she was tired of your quest for knowledge?"

Sara fished her cell phone out of her purse. "I've got to take this." She hurried toward the door. Her phone had not been ringing.

"What's your point?"

"You and that Darrieux guy have a lot in common."

Diane stood in front of the apartment building, stomping her feet in the snow so that she would not get cold.

"You cut your hair," Jim said, slightly out of breath because he had hurried from the T station. He fumbled for his keys, unlocked the door. "That looks nice."

Diane smiled and took off her woolen hat inside the building. Jim pressed the call button for the elevator. "Are you alright? You seem a little pale."

Jim shrugged. "I'm okay." He pressed the call button again.

"What's going on?"

"Do you remember that M.I.T. professor who had a stroke?" Diane nodded. "He lost the prize he'd received in Europe some time ago."

"Did your article do this?"

"I don't know. I hope not."

"But isn't that what you wanted?"

The elevator cab began its descent from the top floor. Jim shifted his weight from left to right, and then left again. "I wanted to have an impact. I'm not saying I wanted to ruin his life."

"You have an odd way to show it."

The elevator passed the ninth, eighth, seventh floor.

Jim pressed his fingers against his temples. "I know we've talked about that before, but can you repeat one last time what you expected me to write about him?"

"Something sad, about a man who finds out that his greatest accomplishment amounts to a mirage, that he spent decades working on a project that won't even be a footnote to history. A man who'd hoped life would give him more and had believed it was within reach but won't ever get it." The elevator stopped on the fourth floor before resuming its descent. Diane unbuttoned her coat. "There was a beautiful story to be told. I don't understand why you didn't see it."

"I guess Andrew McNeill is better at this than I am."

Diane rolled her eyes. "Enough with him already. You'd have written a fine article if you'd tried."

The elevator doors opened at last; Jim and Diane stepped aside to let an elderly couple and a middle-aged woman get out.

"Do you think I have a lot in common with Darrieux?" Jim entered the cab after Diane and pressed the button for his floor.

"You've talked with his wife almost as much as I have. Did you get the feeling he and I would've gotten along?"

Diane frowned – the urgency in Jim's voice had taken her by surprise. The question seemed odd, ill-timed, out-of-place.

"I guess you have the same drive," she said after a while. Her eyes drifted over a flyer taped by the control panel, reminding residents to be considerate of their neighbors at night, keep the music down and refrain from yelling in the hallways. Jim signaled her to go on. "If you'd worked in the same field, you might've been at each other's throats. But since you weren't competitors, maybe you would've gotten along. Yes, I could see that happening."

Jim did not say another word until they had entered the apartment. The closet, the shoe rack, the shelves were brimming with items – it was hard to believe they had stood half-empty only weeks earlier. Jim had made a point of filling the space to forget Diane had ever lived there.

"I'll be out of your way soon," Diane said.

She headed for the kitchen, where she had left cookware in a box under the sink. She had decided against storing them in the friend's apartment where she had stayed at first, while she searched for a permanent home, but she had her own place in South Boston now and the time had come for her to retrieve her belongings.

Jim threw away an empty can of beer that he had left on the counter. Diane cleared her throat. Then she smiled.

Jim rolled his eyes, plucked the can out of the trash, lobbed it into the recycle bin. "So you think we would've gotten along."

"I don't know. You might've. It's a little late to ask yourself that. Darrieux will probably never be again the man he once was, and I doubt his wife will ever forgive you for what you wrote."

Diane dragged a big cardboard box onto the kitchen tiles, peered inside. Cookie sheet, muffin pan, square cake pan, rolling pin – everything was there.

"Let me check I didn't leave anything in the living-room."

She stopped on the threshold – Jim had rearranged the furniture and bought a new DVD reader.

He leaned against the wall. "For what it's worth, I haven't seen any of your stuff lying around. I would've set it aside otherwise."

Diane nodded. She glanced at the trinkets on the shelves, the pile of magazines on the floor – all Jim's. He chuckled wistfully. "It's odd to think that Darrieux and I could've been friends. Maybe we would've written a book on string theory together."

Diane glanced at Jim and shook her head, but she did not make any comment. Instead, she strode toward the bedroom, where she had left her summer clothes in three large bags carefully sealed and tucked in the closet. That room at least looked exactly the same as she had left it – there was not enough space to move the bed, and if the bed stayed where it was, then the shelves could not be pushed around either.

"I might need your help carrying all this to my car." Diane handed one bag to Jim, who swung it over his shoulder.

"His wife started a foundation in Darrieux's name, if you can believe it. She plans to give money to high school students who like physics, or something along those lines."

Diane grabbed the other two bags and returned to the kitchen. She did not seem surprised by the news, which disappointed Jim. "If you can lift the box for me, then we might be able to do only one trip. I can't do it myself, though. It's too heavy for me."

"You're going to find this insane, but I'd like to help her."

Diane raised an eyebrow. "I do find it insane. Anyway, the woman wouldn't be thrilled to see your name among the donors, after what you wrote about her husband. You'd come across as a hypocrite. You should've thought about it earlier."

"But she won't think twice about it if you give money to her charity." Diane blinked. Jim flipped his checkbook open. "Can you do me a favor? Can you donate this to her?" He scribbled an amount and signed in haste. "Wait until the first of the month. I don't want the check to bounce."

Diane gaped when she saw the number. "You don't have that much money to spare. Why are you doing this?" Jim closed the checkbook and folded his arms across his chest. "It's a little late to show remorse. Throwing money at that foundation now isn't going to assuage your guilt."

Jim shrugged. "Just send the money for me, okay? I'll find the address for you."

44

Claire tied her sandals and grabbed her keys on the kitchen counter. Olivia, who sat in her bathrobe with her elbows on the table, read a preprint while slurping coffee; she did not look up. Claire hesitated for a second and then headed for her bedroom, emerged almost immediately with a cardigan that she tied over her short-sleeved top. Olivia took another gulp of coffee and flipped to the end of the paper, drew a cross in the margin next to a reference that held her interest. The door closed.

The balmy spring weather had drawn out joggers and bicyclists, eager to enjoy the mild temperatures while they lasted, before the humid heat had set in for the summer. A group of teens idled in front of the mom-and-pop restaurant where Claire liked to order take-out. A homeless man, slumped against the wall, jingled a few coins in a Dunkin' Donuts cup. Claire caught a glimpse of the white and yellow frame of the #1 bus in the distance and ran to reach the stop before the bus had rumbled past her. It was a close call.

She hopped off at the terminus in Harvard Square. A street musician plucked his guitar; on-lookers huddled around the tables at Au Bon Pain – watching the chess players absorbed in a game, unfazed by the attention. A tourist, camera in hand, lectured his friends on the architectural merits of the Widener Library and the Memorial Church. Claire power-walked through the crowd, past the beggars, across the square, into Brattle Street, until she reached the entrance to the art house theater. Julie and Phil were already waiting by the glass door.

Julie waved at her. "Congratulations, Doctor Warren!"

Claire beamed. "I can't believe I'm finally done, after all these years." She handed eight dollars to the woman sitting in the box office, retrieved her ticket and a quarter. "I keep thinking, no matter what happens next, I'm a doctor now. Nobody can take that away from me." She grinned. The group walked past the snack stand and climbed the stairs to the old performance hall of the Brattle Theater.

"When are you leaving Cambridge?"

"In June, after Commencement. I can't wait."

Julie nodded. "Chicago's nice, especially in the summer."

About two dozen movie-goers had preceded them – it was a good turnout for a matinee, especially with this weather. Claire debated where to sit. Phil pointed at an empty row in the back.

"Actually, I won't move to Chicago before August." Claire plopped into her seat. Julie sat down between her friends. "I just meant, I can't wait to leave. The situation with Olivia has become unbearable." Phil leaned forward, curious to learn more. "She stopped talking to me. Whenever I make the slightest bit of noise – washing dishes, cooking dinner – she glares at me as if I was trying to torture her."

"It'll be over in a few weeks." Julie fished her cell phone out of her purse and turned it off.

"I should've seen it coming," Claire added. "She's always been very hyper when it comes to research. This is a particularly bad time for her, with her former advisor having a stroke and her research going nowhere. But I didn't expect her to make me feel guilty for my accomplishments. It's not my fault she might not get a degree."

"She's a nice woman," Phil said. "I'm sure she's happy for you."

"Where do you know her from?" Julie asked.

"I ran into her at a meeting of the Graduate Student Council, almost four years ago. That must've been right after she moved to Cambridge. We both come from the Southwest. I remember us laughing about the differences with the East Coast."

"She introduced the two of us to each other," Claire told Julie, meaning Phil and herself. "Before we were roommates."

"I used to run into her at concerts in Central Square, dinner parties in Somerville – she had a lot of friends her first year here. Then she dropped off the radar when she became more involved in her research."

"Very withdrawn," Claire said.

"Always backing out of plans at the last minute, unsubscribing from mailing lists, not answering my texts." Phil shook his head. "I tried to stay in touch. I tried."

She had work to do, Olivia kept saying when he called, and she did not have time. It was a pity, Phil had told Claire once, drunk, outside the Temple Bar, that her roommate had not given him a chance.

Julie uncapped her lip balm.

Claire sighed. "She's way too isolated for her own sake. That's not healthy." She untied her cardigan and put it on – the air-conditioning system kept the room too chilly for her. "She spends her days drinking coffee and scribbling equations with bloodshot eyes. She's the most determined person I've ever met, but I don't think that's going to be enough."

"Maybe she'll find something." Phil sounded hopeful.

"Her new advisor is very smart," Claire continued, "but I'm not getting the feeling he's terribly nice. Darrieux was actually a much better fit for her, if you can believe it."

Julie waved a flyer she had picked outside the theatre. "Did you know the movie got five Academy Awards? This is going to be good."

Claire bent toward Phil. "She's in over her head. She's trying to prove something that can't be proved and she refuses to admit it."

"She can't delude herself forever. At some point she'll have to face the facts."

"I'm glad I'm not going to be there when that happens."

The three friends stood up to let a couple reach empty spots on their right, settled back into their seats. Phil admired the heavy curtains that framed the screen – remnants of the days when the room was used as a theater hall. Julie pushed her bag between her feet and turned to Claire.

"Did you find a sublet for your apartment?"

Claire nodded. "First-year student in biochem. She'll spend most of her time in lab – exactly what Olivia needs. Someone who's never home." Julie pinched her lips at the mention of Olivia's name. Phil placed his hand on hers, but the scowl on her face did not soften. "I'm worried about her," Claire explained. "She's headed for a disaster and she's the only one who's not seeing it."

The lights became dim. A hush fell on the crowd.

Phil leaned toward Claire. "We'll keep an eye on her after you've left, if you want."

Julie glared at him in the dark.

Claire shrugged. "There's no point," she whispered as the first pictures flickered on the screen. "She's too far into her own world now."

Olivia knocked on the door and poked her head into Evelyn's office. "The printer's out of paper." The halogen lights accentuated the pallor of her skin, the dark circles under her eyes.

Evelyn turned toward her. "I haven't seen you in a while. How have you been?"

"Busy."

Evelyn waited for a second, then – when it became clear Olivia would not say more – stepped away from her desk and reached for one of the unopened reams she kept on the shelf. "Here." Olivia wrapped her arms around the packet, exposing her bony elbows, and retreated to the door. "You look tired," Evelyn said.

"I'm fine."

"Did you get my email about André? I want to send the department's contribution by the end of next week, Friday at the latest."

Olivia blinked. "I sent my money to Mrs. Darrieux already. I didn't realize it had to go through you." Her cheeks reddened. She was not a good liar.

Evelyn returned to her desk, smoothed the back of her linen skirt when she sat down so that it would not wrinkle. "It doesn't. I'm glad you took the initiative. That's great." Olivia moved toward the door. "How are things with Professor Greenawalt?"

Olivia froze and peeked behind her shoulder. "They're good. We hope to get something published soon."

"Congratulations," Evelyn said coldly.

Olivia stepped into the hallway. "I hope lots of people give money. It's such a wonderful idea. Once I have more savings, I'll be able to contribute more. The scholarship sounds like it's going to be around for many years anyway."

She hurried out of sight.

Evelyn stayed still at her desk until a door at the end of the corridor had opened and closed. Then she shook her head and resumed typing.

She was still typing when Susanna Polits dropped by, check in hand. "That's for André's scholarship. Thanks for the reminder."

Evelyn's face brightened. She opened a drawer, retrieved the envelope where she kept the donations – cash and checks – bound together by a large paper clip.

Susanna eyed the bundle. "How much did you get so far?"

"About twelve hundred. Seventeen hundred with you."

Susanna grimaced. "People tend to wait until the last minute."

"I hope so. They'd be more generous if he was dead," Evelyn said matter-of-factly. "But since he isn't, they find it awkward to help him get his foundation off the ground." She added Susanna's name to the list of donors, placed the money back into the drawer. "She'll send you a tax receipt." She paused. "Seventeen hundred isn't bad, and Hans promised to give me a thousand."

"That's very generous of him."

Evelyn nodded. "Some of André's students gave money too – Patrick, Hyong-Mo. Olivia said she contacted Françoise directly, but I doubt she was telling the truth." Evelyn pinched her lips. "After all the hours I spent listening to her and trying to cheer her up, I can't believe she had the gall to lie to my face like that. Being strapped for cash is no excuse."

"I ran into her in the corridor. She looks like a ghost."

"I don't think things are going well with Tom." Evelyn lowered her voice. "He processed his students' research assistantships for the summer already and she's not getting funded. I know – I handled all the paperwork. I'm not sure if he broke the news to her yet."

Susanna shrugged, unwrapped one of the Hershey's kisses Evelyn kept in a jar by her computer. "I warned her to stay away from Tom. She should've picked another topic, but she didn't want to listen. She only has herself to blame for whatever happens next."

45

Bernard turned the engine off. Françoise, who had been sitting in the back, stepped out of the S.U.V. and opened the passenger's door.

"Look where we are."

André ventured a foot out, clutched his wife's arm. Bernard walked around the front bumper but Françoise waved him away. "I'm fine." She braced herself and lifted André up. Bernard reached for his father's cane inside the Ford Explorer. The Volvo's heating system had broken down at the end of the winter; it had not been worth replacing. Bernard had bought a new vehicle for his parents right after he had moved back from the West Coast – before he had even bought a car for himself, as a matter of fact.

Françoise smiled. "We're at Bernard's old high school. We came here in April to sign the paperwork for the scholarship, re-member?" She scrutinized André's face, in search of a glimmer of understanding.

André nodded. He did that more frequently now, which Françoise viewed as a good sign, although she could not decide what he meant – yes, he recognized the campus, or: enough with the questions already. Maybe he nodded because he realized his wife interpreted any gesture from him in the manner that suited her most.

Bernard placed himself to his left. "We've got the wheelchair in the trunk if you feel tired, Dad." He pressed a button on the remote control. The doors locked with a beep, a brief flash of the headlights. "Just let us know and we'll come back and grab it."

The group inched away. André set the pace, hunched on his cane between his wife and son. He wore a dark grey suit without a tie, Françoise a silk blouse with a maroon shawl and a little hat she had bought for the occasion – someone from the Development

Office would be taking pictures. Bernard, who planned to remain out of the camera's eye, was dressed more casually with a crew neck sweater and khaki pants.

A pop startled them – a baseball rose through the air as a young midfielder sprinted across the athletic fields. Students lingered on the lawn in the quadrangle with book bags dangling over their shoulder. Others read under the trees, their foliage smattered with specks of yellow and red. Boston's Indian summer was coming to an end. Soon it would be a year since André's stroke.

"This campus is beautiful." Françoise made a sweeping gesture with her hand. The red-brick buildings reminded her of Harvard – a prettier version of Harvard without the crowds of tourists and the noise of Massachusetts Avenue. "Every time I visit, I'm amazed by how gorgeous it is." Bernard nodded. His father, looking down, did not react. Françoise pointed at the new science center with a sigh. "Of course, compared to that, we're giving the school small change." The alumnus who had contributed millions of dollars for the building had also written several large checks to Ivy League colleges. Her family could not hope to match his spending.

Bernard shrugged. "It's good for the school to have many donors. That shows broad support for its mission." He slowed down to match his father's pace. André moved with excruciating slowness – making jerky steps, setting the tip of his cane only inches before his toes – but at least his coordination had improved enough that he no longer needed the wheelchair. "People give what they can."

"We're out of that man's league. We're out of all the other donors' league. The staff at the Development Office must wonder why we're wasting their time."

"They think the scholarship's a great idea. Not a lot of people give to high schools. College is what everybody remembers and feels grateful for."

Françoise shook her head. "It's so much money for us, and so little for Danbury Latin."

"It's a lot for the student who's getting the scholarship."

Françoise leaned toward her husband. "Are you looking forward to meeting him, sweetheart? You're making a big difference in that kid's life. He's a budding physicist, even won a prize at the science fair." She chuckled. "I have no clue what his experiment was about, but it seems that he impressed the judges. You would know, though. You would've understood."

A teenager, intrigued by the slow-moving group of visitors, eyed them while he strolled by, on his way toward the language lab, maybe, or the technology center. He stared at André for a second and then turned his head away, his cheeks reddening – Françoise saw pity in his eyes. She felt pity too sometimes, and sadness, and sorrow at all that had been lost, but the scholarship had kept her busy through the summer and those emotions had receded in the background, for the time being.

"The kid's name is Jonathan," she said. "He made the honor roll in every period since he entered the school. His mother's raising him and his two brothers all by herself. She was laid off in March and couldn't find another job that would pay as well. Without you, Jonathan would be back in public school." Françoise paused. "You're giving him a free ride. That will open so many doors for him." She turned to her son. "We'll find the money, won't we?"

"Of course, Mom. Don't worry about it." Bernard spoke quickly. He did not want her to broach the subject near his father.

"It'd be awful if we filled that kid's head with big dreams and then let him down next year. He still has two years to go."

"We won't let anyone down, Mom. It's all under control. We'll find the money."

Françoise pinched her lips. "Maybe next year André's colleagues will contribute more, so that it's not all of our savings, Diane's check and a tiny bit of help from M.I.T."

"We're only getting started," Bernard said. "People never want to give much the first year. They're waiting on the sidelines to see what we do. Once they realize we're serious about the scholarship, they'll be happy to participate."

Françoise adjusted her shawl around her shoulders. "At least Hans and his wife gave a thousand. We weren't in touch for three decades, and yet they came through when it mattered." She cast a side-glance to her son but did not repeat what, out of André's earshot, she had complained about on several occasions: one of André's colleagues had donated twenty dollars. Twenty dollars! That angered her. She suspected the slight had been deliberate, which hurt her even more. One could not even buy a hardcover book for twenty dollars. André, his commitment to research, his dream of making a difference, were worth more than a wrinkled twenty-dollar bill plucked nonchalantly out of Thomas Greenawalt's wallet and forgotten almost immediately. Françoise wished he had contributed nothing, so that she would not have had to send him a thank-you note with an acknowledgement for his tax records.

A boy about to leave the refectory held the door open for Bernard and his parents. André entered first, followed by Françoise, who worried that her husband would miss a step or that his cane would slip on the tiles. But André forged ahead, toward the third floor and the Alumni and Development Office. He had picked up the pace and stamped his cane with more energy on the stairs. Although there was no elevator in the building, Françoise had not dared suggest to the staff that they change the location of the meeting. Her husband was supposed to be doing better. He was said to have read himself all the applications for the scholarship. Would the money mean as much to the teenage recipient if anyone realized André was not as involved in the foundation as his wife and son claimed? It would certainly lower the scholarship's impact on his legacy. Françoise could not let that happen.

"Olivia didn't give anything. It's just as well, because I would've returned her money." Bernard agreed: he would have refused the woman's help too. "I'm glad she's taking a semester off. I hope she won't be back. The department chair assured me this is just a way of easing her out without creating too much drama. Good riddance." Françoise scoffed. "Diane, who didn't even know André before his stroke, gave five hundred dollars. That shows her character." André marked a pause on the second floor and took a breath.

"I told her she didn't have to – I don't think she can afford it – but she insisted."

Bernard frowned. "I don't understand why that woman cares about us so much. Many other nurses helped Dad, and you don't see them keeping in touch with you or contributing to his scholarship. Something's not right."

Françoise shrugged. "She's become a good friend."

THE BREAKTHROUGH

André took a step forward. Bernard, walking behind him, extended his arms to prevent his father from falling if he slipped. The group climbed the last flight of stairs in silence.

When they reached the Development Office, Françoise stood in the hallway for a moment with her eyes on the door. "I wish there was another way to get your father the recognition he deserves," she finally said. "I feel I'm buying his legacy."

"We're changing a student's life too. Maybe Jonathan will become a famous scientist and he'll tell the world, I wouldn't be where I am today if it weren't for André Darrieux. He awarded me a scholarship when I was in high school and gave me the confidence I needed to pursue my dreams."

Françoise made a faint smile, clutched André's hand. "That does sound nice."

The Development Office consisted of a large room with cubicles and one office in the back. A woman looked up from her desk when the door opened. That was Laurie, who had been Bernard's contact person throughout the process and had helped him design the scholarship. She smiled when she recognized the visitors. "How are you? How was the drive?" She greeted Françoise first, then André, and finally Bernard. "Jonathan will be here any second now. He's coming straight from class. We'll have the interview first and then we'll take the pictures. Would you like something to drink?"

André nodded, which surprised Françoise. She found him more alert all of a sudden.

"I'll be right back," Laurie said. "You can wait in the conference room if you'd like."

Bernard flipped on the lights, pulled out a chair. Françoise helped André take a seat at the long, polished oak table and sat down next to him. Bernard walked to the other side. "I don't want the kid to face a row of strangers. That would look like a tribunal."

The silence dragged on.

Bernard folded his arms behind his head. "What made you decide to start a scholarship?" he quizzed his mother. They had rehearsed at home already but one more time could not hurt.

Françoise, leaning forward, rested her forearms on the edge of the table. "André has always wanted to promote education, especially in the sciences." She spoke a little too fast. "For him, his job was always about training students as much as creating new knowledge. After the stroke, education became his number one priority."

"Mom, you've got to sound more natural than that."

"That scholarship means so much to my husband," Françoise continued more slowly. "He enjoyed reading the applications the boys wrote." She would have considered giving the prize to a girl, but Danbury Latin was an all-boys school. "It was so hard for him to make a choice. We wish we could support more students."

"The generosity of André's colleagues has really taken us aback." Bernard tapped on the table with the palm of his hand to emphasize his words. "We knew he was a popular teacher and scientist, but it's been tremendously inspiring to see donations pour in. We're so grateful for the community's support."

Françoise grinned. Bernard grinned in return. "We'll be alright."

The door to the Development Office opened with a jingle.

"Hi, Jonathan." That was Laurie's voice. "They're waiting for you in the conference room."

André turned slowly in his chair, toward the corridor. Françoise looked at her husband, at the hallway, at her husband again. Footsteps grew near – Laurie appeared first, glass of water in hand. A boy in jacket and tie peered behind her shoulder. He had brown eyes, brown hair, freckles all over his face.

"Hi," Jonathan said.

Bernard got up and shook his hand. "Hello, Jonathan. Let me introduce you to my father."

"He's been looking forward to meeting you," Françoise said. "Your experiment at the science fair really impressed him."

The boy stretched out his arm, lightly touched the fingers of André's right hand. For a second, nothing happened. Then André blinked. His lips moved – he mouthed words that no one could make sense of. "He's saying: hi, Jonathan," Bernard said, in a firm voice that would tolerate no second-guessing.

The boy beamed.

THE BREAKTHROUGH

http://www.aureliethiele.com

THE BREAKTHROUGH

5123497R00146

Printed in Great Britain
by Amazon.co.uk, Ltd.,
Marston Gate.